RIKA OUTCAST

RIKA'S MARAUDERS – BOOK 1

BY M. D. COOPER

M. D. COOPER

SPECIAL THANKS
Just in Time (JIT) & Beta Reads

Kristina Able
Alastar Wilson
David Wilson
Lisa L. Richman
Scott Reid
Nick Richard
Joseph Spies

Cover Art by Tek Tan
(Thanks for flawlessly bringing my vision of Rika to life)

Editing by Jen McDonnell
(Extra thanks for the care and attention you give Rika)

TABLE OF CONTENTS

FOREWORD

Rika has a special place in my heart. I don't know why, but she does.

I think that a part of it comes from her original inspiration, which is the character 'Clara' in the TV series *Killjoys*. Clara was a woman who had her right arm replaced by the bad guys at 'The Factory'. It wasn't a voluntary mod, and she's not happy about it, but ultimately she learns how to live with it, and it makes her stronger.

The woman who played Clara in the TV show was very convincing, and I thought, "What would it really be like for someone who has undergone that sort of modification?"

Obviously, for the purposes of a TV series, they can't afford convincing, full-body cyborg alterations—but my (and your) imagination can.

This brings us to Rika. She was born in the Genevian Commonwealth, an interstellar alliance of star systems that fought a desperate war with the Nietzscheans. Her government did not have enough AIs to continue to create combat mechs, and NSAIs were not effective enough...

So they used humans. Unwilling humans.

Rika was one of those humans.

THE AGE OF THE ORION WAR

Humanity has not had an easy time expanding into the stars.

Though no intelligent extra-terrestrials have ever been found, we struggle enough against our selves and our creations. War has forever marred our history, and it continues to do so.

Though conflicts such as the Sentience Wars and the wars of the Sol Dissolution took billions of lives, these wars were contained within a single stellar system, and did not spread across the stars. Without faster-than-light travel, it simply would have taken too long and been too costly to make war on neighboring star systems.

The advent of faster-than-light travel removed that constraint. When the FTL Wars broke out in the late fifth millennia, they devastated humanity.

Wave after wave of dark ages washed over human space, and much of the great knowledge of the past was lost.

In the late ninth millennia, a tentative peace has finally emerged. Accords and Alliances have built up a fragile stability that has allowed humanity to crawl back from the brink of complete self-destruction.

Then a ship from the past is found—a ship containing technology long thought lost: the *Intrepid*.

This one event is the match that lights the powder keg, throwing humanity into the greatest war it has ever seen—a war that spans tens of thousands of star systems across the Orion Arm of the galaxy.

The Orion War

Such a war has many fronts. A conflict spanning hundreds of systems with trillions of deaths is but a skirmish. But to the people fighting those battles, it is not a small event on the edge of space; it is their lives, their families, their very civilizations that are on the line.

The long-running war between the Genevians and the Nietzscheans is one such skirmish. It is here that we find Rika. Her government, desperate to hold back the Nietzscheans, has resorted to barbaric means to achieve victory.

Mechanized humans.

CITIZEN A71F
STELLAR DATE: 09.22.8939 (Adjusted Years)
LOCATION: Tanner City, Kellas
REGION: Caulter System, Genevian Federation

Rika sat behind the grey plas of the defendant's table and looked around the courtroom. Its walls and ceiling were a colorless off-white, with over-bright lighting, and hard concrete floors. She hadn't expected it to be welcoming, but she had thought courtrooms were supposed to look more upscale—another thing the vids lied about.

The tan, one-piece jumpsuit she wore was loose, but still managed to bind in the armpits and groin; Rika shifted on her hard chair in an attempt to get more comfortable. The movement made the chains that connected her wrists to the table jingle, and she felt herself flush. The whole situation was a mistake, just a horrible mistake.

The judge would see that, and in an hour she'd be free and clear.

Rika glanced at the public defender sitting beside her. He was flipping through a virtual stack of pages only visible to him. She had no way of knowing if they pertained to her case, or to one of the many others he was likely tasked with.

He looked sharp in his black court-suit, and the grey wig complimented his heavy brow—beneath which were sharp, blue eyes. His lips were full, just the way she liked them, and Rika imagined what it would feel like to brush hers against them. To press her nose into his cheek and—

Her daydream was interrupted by a voice calling out, "All rise for the Notable Judge Pliskin."

Rika leapt to her feet, eager to show her respect for the judge, and completely forgot about the chains holding her wrists to the table. The cuffs jerked her arms to a stop and she slipped, slamming her face against the table.

"Stupid girl," she heard her defender mutter as he bent over to help her to her feet.

Rika's eyes filled with tears, and she felt a trickle of blood run down her face as she stood and stared at the table, too embarrassed to look up at the judge as he took his seat.

Behind her, a few snickers could be heard from the gallery, and Rika did her best to ignore them, chanting *'back on the street in an hour'* over and over in her head.

Once the judge settled in his seat, the rest of the court followed suit, and Rika carefully lowered herself back to her hard plas chair. Her defender hadn't even acknowledged the blood on her face. Rika bent down and tried to wipe it off, but was certain she'd only smeared it around.

"Case number 823.3234.A433," the court clerk read out. "The commonwealth versus citizen 4C399EB2-76AB-4CB1-AD9D-9F01B69EA71F, who also goes by the name 'Rika'. The charge is theft of a valuable worth over fifty thousand credits."

"What?" Rika tried to rise, but her defender placed a hand on her shoulder, keeping her seated.

"Quiet," he whispered, and glanced at the judge who was giving them a disapproving glare.

<But all I stole was a crate of food,> Rika pleaded with her defender privately over the Link. *<It wasn't even worth five-hundred credits.>*

<That's not what the report says. Says here it was a valuable military-grade scan suite for a patrol ship,> the defender replied. *<I'm going to see what I can do, but you're certainly not getting off for this.>*

Rika was stunned by his response. She had opened the crate; it had been filled with food. There had to be some sort of mistake.

"Seems open and shut," the judge was saying. "You were caught on surveillance stealing the crate, and it was found in your possession. How do you plead, citizen Rika?"

"Plead?" Rika asked, bewildered by the speed at which her fate was being sealed. "I plead innocent of what you're accusing me of. I stole a crate of food, there was no scan suite inside."

"Innocent?" the judge leaned over his high desk. "This is a capital crime, citizen Rika. We are at war with the Nietzscheans, and you have committed a crime against the war effort. The maximum punishment is death. If you plead innocent, this will go to trial and it will be swift—that I can promise you."

"But…but…" Rika stuttered.

This is impossible! I'm only nineteen; there's no way my life— miserable though it's been—can end like this.

"May I have a moment?" her defender asked the judge.

"Very well," the judge replied.

<Look,> her defender said. <*The judge is right. They have you dead to rights on this. Look at the prosecutors; they're not even paying attention to the case. It's a zero-effort win for them. Your only hope is to plead guilty. I'll get the judge to give you a military sentence. You'll do a few years behind a rifle, and then you'll be out.*>

Rika slumped in her seat. She couldn't believe what she was hearing. It was a nightmare. All she had tried to do was get some food, and now she faced death or military service? Which, given how the war was going, was probably also a death sentence.

<*Well?*> her defender asked.

Rika didn't respond, and after a moment he spoke up. "My client pleads guilty, and begs the court's mercy. She will gladly accept a military sentence."

"Will she, now?" the judge asked. "I need your affirmation, citizen Rika."

The judge's words sounded to her like they were coming from underwater, all garbled and warbly—but she understood their meaning, and nodded slowly.

"Very well," the judge replied. "A military sentence of five years is issued. You are to be remanded at once to the Genevian Military Police for processing."

Rika lowered her face into her hands. She wouldn't even get a chance to say goodbye to anyone. Not that many people cared what happened to her. None of her so-called friends had shown up to court today.

She didn't even see the defender approach the judge's high desk and receive an envelope, as rough hands seized her wrists and disconnected her shackles from the table, and reconnected her wrists behind her back.

"This way," a gruff voice said, and she felt a shove on her shoulder.

Rika barely paid attention as she was marched down a long corridor lined with holding cells. She was pushed into one, and the door slammed behind her. Barring a mat on the floor, the cell was completely empty. Rika fell to the mat, curled up in a fetal position, and cried herself to sleep.

Some time later—she was uncertain how long, as her Link access had been severed upon her guilty sentence—her cell door opened, and a stern voice ordered, "Get up, girl. Time to go to processing."

Rika assumed 'processing' was some sort of procedure where the police handed her over to the military, but when her eyes focused on the speaker, she saw that the woman who spoke to her was in a military uniform. Clearly that form of processing had already occurred.

The woman led her through the long hall of holding cells, all empty now. Had they been filled when she came? Rika couldn't remember. Once beyond the cells, they passed through a cold, dark corridor that led to a solitary door.

Her escort grunted softly as she opened the door to reveal dim evening light; as Rika's eyes adjusted, she saw an unadorned bus waiting in an empty parking lot.

The bus was half-full of men and women, and the military woman led Rika to its door. A man with a sheet of plas stood beside the yawning portal and looked up at her, his eyes narrowing with distaste.

"Conscript A71F," her escort said, using just the last four digits of Rika's identity.

"So it seems," the man said with a nod. "Good haul today, eh, Jenna?"

"Decent enough," the woman, who Rika now had a name for, replied. "This one's a bit scrawny, though. Wonder what they'll do with her."

"Who knows," the man grunted. "Can always use meat for the grinder, no matter what it looks like when it starts."

Rika didn't like the sound of that, and she looked at the man, who gave a smile that did not reach his eyes.

"Your new life awaits you A71F, get on the bus."

Rika walked carefully up the stairs. She didn't want to slip again—one smear of dried blood on her face was enough. At the top of the bus's steps she saw an empty row, and slid into the seat by the window. Rain started to fall outside, and she closed her eyes, desperately wishing that someone would walk onto the bus, call out her name, and announce that there had been a mistake and that she was free to go.

Nothing even remotely close occurred.

A moment later, the man who had been outside the bus climbed the stairs and took a seat at the operator's controls. The door slammed shut, and the vehicle began to move.

Rika fell asleep again and when she woke, it was still night. The bus had stopped at a gate, and the operator was talking with a guard outside his window. The door opened, and two soldiers stepped onto the bus. One stayed at the front, rifle held up, stock against his shoulder, while the other walked down the aisle, examining the human cargo.

"All clear," he announced when he got to the back.

The soldier with the rifle nodded, but his weapon remained trained on the conscripts. Only when the first solider passed him did he lower his weapon and walk off the bus.

The door closed, and the operator set the bus in motion once more. It only drove for five minutes before stopping at a large, nondescript building. A group of soldiers stood out front. When the operator opened the doors, another pair of soldiers walked onto the bus.

These two didn't carry rifles—rather, they swung stun batons, slapping them in their hands. One soldier stayed up front, while the other began walking down the aisle.

"Get up, you lazy scum. Your glorious future in the Genevian Armed Forces awaits you. First row, out!" the soldier walking the aisle hollered.

One of the men in the first row didn't rise fast enough, and the woman hit him across the shoulders with her baton, causing him to cry out in pain.

"I said, *Get! Up!*" She screamed right in his face, then grabbed his jumpsuit, lifting him bodily from his seat, and tossed him into the aisle. "Now mooove!"

The man scrambled to his feet and promptly fell down the stairs. Rika stood, ready to get off the bus the moment the woman passed her row. She noted that the stairs would be slippery from the rain-soaked boots of the guards.

"Fucking moron," the soldier grunted. "Not that it matters; you scum will make a proper contribution to the commonwealth soon enough."

Given the other man's reference to 'meat for the grinder', and this soldier's choice of words, Rika's level of concern about what lay in her future intensified.

Once out of the bus, she joined the other conscripts in a long double-row. The rain had lessened, but it was still enough of a drizzle to make them miserable. She saw the first man who had fallen down the stairs standing at the head of the line next to hers. His nose was broken, and blood poured down his face; no one made a move to help him as he sniffled and wiped the blood from around his mouth.

As the bus emptied out, Rika looked over the others. They all wore the bulky jumpsuits, and the least disheveled of them still looked as bad as she felt. She was surprised to see that only half looked like street-rats; the rest of the men and women appeared to have seen baths and good food in recent days. The clean hair and trimmed fingernails were also dead giveaways of a better life.

She did a quick sum as the last woman stepped from the bus, followed by the soldier and her swinging baton. There were thirty-two of them. Thirty-two miserable souls unwillingly added to the Genevian war machine.

The other soldiers formed up around the conscripts, and the baton-wielding woman yelled into the rain-soaked gloom, "Move it, you fucking filth! We don't have all night!"

They marched into the building, and were led down a long corridor to a wide foyer. At the end of the foyer stood a man at a small podium. Behind him were three numbered doors. The man looked the shivering conscripts over for a moment before turning his gaze to a sheet of plas on the podium.

"Conscript B43E, door 1," he announced, and one of the cleaner, though no less miserable, men shambled forward, and stepped through the door as a guard opened it.

The man at the podium carried on, announcing the conscripts' codes and a corresponding door. Rika noticed that there was a clear class preference. The most fit were sent to door one, and the street rats, like her, all ended up going through door three.

It came as no surprise to her when her name was called.

"Conscript A71F, door 3!"

She walked on unsteady feet toward the door, doing her best to hold back the tears that threatened to spill down her face. If she started crying now, she knew stopping would be impossible. Once through the door, she found herself in another long hall, and slowly walked until she came to a bright white room.

Eleven other unwashed scum like her were waiting there, all shivering with cold. After she entered, one more girl joined their number, and there they stood: an unlucky thirteen.

Rika noted that the room was tiled, and drains were set in the floor. Above, there were sprinklers, and along one wall were several large wire baskets on wheels.

A pair of guards entered the room—one with a rifle trained on the conscripts, and the other with a decoupler for their shackles. As he freed each person, the guard with the decoupler gestured for them to stand along the wall near the baskets. Once the last unfortunate soul stood in a ragged line in front of the baskets, he barked one word.

"Strip!"

No one moved for a moment, and he eyed them with an unpleasant stare. "If you sorry assholes aren't butt-fuck naked in one minute, I'm going to have Lars here shoot you all in the kneecaps. Fuck knows you won't need them anyway."

The possible meaning behind his words terrified Rika, but she followed the instructions. Something in his voice made her think he was very serious about shooting them in the knees.

She pulled off her shoes and the jumpsuit, tossing them in the tub behind her. She hesitated at removing her underwear, but despite the guard's hungry gaze, she thought that any ogling from his eyes would be better than bullets from his rifle. As she pulled off her bra, she glanced at the others, who were pulling off their undergarments as well.

Somehow, they all looked better naked than in the ill-fitting jumpsuits. Not that any of them looked great. Most bore the look of hard living on the streets, or in low-rent government housing. Rika had to admit that she looked better than most, though she was shorter and thinner than all but one other girl.

"Get under the nozzles, close your eyes, and clench your dicks, assholes, and pussies. This is gonna sting," the not-Lars guard said with a coarse laugh.

Rika stepped gingerly across the cold tile to the center of the room. She clenched her fists and closed her eyes, prepared for the worst.

When the spray came, it was warmer than she had expected—but it hit hard, scouring every part of her body. Then it began to sting; then burn. She felt like her skin was on fire, but didn't dare to open her eyes. Nearby, a man screamed in pain, and the guard laughed.

"I told you not to open your eyes, fucker. Don't worry, little bitch; you'll get rinsed off in a minute. It'll stop burning, then—mostly."

Rika felt something sliding down her head and shoulders, and she tentatively reached up—her hand encountering a strange, lumpy mass. She recoiled in horror before she realized it was her hair. She touched her face, and found that her eyebrows were gone; she ran her hand higher, and felt her smooth scalp.

"That's it," the guard advised as the warm spray continued. "Brush all that shit off yourselves. The sooner you do, the sooner we can give you the final rinse."

A minute later, the spray changed in pressure and the burning feeling on her skin eased. The man who had opened his eyes a moment before was reduced to a mere whimper, and Rika hoped his vision hadn't been permanently damaged.

"Open your eyes," the guard called out, and Rika tentatively followed his instruction. All around her were the glistening forms of her fellow conscripts. Hairless, with red, irritated skin. "Look at you all," the guard chuckled. "Like shiny little dolls."

"A lot better than the shit-stains that came in here," the guard with the rifle, Lars, spoke for the first time.

"OK, meat," the first guard yelled. "Move!"

At his words, a door opened up on the far side of the room, and the naked, hairless, shivering conscripts filed out.

This time, the corridor was short and well-lit. It opened up into a large room with three long boxy structures running down its center. They looked almost like train cars, though conduits connected to them at regular intervals.

At the near side of each of the long boxes were wide, dark openings, with a pair of technicians standing before them. Rika noticed that no additional guards were present, but she doubted even the two who followed them in were needed. Each member of the thirteen conscripts was utterly cowed, their spirits broken. They would not put up any resistance.

Rika also spotted automated turrets mounted on the ceiling, and knew that any attempts to escape would be met with more force than she cared to encounter.

The technicians on the far right called a citizen number, and one of the men walked over to them.

"Right, then," she heard one of the technicians say to the man. "You're a good size. We'll fit you for the K1R. Good thing, too; we have a quota to fill on those, and you lot rarely live up to the reqs."

The other technician pulled a metal harness along an overhead rail until it slapped the man in the back. Clamps wrapped around his thighs, torso, biceps, neck, and forehead. Without further preamble, it lifted him into the air as he cried out in alarm, and then it pulled him into the dark opening of the long structure.

One by one, the other conscripts were called forward. Each was racked just like the first man as the technicians made cryptic remarks about what they were suited for.

Eventually it was just Rika and the girl who was a hair shorter than her. They stood close to one another; not touching, but taking whatever comfort they could from another human's presence in the hell they found themselves in.

"A71F," one of the technicians at the far-left structure called out.

Rika approached, and the man sized her up. "Hey, Rick, she'll probably work for one of the new scouts, won't she?"

The other man eyed her up and down, likely measuring her with his augmented eyes. "Yeah, she's great for it. Looks like a hundred sixty seven centimeters and just under fifty kilos."

"Has good Link-tech, too," the first technician said. "Won't have to spend too much to make her brain worth using."

"Using for what?" Rika asked quietly. It was the first time she had spoken since the courtroom, and she surprised herself—it was almost as though she had forgotten how.

"You'll find out soon enough," the technician replied as Rika felt the rack slap her on the back.

This one was different than the others she had observed; it clamped tight around the top of her thighs, and again just above the knee. It did the same around her arms—one just above her elbow, and the other uncomfortably jammed up in her armpit. Another clamp wrapped around her head, followed by one around her neck, and two around her torso.

"No!" she cried out, struggling against the clamps. "What are you doing to me? Where am I going? Please, I have to know!"

The technician named Rick slapped her ass.

"Somewhere where *that* will never happen again," he leered.

The rack lifted her up and pulled her toward the dark opening of the long structure, and Rika began to writhe with fear, bucking and straining against the bonds.

"Hey! Stop that!" the first technician called out. "You're gonna miss the—aw, shit."

Rika felt something hit the clamp on her neck and slip to the side. She wasn't certain what she had just avoided, but she was glad—until she heard the technician named Rick laugh behind her.

"Well, I guess you don't want the anesthetic, then! Don't worry, the pain will make you pass out soon enough."

"What?" Rika cried out, and then she felt something hot against her elbow. She strained her neck, trying to get a good view, and shrieked in terror and pain as she watched a laser slice her arm off at the elbow. The light from the opening was fading, but she could still make out her forearm, falling free from her body and landing in a pile of limbs below her.

The scream that tore from Rika's throat was cut short by her collapse into blessed unconsciousness.

"See?" Rick told the other technician. "I told you she wouldn't make it past the first limb."

"Good for her; would have sucked if she was still awake when it started cutting her skin off."

A thud came from behind the pair, and they turned to see the thirteenth conscript unconscious on the ground.

"Well," Rick laughed. "At least we don't have to worry about her struggling."

MECHANIZED

STELLAR DATE: 09.23.8939 (Adjusted Years)
LOCATION: GAF Base 99A1, Kellas
REGION: Caulter System, Genevian Federation

Rika woke with a strangely muffled scream, and began thrashing.

It took a moment for her to realize that she could move her limbs; then a moment more to realize that everything felt wrong. Her eyes were open, but she couldn't make out anything around her. She blinked rapidly, the motion of her eyelids coming down strange, like her eyes were too slick.

Around her, a room slowly resolved into view. Coupled with the feeling of something cold and hard against her skin— which felt coarse and almost numb—she inferred she was on a table. She looked around and the vague shapes slowly solidified into stacks of equipment. Not medical equipment; more like what would be found in some sort of workshop.

She tried to sit up, and was served with the brutal reminder that she was missing her arms from the elbow down. She lifted a leg and saw that it too had been severed, now ending at the knee.

Rika closed her eyes tight, and a whimper escaped her. She laid her head back and shook it.

No no no no!

After a minute, she opened her eyes again and looked at her arm. That was when she realized why her skin felt coarse and numb—where there should have been pink flesh, there was only a matte grey covering.

She rubbed her stubby arms against her torso as tears began to streak down her face. As she did, there was a moment of incongruous relief as she realized that her breasts

21

were still present; though they were little more than nondescript lumps under her artificial epidermis.

The end of her arm stumps were cold against the 'skin' of her torso, and Rika realized that her limbs were capped with steel, from which protruded small, ridged cylinders, roughly four centimeters long and three across. When she attempted to bend her elbow, or gave what she assumed was the mental equivalent of moving her elbow, the small cylinder moved. She realized it must be mounted to a ball-joint of some sort inside her arm.

It took her a few minutes to grasp what this all meant. She had been prepped for cybernetic limbs. Rika had seen soldiers in combat vids with cybernetic limbs, but never all four—and she had always assumed it had been a voluntary modification.

Apparently she had been naïve.

Rika lifted her head as much as possible, and pushed her pelvis up. She took a moment to realize that putting pressure on the ends of her limbs didn't cause any pain—there were some small miracles, at least.

A glint of light caught her attention, and she noticed a metal port in her stomach where her belly button used to be. She took more care to examine what was left of her body, and saw another pair of ports at the bottom of her rib cage, two more in her thighs, and another pair on her biceps.

Careful examination with her arm-stub led her to discover that there was one at the base of her neck, as well. Her movements on the table also revealed that there were several more ports running down her spine and, she noted with a grimace, another between her ass cheeks.

"Oh, shit, you're awake!" a voice nearby said, and Rika turned her head to see a man approaching. "Must have screwed up the sedation. I hate it when they do that."

The man was young, not too much older than Rika. He held part of a sandwich, of which he took a final bite, chewing rapidly.

"I wish they'd at least tag you when that happens. Then I'd know you were gonna wake up," he said around the mouthful of food.

Rika attempted to speak, but found that she couldn't part her lips, or move her tongue—or her jaw. She had another minor freakout, and the man placed a hand on her stomach. The sensation of human contact was calming and welcome, though it felt oddly muted through the matte grey material that covered her.

"Easy now, you can't talk anymore. I'll get your Link back up in a bit. You're probably hungry, too; let me give you something—not too much, mind you, I don't want you to get queasy."

He grabbed a tube from beyond her field of vision, and attached it to the port on her stomach. A strange sensation of her stomach filling came over her, though she had not swallowed anything.

"I'm really excited," the man carried on as he detached the tube. "You're the first of the SMI-2 scout models I've had the opportunity to build. They're new and super-advanced. You're going to love it, I bet."

Rika desperately wished that she could tell this 'assembler' that she would love to have her limbs back, but that wasn't possible. She made *hmmmm*ing noises out of her nose as loud as she could—which also felt weird, for reasons she couldn't identify—but the man just patted her on the stomach again.

"Don't worry, you're in good hands. I've put a thousand of you guys into mechs. You'll be up and ready to fight in no time. I have to admit," he said with a hungry smile as his gaze swept up and down her body. "It's gonna be handy to have you conscious, being my first scout mech and all. We can make sure the fit is good."

The assembler touched her stomach again, running his hand across it. "This new carbon-polymer is really great, too. No more of you mech-meats having stinking skin that needs to be cleaned all the time. Pretty sexy, if you ask me. Too bad they sealed up all your useful bits down here."

As he spoke, the man reached down and patted her crotch.

She jerked away, recoiling from his touch, though she could instantly feel that there was nothing there; she was smooth as a child's doll between her legs. Rika lifted her pelvis up, trying to get a better look at this new indignity that had been bestowed upon her, while the man walked toward a rack and lifted up a long item, carefully unwrapping its plas covering.

Rage and shame mingled together. She was just a thing to him; an object that deserved neither respect, nor remorse.

If I had my limbs, I would—

"Oh," he said while looking over his shoulder. "Once you're built, don't even think about hitting me or anything. You'll regret it if you do."

Rika couldn't help it; she was already thinking of beating him senseless. Searing pain tore through her mind. She would have screamed if it had been possible, but she only managed to make loud, breathy grunts as her chest heaved from the shock.

The assembler chuckled. "Gets 'em every time. You have a compliance chip in your head now, Mech A71F. You'll never have an unsavory thought about anyone in charge of you again."

He held up the object he had unwrapped. It was a leg, a long one. It looked strange, and Rika realized that was because it was shaped like a horse's hind leg: double-kneed, with the first one bending backwards. The foot, if it could be called that, was more like a three-taloned claw, with two on the front, and one at the back for the heel. The limb appeared to be made of some sort of dark carbon-fiber material, and had overlapping ridges where the joints were located.

"Lay still," the man said, and Rika felt her muscles stiffen and was suddenly unable to move. The assembler lifted the limb in the air and spoke again. "Raise your right leg."

Rika found that she could move her leg now, and lifted it into the air.

"Think like you're pointing your toes," her assembler said, and then nodded with satisfaction when the cylindrical nub on the end of her thigh pointed straight out. He then slid her new leg into place. It covered her whole thigh and seated into the cylindrical protuberance with a satisfying *ssshhhhuck* sound.

"Looks pretty good," the man said with a nod, and he lined up a pair of rods, each with two holes, across the thigh-section of the attachment. He shoved them into the holes, and Rika felt them slide through her leg. They must have passed right through her femur and out the other side. She realized that's what the ports she had seen were for. He ran another pair of rods through the back of her leg using a set of ports she hadn't spotted, and then turned toward a console.

"OK, I'm going to connect the leg to your nervous system, then we're going to put it through some tests."

The next hour was filled with Jack—which was the assembler's name, as she finally learned—slowly adding limbs, and testing out every possible piece of functionality.

When he was done, she stood on the floor in front of the table, flexing the joints on the double-kneed legs that were attached to her thighs—which still felt awkward to walk on, but Jack said she'd get used to them before long.

Her left arm, thank the stars, was relatively normal, with a three-fingered hand at the end of a nondescript limb. Jack had explained that it was useful for a mech to have a hand so that it could do things like operate doors, or manage its own feed and waste tubes.

During the fitting, he had continually referred to her in the third person as 'the mech', and she slowly had begun to think of herself as nothing more than a piece of hardware. A part of her mind screamed that this was mental conditioning—likely enhanced by the compliance chip in her brain—but there was really nothing she could do about it.

Her right arm ended in what Jack referred to as a 'multi-function weapons mount'. Currently a long sniper rifle was attached to it, and she practiced aiming while Jack lifted another object off the rack and set it on the table.

"This is a bit different. Since you don't have skin to clean anymore, it's going to fit a lot tighter—but it's more flexible, too."

He lifted up two pieces of a shell that would wrap around her torso and between her legs. It had an almost chitinous look to it, with the overlapping plating. Jack pressed the front piece against her torso, and studs protruding from the armor—for that's what it was—sunk into the ports there. He repeated the process with the back, and then fiddled with an overlapping plate between her legs, finally driving a long shaft into her pelvic bone to pin the armor in place.

Next he placed chest armor over her upper torso, front and back, and anchored it into place as well. The chest armor was less flexible; only a small bulge revealed that under all the steel and carbon fiber, she was still a woman made of flesh and blood.

"Can the mech bend over?" Jack asked. "I want to test full range of motion. Touch your toes...or your claw-feet things..."

Rika did as instructed and bent over, touching the front claw on her right foot with her right hand, and then tapping the muzzle of the rifle against the other.

"OK, good," Jack said. "Now twist side-to-side…OK…then arch your back."

Rika followed the directions without pause. She had received two additional mental shocks from the compliance chip for responding too slowly, and she wasn't about to let that happen again.

"Hmmm," Jack muttered. "A bit of slippage when you arch backwards; but I suppose you won't do that much, and your skin underneath can still stop a bullet."

He turned to grab one more thing from the rack.

"And now for the mech's grand finale!" He turned and showed Rika a featureless black oval, which he deftly split in two. "Your helmet."

Rika twitched backward. The helmet looked like it belonged on a robot. It would take away the last appearance of her humanity, and make her nothing more than a machine.

"Don't move," Jack said sternly, and Rika found herself paralyzed once more. She blinked rapidly, the only movement she could make, as Jack placed the back and then the front of the oval around her head. It was dark inside, and her breathing was loud in her ears—until something snaked into her ear canals and all sound ceased. She felt something wrap around her neck, and knew she was now completely entombed in her matte grey shell.

<OK, Mech.> Jack's voice came over the Link; the first time she had received any mental communication since the courtroom.

Rika realized that with the Link, she had access to basic information like the date and time. She saw that her sentence had only been commuted three days prior.

Three days…

It felt like a lifetime had passed; like the Rika then was another person.

All that remained now was Mech A71F.

<I'm going to activate your helmet's visuals and swap out your natural optics. They'll still work as a fallback, but you'll default to external sensors now.>

The black interior of the helmet was replaced with a full three-hundred-and-sixty-degree view of the room. If Mech A71F hadn't been locked stock-still by Jack's order, she would have fallen to the ground as waves of dizziness came over her.

<Wha...I can't tell which way is forward,> she said in a near panic.

<Easy now, Mech. There are indicators on your HUD, and it will feel perfectly natural in no time. Give me a moment while I put on your external power pack and remove these hookups. You have SC Batts inside, too, but this external one has a lot more juice.>

She watched with startling clarity in the dimly lit room as Jack disconnected the power cables that had been attached to her limbs, and placed a small, oval battery pack on her back. A readout appeared on her HUD showing that the external battery was 98% charged, and would last fourteen days at its current drain. Estimates appeared beneath that data showing that under strenuous activity, the battery would only last five days.

There was a brief snapping sound in her ears, and Mech A71F realized she could hear sounds in the room again, but not with her ears. The sounds were fed directly from the helmet's sensor array into her brain.

"Can you hear me?" Jack asked.

<Yes,> Mech A71F replied. <Loud and clear.>

"Good," Jack replied. "Run full diagnostics."

She wasn't sure how to, at first; then suddenly she knew exactly what to do, and she ran the diagnostic routine on her armor. It showed green across the board, and she reported that to Jack.

"Good. Mech A71F, you are ready for combat. You will receive final subliminal training en route to the front. Exit this room and follow the route highlighted on your HUD. It will take you to your transport."

<*Understood,*> Mech A71F replied, and took her first faltering step toward the door—and the rest of her life.

* * * * *

Author's Note:

If you haven't read the Rika prequel, *Rika Mechanized*, you may want to do so at this point. It tells a story of Rika's time in the Genevian military, and paints a picture of what she had to go through to survive the war that her people ultimately lost.

Buy Rika Mechanized for only $5.99

However, it is not necessary, and you may read on to see what is in store for Rika next...

DEKAR'S DREGS

STELLAR DATE: 07.02.8948 (Adjusted Years)
LOCATION: Dekar Station, Merchant Docking Ring
REGION: Outer Rim of Parsons System, Nietzschean Empire

Nine years later...

"Hey, Rika, you have a ship to load! Get your tinhead out of the stars and get that shit loaded, or I'll dock your pay!" Bay Chief Hal yelled at Rika from two berths over.

"Not a tinhead anymore," she muttered in response.

"You'll always be a tinhead to me," he called back.

"Damn, Chief Hal has good hearing," Chase said from across the stack of pallets. "Guy can hear a mouse across the bay."

<Yes, I can.> Chief Hal spoke into their minds over the Link. *<Now get that damn ship loaded. You have ten minutes. After that you eat into their departure window, which means they might get fined, and if they get fined, they sue me, and if they sue me, I take it out of your pay; so **move**!>*

Rika let out a long, silent breath, resisting the urge to walk over to Chief Hal and slap him clear across the bay.

<Not worth it,> Chase said privately, apparently reading her expression all too easily.

<But, damn, it would be satisfying,> Rika said with a mental sigh.

<No argument there.>

Rika stepped up to the cargo stack and slid the rods protruding from her forearms into the slots on the top of the crate, hefting its three hundred kilos with ease.

She noted that the crate was stamped with a Nietzschean logo, indicating that it was confiscated material, seized as the spoils of war.

The war her people had lost.

'My people'.

Rika no longer considered the Genevians 'her people' any more than she did their Nietzschean conquerors. The Genevians had taken her body from her, thrown her into desperate battle after desperate battle, and made her kill thousands of enemy troops.

All for an unwinnable war, where the high command squandered the lives of the mechs—and the soldiers fighting alongside them—until there was nothing left.

When the Genevians finally surrendered, the peace turned out to be no better than the fighting.

That the Nietzscheans despised the Genevians was no secret; their actions during the war did not belie their hatred in any way. Rika had believed that the only thing they hated more than Genevians were their mechanized warriors. As one such warrior, Rika had expected to be executed when the change of masters had occurred.

Some of the mechs *had* been killed, but only the ones who had gone insane with rage and hatred and could never be integrated into any society again.

The rest—Rika included—had spent some time in internment camps, but eventually had their compliance chips and military hardware removed, and were set free.

'Free'.

Whatever freedom was, Rika was certain it was not present where she had ended up.

What Rika had learned in the five years since the end of the war was that, though the Nietzscheans hated the Genevian mechs because of the destruction they wreaked during the war, they respected them as warriors for rising above their circumstances. That respect had translated into their release back into society.

However, the Genevians felt great shame for what they had done to their own citizens. Unfortunately, that shame did not include any form of respect, acceptance, or financial aid to help rebuild the mechanized warriors' organic bodies.

Those conditions made for scarce work. Rika had moved from one manual labor job to another, until she finally ended up at Dekar station on the outskirts of the Parsons System.

It was surreal to be here, slinging cargo in a system where she had fought so many battles—many of them victorious.

But every hard-won ground battle was balanced by a loss in space; Rika still remembered boarding one of the last ships that had evacuated the Parsons System, when the Genevian fleet retreated and abandoned it altogether.

An abandonment that had not hurt Dekar Station in any way.

Though the Genevians had lost the fight in the Parsons System, Dekar had prospered. The station was on the fringes of the system, and when the Nietzscheans had attacked seven years ago—just over two years before the end of the war—Dekar had surrendered without a fight.

There was no profit in fighting against a superior enemy—especially when your own space force ran from almost any conflict—and the owners of the station were far more interested in profiting from war than actually fighting a war.

Fleecing refugees had also become a substantial business on Dekar as the years passed.

It sickened Rika to be here in their company. But where the denizens of Dekar were cowardly, they were also pragmatic. It hadn't taken long for Bay Chief Hal to realize that, with her mechanized body, Rika was stronger than ten fully organic humans and far more versatile than a bot.

The icing on the cake was that, unlike with a bot, he didn't have to pay for repairs when her robotic components suffered damage. *She* was responsible for that.

Which was the reason Rika was so deep in debt.

Well, part of the reason.

Rika had spent most of her initial earnings on getting her face reconstructed after what the Genevians had done to it. It was no small expense, but well worth it.

From the neck down she was still covered in her matte-grey skin—no longer sheathed in armor—but her head looked as it had before that fateful night when she'd been sentenced and ended up in the Genevian military's human chop shop.

She allowed her thoughts to continue to wander, and it helped pass the time as she and Chase loaded the freighter. He worked the loader, pulling the crates off the bay's grav conveyers, and Rika carried them into the ship's main cargo bay, stacking them according to the Supercargo's directions.

Even with her slow start, Rika finished the job just under the ten-minute deadline set by Bay Chief Hal. Without a word of thanks, he assigned her three more ships to load; when that work was complete, another two.

The workload wasn't unexpected; they didn't call Bay 1217 'Hal's Hell' for nothing. He ran it with a ruthless efficiency, and many discerning captains requested berths in Bay 1217, keeping it busy at all hours—much to the dismay of his dockworkers.

Chase wrapped up his shift seven hours later and passed Rika a message as he left, <*Gonna be at Krueger's tonight. Stop by when Hal finally cuts you loose.*>

<*Thanks,*> she replied. <*Maybe I'll do that.*>

<*Maybe I'll see you, then.*>

They both knew she wouldn't show up.

Chase had always been kind to her, but he had grown even friendlier since her facial reconstruction surgery, asking her to join him for drinks nearly every night.

Rika didn't fault him for not finding her attractive when her head was just a faceless orb with two eyes and not even a nose; but the fact that he had only asked her out after her surgery hurt more than she cared to admit.

"Pining after a real boy?" Hal's voice sounded nearby, and Rika looked back, staring down at him from her 2.3-meter height—towering over him.

"Haven't seen one," Rika replied. "Just talking assholes around here."

Hal snorted. "Have it your way, Rika. Another ship just came in. Needs to be cleared out and loaded back up in two hours. You just bought yourself that job."

Rika bit her tongue and nodded as she walked to the ship that Hal pointed at, examining the work order he passed her over the Link.

Getting it done in two hours by herself was going to take a miracle.

A DANCE WITH DENNY

STELLAR DATE: 07.02.8948 (Adjusted Years)
LOCATION: Merchant Docking Ring, Dekar Station
REGION: Outer Rim of Parsons System, Nietzschean Empire

Rika walked slowly through the warrens of Deck 741, one hundred levels down from Hal's Hell, and just three away from her quarters. The wide corridor was crowded with other workers heading home or up to the docks to begin their shifts. Refugees, long-since turned to beggars, huddled along the bulkheads; the poor and unfortunate who had fled the fall of the Parsons System, only to make it to Dekar and no further.

She felt pity for them, but not so much that she could afford to share any of her spare credits—were she to have such a thing. The war had taken everything from her, too. These beggars may think they lived in a hellish afterlife, but Rika knew that even their blighted existence was far more desirable than hers.

An indicator flashed on her visual overlay reminding Rika that her internal batteries were down to ten percent. Back when they were new, the batteries could hold a charge for far longer, under a lot more strain—but now they were showing their age. Just a few hours of overtime, and she was running on her last joules.

Maybe it would go better if I didn't antagonize Hal so much, Rika thought, shaking her head with a rueful smile on her lips.

A dozen meters down the corridor stood her favorite food stall—well, her favorite stall that served any food she could afford. Jessie, the owner, would also let her plug in for a quick charge while she ate.

As Rika approached the stall, she saw a few members of Pinky's gang further down the wide passageway, alternately mocking and extorting refugees and passersby.

Rika did her best to ignore them, hoping they wouldn't spot her. No small number of local gang leaders were constantly pressuring her to join their ranks. They promised parts and power, but little respect.

"Long shift," Jessie commented as Rika approached and leaned an elbow on the counter.

Rika smiled at the pink-haired proprietor. The fact that Jessie never mentioned Rika's mechanized body, and always looked her in the eyes—even before her surgery—was the other reason why Rika frequented her stand.

"You too," Rika replied. "You were here when I left for my shift this morning."

Jessie shrugged. "Yeah, Annie ditched me again today; said that she had some sort of ache or pain. I kinda don't mind, though. She's a shit worker, and if I don't have to pay her ass, it's a win for me."

"Yeah, she can't flip a burger for the life of her," Rika replied. "And now that I can eat burgers again, I hate having to settle for what she can produce."

"Never fear, Rika—your favorite mystery meat delight is coming right up. Maybe someday, both you and I can get off this shit station, and I'll cook you up a real burger."

"I'd like that very much," Rika said as she spooled out her charge cable and handed it to Jessie, who plugged it in behind the stand's counter.

Rika felt a sense of relief as her charge meter showed the power trickling back in. Running out of power in the warrens was one of her worst fears. She harbored no illusions about what would become of her should that happen down here.

With power, she was one of the most formidable people on the station. Without it, she was scrap metal waiting to be picked clean.

A memory of being racked for transport came back to her; how the military removed her limbs and left her helpless, little more than a piece of equipment stored on a shelf.

She would never let that happen to her again.

If there was one thing she was thankful to the Nietzscheans for, it was the removal of her compliance chip. Her future was grim, but at least she was in control of herself again.

Jessie poured Rika a cup of black coffee, and she inhaled the aroma, savoring the eight ounces of joy that was waiting for her.

"I still don't know how you get coffee here," Rika said after she took her first sip.

"Everything comes through Dekar," Jessie shrugged. "Just have to know the right people."

"Those have to be some people," Rika chuckled. "Even Hal bitches that he can hardly get coffee."

"Well, I wasn't always running a food stand down in the warrens," Jessie replied with a sardonic laugh.

"You've mentioned that before," Rika said. "What was it that you used to do?"

Jessie gave Rika a sad smile as she slid a plate holding a burger and fries onto the counter. "Maybe I'll tell you sometime, Rika. Not today, but sometime."

Rika picked up the burger and took a bite, enjoying the savory flavor as it hit her tongue.

"Mmmm…tastes better every day," Rika said.

"You're crazy," Jessie laughed. "But I'll take the compliment."

Rika swallowed her bite and picked up a fry. "Best oatmeal fries this side of Parsons, too," she said before popping it into her mouth.

As she ate, a loud bang sounded down the corridor, and she turned her head to see one of Pinky's gang members holding a gun on a refugee. No one appeared to be harmed, so

Rika surmised that the first shot must have been fired as a warning.

"Fuckers," Jessie swore. "Can't rise to your feet around here without someone trying to push you back down."

"They bother you at all lately?" Rika asked.

Jessie smiled broadly and shook her head. "Nope, not since you caved Begee's face in last month. They give me hella dirty looks, but everyone knows that if they mess with me, they're gonna get a visit from you.

"Good," Rika said around a mouthful of burger.

"Not that I need it," Jessie said with worried eyes. "I have enough connections that Pinky may mess with me, but she's not going to do anything too stupid. You, on the other hand…your bleeding heart shows too often. One of these days, someone's going to take advantage of that and cut it out."

Rika sighed. She did her best not to give a damn, but it didn't always work. Jessie was right, though. One of these days, it was going to bite her in the ass.

"I'll have one of your fine cups of coffee, Jessie," a voice said to Rika's right, and she turned to see the sneering face of Denny, one of Pinky's lieutenants.

"Oh, hey, Rika. Thought you were just some dirty parts someone had dumped in front of Jessie's stall…well, I guess I wasn't really that wrong."

"Fuck off, Denny," Rika growled.

"Rika! I'm here to spend my hard-earned credit on some of Jessie's fine brew. Best on the station, if you didn't know."

Jessie gave Rika an imploring look, and then gave Denny a long-suffering one. "Payment up front, and you can have all the coffee you want," Jessie bargained.

Denny's face adopted a wounded expression and he touched a hand to his chest. "Jessie! Are you calling me unscrupulous? You cut me deep, cut me to the quick!"

"Yeah, I am," Jessie said. "Credit."

Denny muttered something incomprehensible as he fished in his pocket for a hard chit. He finally pulled one out and slapped it on the counter.

"Man of my word," he said. "I'll take a large."

Jessie turned to grab a cup, and Denny stared longingly at her ass.

"See that, Rika? Jessie's built all nice and proper. Not like your hard, carbon-fiber rear end. I bet she gives a good fuck, too—though I suppose you'd be good for something, now that you have lips again."

Rika took a bite of her burger and did her best to ignore Denny. She knew he was just trying to egg her on; he had checked her out on more than one occasion. Though there were augmented bones and muscles underneath her matte-grey skin, her ass didn't look that far off from its original appearance. It wasn't covered in skin, but that wasn't so unusual.

"No comment, Rika?" Denny smirked as Jessie wordlessly handed the gang member his coffee with one hand, and took the credit chit with her other.

"You hear something, Jessie?" Rika asked with a wink.

"Yeah, some sort of dripping," Jessie replied. "Like a leaky faucet, or something."

"A snot faucet, maybe," Rika said with a laugh.

"Watch yourself," Denny cautioned, his voice dropping, and even managing to sound a bit menacing. "Pinky wants to play a long game with you; get you over to her side through slow persuasion. Me? I don't see the appeal so much. Maybe I'll just take you out of play right now."

Rika looked down at Denny, and slowly raised the remainder of her burger to her mouth, popping it in and chewing slowly.

"Maybe you should try," she said around a mouthful of food. "Then I can punch your mouth off the shit lump you call a face, and no one will have to listen to you anymore."

As she spoke, a small voice was wailing in her mind, reminding her that she only had fifteen percent charge, and that a fight in the warrens was not what she needed right now; but another part of her just wanted to do the universe a favor, and wipe the stain that was Denny from existence.

"Fuck you, Rika!" Denny shouted as he took a step back and pointed a ballistic pistol at her. "I'm sick of your superior attitude. You're shit, just like the rest of us, and you can still bleed and die."

While Denny pontificated, Rika reached down and unplugged the charge cord from her side, then took a step away from Jessie's stand.

Denny kept the weapon trained on her head, while Rika kept one eye on his trigger finger and the other on his feet as he twisted to track her.

After a minute, Denny seemed to reach a decision. His brow furrowed an instant before he pulled the trigger. It was all the tell Rika needed—she jerked to the side, and the projectile flew through the air where her head had been.

Her arm shot out, and her steel fist slammed down on Denny's right wrist, shattering the bones within.

The gangster screamed and dropped his gun, but his look was not one of defeat; more like pained joy.

Rika turned to see seven more members of Pinky's gang approaching—each one of them armed, and all appearing to be spoiling for a fight.

"Gonna get it now, bitch," Denny hissed as he dove to the side of the corridor.

Rika dropped as well, reaching for Denny's discarded pistol as a hail of bullets and pulse rifle blasts flew overhead.

She scampered behind a pillar and double-checked her body's readout.

She had been hit in the side and the leg by three ballistic projectiles, but none had done any damage. The low caliber weapons the gang employed wouldn't be able to penetrate the artificial skin covering her body. But without the plating on her cyborg limbs—taken by the Nietzscheans at the end of the war—a lucky shot could wreck a knee or an elbow joint.

"You sure you want to do this?" she called. "It's gonna get messy."

"Fucking kill her!" Denny shouted before anyone had a chance to respond—not that Rika expected any of the gang members to argue for clemency.

Rika knew that the pillar would only protect her for another minute before the attackers surrounded her. The corridor offered little cover, which meant that her best defense was a strong offense. One that involved taking a better weapon than the pistol she now held.

She peered around the pillar and quickly scanned the corridor with her eyes, wishing that she had just *one* of the drones she used to carry back in the war.

Three goons on the right, which meant the other four were on the left. She jerked her head back as a round struck the pillar, just three centimeters from her eye.

She responded by reaching her arm around the pillar and firing back at the approaching attackers, her visual overlay providing targets based on the gang members' most recent positions.

Two separate screams let her know that her predictive algorithms were working just as well as ever. She estimated that her enemies were within two meters on the left side. Rika took a steadying breath, dropped to a crouch, and then leapt out around the left side of the pillar, kicking at the legs of the closest attacker while firing into the torso of another.

The pistol got off two shots before it jammed, and Rika threw it aside as several shots struck her chest. She saw that the shooter was one of the gangsters on the right side of the pillar.

She leapt to her feet, grabbed the man she had shot, and flung his body at two of the attackers, then delivered a roundhouse kick to another guy, shattering his ribs and probably his spine with her three-clawed foot.

A spray of bullets hit the bulkhead nearby, and Rika threw herself at the shooter, breaking the woman's neck with a well-aimed blow.

The rest of the fight passed in a blur, and less than a minute later, Denny's accomplices were either dead or drawing their final breaths.

Rika cast her eyes about, searching for Denny—the piece of shit who had started this, who had brought out the killer in her.

As she looked for him, Rika realized that the corridor was nearly empty. The refugees and other passersby had cleared out to avoid getting caught in the crossfire.

A wave of sorrow hit her with the realization that her months of careful control—when she had thought that she was improving, becoming human again—had really just been a thin veneer over the vicious machine that still lay underneath.

The sound of shuffling feet reached her ears, and she turned to see Denny sliding out from behind a pillar several meters away, still cradling his shattered wrist. His wide eyes stared at her with fear, and she saw tear streaks down his dirty cheeks.

"Get out of here," Rika said wearily. "Tell Pinky I don't want to see her dicks down here anymore."

Denny nodded manically and then turned and ran.

Rika let out a long breath and took a step; that's when she realized that the fight had not been entirely one-sided. An actuator in her left knee had been hit by a bullet at some point, and she had limited motion in the limb.

She would have to pick up a new one from a nearby mod-shop. They wouldn't have one with the right specs for her, but she should be able to retrofit one of their civilian models.

Rika hobbled back to Jessie's booth and leaned heavily on the counter.

"I think I'll need another coffee," she said.

No response came, and she realized that Jessie was nowhere to be seen. The stall was small, so Rika leaned over the counter and peered into the corners around the stove, table, and chill-unit.

Her breath caught, and a choked gasp escaped her throat when she finally caught sight of Jessie.

The stall owner had hidden underneath the front counter, and a stray shot had passed through the thin walls of her stall. The wound on her forehead was small, but the back of Jessie's skull was a tangled mass of blood, pink hair, and grey matter.

Rika turned aside and threw up; spewing out her burger and coffee, followed by whatever else was left from her lunch earlier in the day.

She tried to hold back the tears, but it was impossible. She collapsed to the ground, sobbing uncontrollably.

Which is where the station security found her eleven long minutes later.

P-COG

STELLAR DATE: 07.09.8948 (Adjusted Years)
LOCATION: Combat Information Center, MSS *Foe Hammer*
REGION: Interstellar Space, near the Praesepe Cluster

David eased back into his seat in the *Foe Hammer's* CIC and set his coffee pouch in the pocket on the side of his chair. If there was one thing that the Marauders had over the military, it was that the Old Man let people drink coffee at their posts.

Not that coffee was the *only* thing better than the Genevian Armed Forces—but it certainly ranked high on the list, as far as David was concerned.

He pulled up the logs he was reviewing and gave them a visual scan, looking for patterns that may not be apparent to others. He spotted a few interesting alignments in timing, data size, and destinations.

Probably nothing nefarious, but still worth checking, he thought before pushing them into one of his analysis matrices.

As a P-Cog, or Pattern Recognition Specialist, David's job was to look for things others missed. Even though a dozen other humans and AIs had been over these logs, there was always a gem nestled in them for a P-Cog to pick up.

It was his special gift from the Genevian Armed Forces during the war with the Nietzscheans. Some draftees—conscripts, if he was being honest—got the real shit mods, like the mechs; especially the K1 models. But other poor saps, like himself, got their heads jammed full of upgrades that served other purposes.

David's upgrades were dedicated to spotting patterns and ferreting out connections between seemingly unrelated things.

Massive NSAI grids usually performed tasks like that, but some wiz in the GAF's R&D division decided to capitalize on the one thing that humans had in spades over NSAI: intuition.

David had known all his life that he had good intuition. He could talk his way out of almost anything, and spot good and bad deals a mile away. It had made him a great contract negotiator before the war, and his services were always in high demand.

When he was drafted, the aptitude tests had picked up on his abilities, and he was shipped off to a lab filled with a lot of unfriendly-looking folks in gleaming white coats.

That was when the poking and prodding inside his brain had begun. Thankfully he remembered little of it; though there had been lucid moments. Moments punctuated by fear, terror, and agony.

In the end, he had come out packing a lot of extra hardware between his ears. Enough that his skull needed passive cooling—which accounted for his lack of hair and the addition of cooling fins on his head.

The adaptation had earned him the nickname 'Sharkie' in the military—even though he'd never seen a shark with seven fins.

After the war, David had attempted to return to his prior work, but because of the mech-conscript program, most Genevians assumed that any GAF-modded person was a criminal conscript, not a draftee.

Few people would hire him, and those who did wanted to use him to hide criminal activity—not seek out wrongdoing.

That was when a friend from his division had told him about the Marauders, and how the group was almost entirely filled with Genevian Armed Forces vets who were trying to find a place after the fall of Genevia.

David had enlisted as soon as he could travel to a recruitment center, and look where he was now: working in the CIC of the Old Man's flagship.

A yawn escaped his lips, and David picked up his coffee pouch and took a long draw of the bitter drink. At least here in the Marauders when he found something wrong, he could do something about it. Most often, the wrongdoers were unsavory types that would see the business end of a Marauder rifle before long.

Until this operation—the goal of which was the overthrow of the Theban leadership, and facilitate the forcible annexation of Thebes by Septhia.

As far as David could tell, both the Septhians and Thebans were good people. Sure, they had their issues; but on the whole, their governments represented the people, elections were as fair as any, and the populace was content and prosperous.

He understood that the Septhians were worried about Nietzschean expansion—everyone spinward of the Pleiades was. It seemed like nowhere was safe from the specter of war anymore. All of the major empires and federations in the Orion Arm were gobbling up their smaller neighbors at an alarming rate.

Though the Praesepe Cluster was small—less than one hundred light years in diameter—it contained well over a thousand stars; the nations within its bounds were tightly-knit, possessing great strength in numbers.

That is what made David wonder about the Septhian desire to attack Thebes. Septhia was a much larger alliance, with over fifty member systems compared to the Thebans' five; but there was no reason he could see why the alliances couldn't work out mutually beneficial treaties.

Over the years, the Septhians had made frequent overtures to the Thebans, offering them a place in the alliance—but the Thebans had declined each time. David could see why. Thebes was on the edge of the cluster, facilitating trade with systems deeper within Praesepe.

They also controlled one of the few areas in the cluster with less dark matter, making Thebes a gateway into the star cluster.

David pulled up a map of the cluster on his console, overlaying the stars with the latest dark matter dispersion maps. Dark matter was the Praesepe Cluster's greatest strength, and its most vexing problem.

Outside of star clusters and stellar nurseries, dark matter was only found tightly packed around stars. But in clusters like Praesepe, it was everywhere—making FTL all but impossible.

Without entering the cluster through a region of space like the one Thebes controlled, it could take decades, even up to a century, to travel to the cluster's inner reaches.

While there were two other alliances in the cluster that controlled regions of space with sparse dark matter, they were on the far side. Thebes controlled the clearest dark matter region near the Nietzschean border—a border that was only thirty light years away after the Niets' conquest of Genevia.

David ran a hand across his head, tracing the grooves between the cooling fins—a pensive habit he had picked up after getting the mods, and constantly worrying that his brain was somehow going to hemorrhage from all the alterations.

He was not the first person to see this obvious connection. If the Nietzscheans were planning to annex the Praesepe Cluster—an act that would expand their empire tremendously—then Thebes was the obvious place to start.

But rather than attack, a far better plan for the Septhians would be to convince the Thebans of this possibility, and aid in bolstering their defenses.

Scuttlebutt amongst the Marauders maintained that the Thebans must have received such an overture, and viewed it as the first step in a slow takeover after all the other diplomatic attempts had been rebuffed.

David could see that possibility, but all his intel on the Theban President, a woman named Ariana who was just now entering her seventh term, showed her to be a competent and reasonable person.

Would the Septhians really resort to toppling the Theban government just to secure the rimward edge of the Praesepe Cluster against the Nietzscheans? They must have made a very convincing argument to the Old Man for him to engage in this sort of subversive action—an action that had Marauder teams operating as assassins within Thebes.

One thing was for certain: if the Nietzscheans got wind of this before the Septhians had secured Thebes, the Niets would undoubtedly strike, and strike hard.

Which was one of the many things David was keeping a keen eye out for. There could be no leaks from the Marauders that the operation was underway.

Thus far, there had been no leaks that he could see. Not that David was surprised; if there was one thing the Marauders had in common, it was a deep hatred of the Nietzscheans.

But something was tickling in the back of David's mind. There was a thread that he couldn't quite see, waiting to be found and pulled. Something didn't feel right about the arrangement with the Septhians, with the whole plan in general.

There was a piece missing, or out of place, or both.

David brought up a new set of logs. The details and content of the Old Man's arrangement with the Septhians was not accessible to him, but the logs of the communications themselves were.

He spread out a holographic matrix and began filtering the logs into the framework, looking for patterns that only a P-Cog would spot, searching for that clue that would explain to him what was really going on.

KRUEGER'S
STELLAR DATE: 07.02.8948 (Adjusted Years)
LOCATION: Rika's Quarters, Dekar Station
REGION: Outer Rim of Parsons System, Nietzschean Empire

Rika lay on her hard bed, trying not to think about the last few weeks. She had seen a lot of death over the years—a lot of it caused by her. She had watched teammates die in her arms, and witnessed the enemy cradle their dead comrades.

Somehow Jessie's death was worse.

Jessie was just a woman trying to make the best of a shitty situation in a shitty world.

She had died because of Rika. Because Rika had let Denny—one of the most pathetic examples of humanity ever to breathe air—get the better of her.

Rika felt as though darkness was pressing at the edges of her vision, and she knew she was slipping into a deep depression.

While the Nietzscheans had pulled her compliance chip, they had left the other mental augmentations the GAF had inserted into her head.

Those augmentations had dosed her with drugs, and given all of the counseling that a non-sentient AI could provide; but it still wasn't enough. Rika knew that she needed human companionship to help pull her out—but that was just the sort of thing that got her in this mess.

She remembered what Silva—scout team Hammerfall's leader, and her dear friend—had told her when the war had ended: *"Rika, things are going to be hard for us, maybe harder than the war. There's no place for us out there, back with…people. But we have to try. If we shun humans…that's when we stop being human."*

Rika and Silva had been separated by the Nietzscheans when the Genevian military had surrendered. Rika had searched long for her former team leader, but it was as though the woman had disappeared.

Rika feared that the Nietzscheans had found Silva unfit for a return to normal society, and had killed her.

She sincerely hoped that had not occurred. Silva had always struck Rika as the most well adjusted member of Hammerfall. If the Nietzscheans had found Silva unfit for reintegration, Rika couldn't imagine how they'd given her a pass.

"Enough!" Rika said aloud, and sat up, grabbing a cloth to rub her eyes. The action sent a new wave of sadness through her.

It was the little things she missed the most. No one ever thought about how a mech, with cold steel hands—which Rika's angular steel appendages barely counted as—couldn't even *rub their own fucking eyes!*

Not unless they wanted to accidentally gouge them out.

Maybe getting my face back was a mistake, Rika thought; not for the first time, either. The debt she was under was crushing, and the repairs from the fight with Denny and his thugs a few weeks back had pushed her under even further.

Rika had been forced to reach out to Pierce, a loan shark—no, a loan megalodon—to get the money to repair herself so that she could get to work at the docks, and slowly wear herself out for the next pending repair.

Pierce had demanded a consolidation, saying that there was no point in her being last in line to pick Rika's sorry ass clean when she reneged on her obligations.

She had paid off all Rika's other debtors, which had an upside: none of the small fish were going to ask for a little something extra when Pierce came around to settle up.

Of course, the downside was that Pierce pretty much owned Rika now. For all intents and purposes, Rika worked for her.

As if her existence couldn't be any shittier.

"No!" Rika shouted. She wasn't going to fall into this trap and cry herself to sleep *again*. A walk around the station—the parts of the station worth walking around—was just what she needed.

She looked at her jacket, torn from where her arm had caught on it earlier that day, and decided not to bother donning it. It had been her last piece of clothing; the loss of which contributed to her current spate of melancholy self-loathing.

Rika rose and walked the two meters from her bed to the san unit, and picked up her brush, running it through her hair, and then wiping her face clean. She reset her makeup—another expenditure she had wasted money on after getting her face back—to be a touch darker than she wore at the docks.

Satisfied with her appearance from the neck up, she examined her body, ensuring that no bits of mattress or dirt were stuck in it.

Rika allowed a small smile to grace her lips. It wasn't all bad, if one ignored the fact that her arms and legs were hard steel, and glossed over the armor mount points on her hips, shoulders, and elsewhere; the organic portions of her body were rather attractive, the matte grey 'skin' the military had given her was smooth and perfect, bulging slightly where her augmented muscles rippled beneath.

"OK, Rika. Let's go have a nice walk, look at the stars, and take our mind off what a shitbucket our life is."

She barked a laugh. *Talking aloud in the third person is probably not a good sign.*

Rika left her small room and walked through the narrow passageways toward one of the larger thoroughfares with walkways along the side, and room for groundcars in the center.

When she reached the broad corridor, the station was alive with light and life as people went about their business. It had reached the end of the second shift, and everyone was enjoying as much revelry as possible before the next day's drudgery was upon them.

Rika passed a couple wrapped in a passionate embrace. Their lips were locked together, bodies ignoring the world around them, and Rika's thoughts flashed to Chase; he was probably still at Krueger's, where he had invited her once again.

A maglev train screamed by, hanging from the overhead, far above the street traffic flowing around Rika, and she decided it was time. She had enough credit for one drink, and having that in the company of friends was just what she needed.

She strode down the walkway, threading her way between the other pedestrians. Most made way for her—bumping into a mech was not usually an enjoyable experience—but she had to skirt around some groups who gave her steely looks and refused to move.

Before long, Rika reached a maglev station and boarded the train that would take her to the outer docking ring where Krueger's was located. It was close to Hal's Hell, but not too close—which suited her just fine.

She doubted sleep would come to her tonight. Maybe after having a drink with Chase, she could start her shift early and put in some extra hours to catch up on her already-late payments to Pierce.

The maglev station where she disembarked was only one hundred meters from Krueger's, and as she stepped out onto the docking ring, Rika could hear the boisterous revelry spilling out of the establishment.

Krueger's was frequented by an equal number of merchant crews and locals, and it was always full of happy, and some not-so-happy, drunks. Tables surrounded the bar's main entrance, with umbrellas over each—a silly affectation within the station, but it did serve to add a more welcoming feel.

Rika looked for Chase around the tables outside, her augmented vision scanning the patrons, and highlighting those who gave off excess heat or heavy EM fields as heavily-modded. Most had a yellow glow surrounding them, but a few were outlined in red, and Rika subconsciously cataloged their threat levels and potential responses.

Chase wasn't outside, so Rika strode past the tables toward the entrance, catching a few catcalls.

It was nothing new. Though her nethers were still sealed under the more durable skin the military had given her—and unseen by even *her* in years—it didn't change the fact that, without the jacket she'd left back in her quarters, she was essentially naked.

"Look at that!" a man called out from a nearby table. "Now that's what I call a cargo loader!"

Rika winced, but kept walking.

Her enhanced hearing picked out the man's voice as he turned to his friends. "Saw her working in Hal's Hell earlier today. Imagine having her on board? Work all day, and still have enough charge for play!"

The taste of blood entered her mouth, and Rika realized she was biting her cheek. Maybe her torn jacket would have been a good idea—it didn't typically affect the number of comments she heard, but it did cleanse the content a little.

They'd say stuff like that to anyone. It's not because you're a mech, she thought to herself. *Don't let it get to you, Rika.*

Once inside the bar, the crush of bodies shielded her from most eyes, and she relaxed in the anonymity. She scanned the crowd and saw Chase down at the end of the bar with two of his friends—a man named Terry, and Terry's sometimes-girlfriend, Trina.

As Rika approached, Chase caught sight of her and his face lit up with a brilliant smile—the sight of which washed away the filth she felt from the man's comments outside the bar.

Chase rose from his stool and held out a hand to welcome her. "Rika! I was starting to think that you were allergic to something in here! Really glad you could make it."

Terry gave her a kind smile, but Trina's eyes narrowed and her lips formed something closer to a smirk than a smile.

"Great to see you again," Terry said. "Chase is always talking about you, you know—all good things, of course."

Rika saw Chase flush, and noted that his pulse had quickened.

"Well, she *is* amazing," Chase said with a genuine smile, apparently going for broke. "I wouldn't be able to survive Hal's Hell without her around. Rika's like my guardian angel."

It was Rika's turn to flush. Chase's acceptance of her was one thing, but she didn't think anyone had ever called her an angel.

"Thanks, Chase. I wouldn't have made it through my first day in there without you," she said with a small smile.

"What do you drink?" Chase asked.

"Or do you drink at all?" Trina asked with a smirk. "Other than oil, of course."

Terry elbowed Trina, and Rika ignored the woman, determined not to lose the little high that Chase's statements had given her.

"I've got enough credit for an amber ale, if they have any," she replied.

"Rika, seriously, your money is no good here," Chase said as he leaned over the bar and shouted for something called a Rikers Amber. "You'll like it," he said with a smile.

"Thanks, Chase. I really appreciate that."

"Nonsense, Rika. I've been saving some credit to buy you a drink for months. These chits have been so sad, trapped in the depths of my accounts, I have to set them free."

Rika laughed, the sound almost foreign to her ears.

"You don't do that enough," Chase echoed her thoughts. "Maybe if you start coming out with me, I'll get to hear it more. It's certainly worth the price of a few beers."

Rika felt her flush deepen, and a strange feeling crept into her heart. Just a sliver, but she knew what it was: happiness.

Chase bought her more drinks that night, and though her enhanced metabolism kept her from becoming drunk, she enjoyed the buzz. Terry was pleasant company as well, and even Trina kept her snarky comments to a minimum.

As the time slipped well into the third shift, Terry and Trina left, and Chase began to look tired.

"I can't tell you how great it's been having you here tonight, Rika," Chase said, his words slightly slurred. "Being with you is like a dream come true."

"Chase," Rika said with a smile. Though her heart soared to hear his words, she demurred, "I'm nobody's dream."

"Are you kidding?" Chase asked, as his eyes slid down her body and up again—something that they had done a few times during the evening. It wasn't leering; it was appreciation—something she was all too eager for him to feel.

"Rika, you're a goddess. You're the epitome of perfection. And I'm not just talking about your smoking hot bod…" he flushed at that, and Rika was glad that the alcohol had elicited that unfiltered comment from him.

Rika smiled. "Do go on."

"Uh, yeah, what I mean is that there's so much strength in you. You got dealt one of the shittiest hands ever—and I don't even know the half of it—but you're so *strong* in there." As he spoke, Chase touched a finger to her head. Then he lowered his hand to rest above her breasts.

"And here."

Rika leaned forward and closed her eyes, silently begging whatever stars may still care about her to show Chase what to do.

Either they were listening, or Chase didn't need any prodding; his lips met hers, and he leaned forward, wrapping his arms around her. She slowly embraced him, taking care to keep any pointy or sharp edges facing outward.

They moved into a back corner of the bar, Chase pushing Rika against the wall as they continued to press against one another. Chase explored her body, commenting with a laugh that her armor mount points made for useful handles.

Rika wished that she had managed to save enough money to reconstruct her nethers. If she had been able to have sex, she would have taken Chase right then and there in the back of the bar.

Though that was not possible, it didn't seem to diminish Chase's hunger for her, and they pleasured one another as much as they could. Eventually Rika felt a tap on her shoulder, and she turned to see one of the bar's staff.

"We're closing up now," the woman said, her smile not unkind. "You two lovebirds are going to have to take that somewhere else."

"Ah, shit," Chase sighed. "I was hoping we were stuck in some sort of temporal disturbance, and this could last forever."

"Well," Rika said as she gently ran a steel finger down Chase's chest. "There's always tomorrow night."

"C'mon, guys, I gotta clean up," the woman said.

"OK, OK," Chase said as Rika stood and helped him to his feet. "Damn, girl, you're not even tipsy."

"Takes a bit more than a dozen beers to set me back," Rika said with a giggle. *A giggle!*

She helped Chase walk out of the bar and onto the docking ring. They both took a long breath, soaking in the myriad scents of Dekar's ring, and Rika smiled.

Maybe things weren't so bad after all.

Chase took her hand—growing steadier as they walked—and led her toward the maglev station.

"Why don't you come back to my place?" he asked as they reached the platform.

"Oh, stars, Chase," Rika whispered. "I can't think of a damn thing I'd rather do right now. But your shift starts in six hours, and I need to put in some extra time to get caught up with Pierce."

"Fucking work. I'd rather work at fucking," Chase grinned.

Rika's face fell; the sorrow she thought was gone crept up on her once more.

Chase stepped forward, a look of concern on his face. "Oh, shit, sorry, Rika. I know you can't, and I'm perfectly OK with that. I'm into *you*. All of you, the total package." He stroked her cheek. "Don't you worry about that at all."

They kissed again.

"I'll see you in a few hours," Chase said, and boarded the next maglev car as it pulled up. She watched him take a seat, still a bit wobbly, and then the train whisked him away.

A smile tugged at Rika's lips, and she let it spread across her face. *Have I found love? Is just the alcohol, or does Chase really feel so strongly about me?*

Though he didn't start asking her to Krueger's till she had a face, he had always been nice to her. But she had thought maybe he just had a fetish for mech girls.

She chuckled. Maybe he did, but his affection for her seemed genuine; if he got turned on by her machine parts, maybe that was just fine. They weren't going anywhere soon, anyway.

A thought occurred to her about Chase's invitations to the bar. *Maybe he didn't invite me before I had a face because I wasn't able to drink! Was his change in behavior more to do with compassion than an appreciation that was only skin-deep?*

How did I stumble across someone so amazing in a place like Dekar?

Rika turned and walked back onto the docking ring's main sweep, whistling a tune—so happy that even the thought of sixteen hours in Hal's Hell couldn't put a dent in her joy.

"Rika!" a voice called out from behind her, and she turned to see a dozen men and women approaching. The joy that had filled her so fully evaporated in an instant, replaced by dread.

These were Pierce's enforcers.

"Pierce wants to see you," one of the men said. "You're late, and it's time to pay up."

"What? No!" Rika cried out, taking a step back. "I'm just a week late, and I get paid after my shift today! I'll be square!"

"Too late," one of the women said with a cruel grimace. "Come quietly. You may be tough, but we're ready for you. Won't be like when you fought Denny and his asswipes."

Rika could see that. Every member of the group was armored and held serious weapons—not to mention net-casters.

She lowered her head and nodded. "OK, lead the way."

"Good call," The first man said, and the group formed a box around her, marching her back to the maglev station.

They took a train halfway around the docking ring and then led Rika through a maze of corridors until they came to a manufacturing district.

Rika was led into a warehouse, past stacks of crates, to a small office along one wall. Standing in the entrance to the office was Pierce.

"Rika, Rika, Rika; what am I to do with you?" Pierce asked, her ruby-red lips pressed into a thin, disapproving line.

"Pierce!" Rika said. "I tried to tell your people I'm getting paid today. I was going to work a double to get enough money. You'll get it today, I promise!"

"Oh, don't worry," Pierce said with a chuckle. "I know I will. Hal will turn over what pay is owed you, but your time slinging cargo is over. You see, you misread our contract."

Rika frowned. The contract had been simple—just one screen. It had outlined the amount of debt, the transference from other lenders, and the payment schedule. What could she have missed?

"I can see that you're confused," Pierce chuckled. "I'll admit I did it deliberately. You see, there was a clause in there—a particular form of legalese used here on Dekar—that means if you fall more than a week behind…well…I own you."

Pierce finished the statement with a broad smile and spread her arms wide.

Rika felt like she'd been hit by a tank. "Own?" she asked.

"Oh, yes, 'own'. I gotta say, I love the Nietzscheans. They don't endorse slavery, but they figure if you're dumb enough to get made a slave, then that's all you're good for," Pierce replied, and let out another throaty laugh before continuing. "Now, I normally don't care for owning people. Messy business. People have all these needs, and you have to care for them; the ones dumb enough to get made slaves usually aren't worth it."

Pierce stepped forward, her eyes walking down Rika's body and then back up, boring into Rika's eyes.

"But you…you are a prize worth having. An SMI-2 scout mech. Top of the line. Sure, you don't have a lot of your military hardware anymore, but you have the internal mods and augmentations. I know; I saw the recordings of the fight with Denny and his pack of morons. You're not a woman, honey; you're a weapons platform. One that people are willing to spend top dollar to get their hands on."

"What?!" Rika shrieked as Pierce's words sunk in. "You're going to *sell* me?"

"Yup! Auction's tomorrow. I could have nabbed you sooner, but I figured I'd let you work your last few days with Hal so I could collect your pay." Pierce tapped her head. "Always thinking, always taking opportunities. Not like you, Rika. You may have been great at war, but you suck at life. There were opportunities all around you; you could have been a queen on Dekar, but you allowed yourself to be chattel. Being a slave is your lot, little Rika. You're just a killing machine, and there's a lot of killing that needs to be done out there."

Rika's vision swam as rage filled her. She would not be sold; she would not kill on another's orders ever again.

Of her own volition, though—now that was another story entirely.

She took a swing at Pierce, but the woman had been ready for it, and danced back as a series of pulse blasts hammered into Rika from behind. Then one of the net-casters fired, and Rika was wrapped in carbon-fiber strands.

"You fucking *bitch!*" Rika screamed. "I'll kill you for this! Kill you! You hear me? I'm going to tear you limb from limb!"

"Rika!" Pierce said with mock concern. "You always seemed so calm, so levelheaded." Then Pierce's brow lowered, and a wicked smile spread across her lips. "I'm glad there's still a killer in there, though. That'll bring top dollar for sure."

Rika struggled against the net, feeling it begin to give against the power that surged through her limbs. "Better run, Pierce," she grunted as a part of the net tore open. "I—"

Her words were cut short as she felt a stinging sensation in her neck. She reached up and pulled out a tranq-dart, then yanked more of the net apart and climbed to her feet, fighting the waves of dizziness that threatened to topple her.

"I—" she began to speak, but two more darts hit her, and then a fourth.

She took a step, but the ground was in the wrong place; she realized that the darts contained nano, not drugs. Her foot seemed to be floating above the ground, and then her face smashed into the deck.

Pierce approached and leaned over, her face close to Rika's.

"Should never have got your face back, Mech A71F. It made you weak, and exploiting weakness is what I do best."

Rika tried to reach out and grab Pierce, but her limbs wouldn't respond. As her vision went black, she heard Pierce issue an order to someone nearby.

"Get a compliance chip back in her. I want her under control for the auction."

AUCTION

STELLAR DATE: 07.02.8948 (Adjusted Years)
LOCATION: Pierce's Warehouse, Dekar Station
REGION: Outer Rim of Parsons System, Nietzschean Empire

Rika woke with a start, as though the nanotech suppressing her conscious mind had shut off at a pre-programed time—which was probably the case.

The room she was in was small and spare, with a few crates stacked along the walls, and a door to her right.

She tried to move and realized that she was mounted on a rack; its hooks set into the hardpoints on her back. Rika considered attempting to tear herself off it when she felt a familiar tingle in her mind.

A compliance chip.

The vague memory of Pierce ordering someone to install a new one came to her, and Rika let loose a string of curses that would have impressed even her most foulmouthed teammates back in the military.

<Ah, you're awake,> Pierce's voice entered her mind over the Link. *<And right on time, too. Gotta love it when tech works. You'll be happy to know that the auction is underway, and more than a few people have shown up to bid on your lot. I have to admit, even I didn't expect a payday this big off your sale—if I had, I might have put you up for auction sooner.>*

Rika didn't have anything to say to the woman speaking in her mind. Nothing that wouldn't make her sound like a raving lunatic, at least.

<No rejoinder? No threats to kill me?>

<No,> Rika replied. *<I hope you have a big celebration tonight, basking in the joy of selling off a fellow human being—and then choke and die on your favorite dish.>*

<Oh ho! There we are; love that spunk, Rika. Don't worry, though. I'm not getting joy from selling a human being—you're just mech-meat. Surplus military hardware that I picked up for a song. Pull yourself together, now. Your lot number is up soon. Or throw a tantrum and give me an excuse to show off how well the discipline system works—I'm OK with either.>

Rika seethed but she didn't respond, and she felt Pierce leave her mind a moment later.

Her thoughts drifted to the previous night, to her time in Chase's arms. *Why did I wait so long?* To just have one night of happiness, and now to descend back into hell was too much, far too much.

Rika forced herself to calm down, taking deep breaths, remembering how she used to make her mind go still—how she would focus on a point of light within herself, and push away all her fears.

It was working, sort of, when the door opened, and two of Pierce's guards entered wearing powered armor. She suspected that they weren't taking any chances.

One stood in front of her and smiled. "You're a serious piece of gear, Rika. I was half-hoping that Pierce would keep you around. I bet folks wouldn't miss a payment if they knew you were coming by."

"Yeah, but you saw all the people interested in her lot. Boss said she'd give everyone on the takedown team half a percent. That's gonna be some serious coin."

"Hey," the first guard said as he released the locks on the rack and pushed it toward the door. "I said 'half-hoping'."

The other guard chuckled as he held the door open, and Rika considered reaching out and slamming his head against the door frame, but thought better of it as the tingle of discipline rose up in the back of her head once more.

The guards wheeled her down a short hall and then through a doorway and onto a raised platform.

Rika realized that she was still in the same warehouse as the night before, but the stacks of crates had been moved to create room for the nearly one hundred people who were gathered in front of the platform.

Some sat in rows of chairs, while others stood behind the seats and along the sides of the room. Each held a sheet of plas with a number on it, and Rika could see that many were adjusting their posture, readying to raise their plas in the air.

Humiliation flooded through Rika; to be wheeled out on the platform like she was a *thing*—which is exactly how they viewed her—was almost too much to bear.

Only the memory of the previous night kept her from breaking down. Chase saw her as human, as a person. That meant she was, no matter what these people thought.

"You can see here that we have a fine specimen of Genevian mech technology, manufactured at the height of the war, with all the latest enhancements government money can buy," the auctioneer began, smiling as he walked in front of Rika and gestured to her body.

"It has augmented muscles, an upgraded skeletal system, military neural mods, and," the auctioneer gave a soft chuckle, "a compliance chip."

The sound of soft laughter came back from the crowd, and Rika grimaced, turning her head to the side.

"Don't let her demure attitude fool you," the auctioneer cautioned. "You have all seen her combat record, and the footage of the recent fight on Dekar. Mech A71F is top-notch and ready to roll."

The pair of guards walked back onto the stage, carrying a crate between them. They set it down next to Rika, out of her field of vision, and began to open it.

"But that's not all!" the auctioneer cried out. "The seller has managed to secure an OEM multi-function weapons mount for our little mech, here.

One of the guards stood holding the tool necessary to remove Rika's limbs. He slotted it into her left arm and released the locking bolts, sliding them out and slipping them into a pocket. He gave a twist, and pulled.

Her days in the military flooded back—the numerous techs who had repaired and rebuilt her time and again. She chuckled. "Gotta twist it a bit harder than that, you fucking squishie."

There were a few chuckles from the crowd, and the man flushed, giving her a dirty look. He twisted again, harder this time, and her arm came free. Rika stared down at the stub of a limb that remained.

The man lifted up a weapons mount attachment, complete with a GNR-41C sniper rifle, and slid it onto her arm, twisting hard in the other direction.

The new appendage clicked into place, and Rika saw the weapons specs and loadout appear on her HUD as the guard slid the locking rods through.

"Look at that!" the auctioneer cried out. "Is that a war machine, or what?"

Rika saw nods of approval and shook her head. "Except that I'm a fucking lefty. I need this hand for a handheld weapon. You got a gun mount for the wrong arm."

"I imagine you'll adapt," the auctioneer said, and shrugged before turning back to the crowd. "Let's start the bidding at fifty-thousand Nietzschean credits!"

Rika knew he'd start there. It was the amount she owed Pierce and, by law on Dekar, bidding had to start at the amount owed. Sadly, she would not get to keep any excess.

Plas placards flew up around the room, and the auctioneer continued to raise the bid until it was close to a million credits. Around that point, Rika saw Pierce step out from behind a stack of crates wearing a cheek-splitting grin, and she wished she could get off the rack and tear that smile right off Pierce's smarmy face.

As the bid amount closed in on one and a half million credits, many of the bidders fell out of the race. Only two remained.

One was a slender woman with a glowing red tattoo over her right eye, and the other was a cloaked figure in the back of the room, his face shrouded by a hood—though Rika's enhanced vision could make out a bearded chin and sharp nose beneath the cowl.

The woman bid up to one and a half million, and the auctioneer scanned the room.

"We have one and a half million Nietzschean credits for the SMI-2 mech. Do I hear one point five-five million? Going once…"

"Two million!" the shrouded figure in the back called out.

"Two million Nietzschean credits!" the auctioneer cried out with glee, looking to the woman with the red tattoo. She shook her head and lowered her placard. "Sold to the man with placard number forty seven!" the auctioneer shouted.

The two guards had carried off the crate that held her arm, and now returned to wheel her off the stage.

"Nice haul, Rika!" one of the guards whispered. "Gonna buy a new rifle with my take. Thanks a mil!"

"Or two mil," the other guard laughed.

They returned her to the small room where she had first awoken. The man who fitted her before pulled out the limb removal tool, and slotted it into her left arm, removing the bolts, and then the multi-function weapons mount and GNR-41C sniper rifle.

Rika hoped against hope that he would put her regular arm back on, but her worst fears were realized when he instead slotted the removal tool into her right arm.

"Hey, you don't need to do this," Rika said. "I have the chip; I can't hurt my...owner."

"Pierce's orders," the man said with a shrug. "I think it's because she got a really small cryopod for transport. Cheaper that way."

He pulled off her other arm and then moved to her legs. A few minutes later they were both laying on the floor, and Rika's HUD switched off the overlays that monitored those systems. It felt empty, seeing the world without all of her peripherals data framing it. Now all that remained was her charge readings and standard bio-data.

One of the guards flipped open a crate, and Rika saw a small cryopod within. He keyed in a code, and the pod's lid split open and slid aside. Then the guards lifted her off the rack and carefully carried her to the pod.

"Shit, Rika, you're heavy. What did you eat last night?" one of the guards asked.

"Don't be such a pussy," the other said as they lowered her into the pod.

"Speaking of pussy...I sure wish she had one," the first guard said as they stood back. "Look at her. Without limbs, she looks like a little grey puppy. Stars, I'd fuck her sideways all day."

"Shut up and—" the first guard's words were cut short by a scuffle in the hall, and Rika peered up to see Chase burst into the room.

"Rika!" he cried out. "No, Rika—when you weren't at the docks today...shit, Rika, they sold you!"

"Chase, please," Rika whimpered, humiliated that Chase had seen her like this—just the shell of what was once a person.

"Hey, dickhead, get out of here," the second guard yelled, turning to Chase and shoving him backward. "Deal's done. She ain't your girlfriend no more.

"Get off me!" Chase yelled and shoved back, only to get a fist in his mouth, followed by another in his solar plexus. He fell to the ground, gasping for air, his eyes locked on Rika's.

"Go," she mouthed the words, not trusting her voice. *"Please go."*

Chase's eyes were filled with pain, and tears formed in their corners.

"I'll find you, Rika. I don't care where they take you; I'll find you and I'll set you free. I promise!"

"Yeah, right, loverboy," one of the guards said as he kicked Chase in the stomach. The other guard reached down and grabbed Chase by the hair, dragging him bodily into the hall.

The first guard turned back to Rika and pushed a button on the cryopod. As the lid closed, she caught one last glimpse of Chase—he had been thrown against a wall and was getting punched in the stomach.

Then Rika's view of the first man who had ever treated her like a person was cut off, and everything went black.

THEBES

STELLAR DATE: 12.15.8948 (Adjusted Years)
LOCATION: Warehouse on the northeast edge of Berlin
REGION: Pyra, Albany System, Theban Alliance

Rika felt the slow return of consciousness that followed cryostasis. She had been through it before, and it was just as unpleasant as she recalled. The process was akin to becoming un-drunk over the course of thirty seconds.

As her brain began to accept stimuli from her eyes, she saw that she was in a room with a wooden ceiling. Wood. Dust. She was planetside somewhere.

Sounds reached her ears: scuffling, something being dragged around, low voices.

"This isn't right. Does she get paid, at least? How can she be on the team if she doesn't get paid?" one voice said. Female. Soft, but with a rasp.

"She's not really a person, she just needs parts and power. She belongs to us now."

The second voice was male. It was low, and even though the words were spoken softly, they still carried a deep resonance.

"Shut up, you two, she's waking up," said a third voice. Also male, but a touch nasal—like the owner had a sinus issue of some sort.

Rika closed her eyes and rotated her neck around, getting a feel for moving again, before opening her eyes again to see yellow eyes peering down at her from a dark-skinned face, framed by long black hair and a warm smile.

"Good morning, Rika. I'm glad you made the trip without any trouble. Sorry about the mode of transport; it gets a bit tricky to bring military hardware like you into the Theban Alliance."

"Thebes?" Rika asked, trying to remember the Alliance's systems and worlds.

"Yeah. We're on Pyra, their capital world. In the Albany System."

Rika closed her eyes and nodded, finally recalling the interstellar cartography of the Theban Alliance.

"Jerry, give me a hand here," the woman said before looking down at Rika. "Oh, by the way, I'm Leslie. We're glad to have you on the team."

"Stop talking to her like she's a person," the deep voice said. "She's 'on the team' like my rifle is 'on the team'."

Leslie grimaced. "You're going to have to ignore Barne. He's not really good at anything but shooting."

Another face appeared over Rika, and she saw a mess of blond hair atop a grizzled face.

"Lieutenant Jerry," he said with a nod.

"Lift your…arms, and we'll pull you out, and get you on the rack," Leslie added.

Rika nodded and allowed herself to be lifted out of the cryopod; though it was not as if she had much say in the matter. Not unless scurrying around on the floor and biting ankles could be considered a viable escape plan.

As they carried her to the rack, Rika confirmed that her location was indeed a warehouse; one filled with old wooden crates, amidst which appeared to be a small staging area filled with surveillance equipment and no small number of weapons.

Leslie and Jerry grunted as they lifted her high and set the rack's hooks into her hardpoints.

Leslie gave a long exhale and leaned against the rack. "Stars, you're heavy."

"I've heard that," Rika said. "Who are you, if you don't mind my asking? You don't look like the guy that bought me."

She saw Leslie wince and give a meaningful glance at Jerry, who looked away.

From behind her, Barne, who she still hadn't seen, gave a throaty laugh. "That was probably Gregor, our outfit's quartermaster. He always gets us the best toys."

She could tell that Leslie and Jerry weren't fully comfortable with the idea of having a slave on their team—though Barne was coping with the idea easily enough by treating her as an object to be bought and used.

Rika found it ironic that of the three, his reaction was the easiest to deal with. The way Jerry and Leslie were behaving made her feel ashamed. Barne just made her angry. Anger was something she could use.

Her anger at Barne and the situation she was now in could mask the sorrow she still felt from her final moments on Dekar Station; final moments that were, for her, just minutes past. She could still hear Chase's grunts as Pierce's guards beat him, and the painful lump was still in her throat, threatening to unleash the type of emotional outburst that would not serve her well in her current situation.

Rika knew that she was in the midst of a professional crew. If they had any reason to believe that she would be a hindrance to their mission, they would put her right back in the cryopod. Rika would do just about anything to keep that from happening.

Strength and surety were her best allies now.

With a conscious effort, Rika pushed down her emotions and drew upon the pre-battle calm she had worked so hard to develop during the war.

She took a deep breath. "You're a mercenary crew," she said, peering around at the crates of weapons, munitions, and intelligence gathering equipment.

"Yes," Leslie replied. "We're with the Marauders. This is Team Basilisk—we're a spec-ops group."

Rika had learned of the Marauders not long ago. One of their recruiters had passed through Dekar looking for Genevian veterans to join the mercenary outfit. He had called Rika more than once over the Link, but she had ignored him.

For whatever good that had done.

"So, Rika," Leslie said. "Let's put you back together."

"You sure that's wise?" Barne asked. "Mechs are psychos, every one of them. We put her together, what's to stop her from killing us?"

"Relax, Sergeant. I have the tokens for her compliance chip," Jerry said, stepping around Rika to look her in the eyes. "But I won't need to use them, will I, Corporal Rika?"

Rika took a deep breath, the words flowing from her mouth by rote. "No, sir. You won't need to."

"See?" Jerry said with a smile. "Been out awhile, but you still remember your place."

"If only our space force had the guts you mechs had," Leslie said, more sympathy than admiration in her voice.

Rika snorted. "Mechs get in the fight while the spacers take flight."

Barne barked a laugh, finally walking around to eye her from the front. "Is that what you little mechs all told yourselves?"

Rika noted that Barne looked like he sounded: a large man, dark-skinned and barrel-chested. His right arm was robotic, but skinned with a smooth metal that flowed and rippled in the light.

"Like it?" he asked, holding it up. "Lost this to a K1R that the Nietzscheans captured and turned. Fucking mechs; no real soldier would turn on his own."

Rika wanted to tell the man that a slave has no loyalty to its owner, but knew that making such an utterance here and now would not bode well for her future.

"Seriously, Sergeant," Leslie said, casting a caustic scowl in Barne's direction. "Stop waving around that bullet magnet you call an arm. Give me a hand with the crates."

"Fuck no. I still say that we do this without her. You put the tin soldier together if you think she's so special," Barne said as he skulked out of sight.

"Orders say we use her, so we use her," Jerry said. "The Old Man didn't dump millions of credits on all her hardware just to leave it—and her—in crates."

Barne only grunted, and Jerry shook his head. Leslie opened a case, and Rika saw her legs. Leslie and Jerry carefully lifted her right leg out of the case and aligned it with the socket on the end of her thigh.

"Turn it right," Rika said. "Yeah, like that; then push and twist."

The pair followed her directions, and before long, both her legs were in place.

"OK," Leslie said as she kicked open another case. "Now for your gun-arm...or, I guess it's called a 'multi-function weapons mount'."

Rika chuckled. "I rather like 'gun-arm'. But is there any chance you can give me both my regular arms right now? I can swap over to my gun arm when we need it."

Leslie looked up at Rika. "You don't want it?"

"I'm left-handed," Rika replied. "That gun-arm is a left-side one...makes life miserable for me. Back in the war, I had a right-mount GNR."

Leslie glanced at Jerry, who shrugged. "Makes sense to give her regular arms—especially if we need to go out on any more recon. A meter-long rifle barrel kinda gives you away."

"OK," Leslie replied. "Two regular arms coming right up."

After a few false starts, they got both her arms on, and Leslie lowered the rack, allowing Rika to settle on her own feet.

"Thanks," Rika said. "Feels good not to be hooked up on that thing.

"I'll bet," Leslie said. "We have something else for you."

Jerry walked over to where Barne was preparing a meal, while Leslie led Rika over to another case, and flipped it open. There, with its various components set in shipping foam, was a set of SMI-2A9 armor in what appeared to be pristine condition.

The emotions that Rika felt flow within her were far different than she expected. Rather than revulsion, she suddenly wanted to be wrapped in the armor—to feel its protective shell around her, keeping her safe, making her invincible.

"You look pleased," Leslie said quietly, her yellow eyes serious. "I wasn't sure you would be. I—I knew a few mechs back in the war. They weren't really happy people."

"Not a lot of happy people in the war, if I recall," Rika said. "Still…I know this is crazy, but I'm looking forward to putting it on."

Leslie reached up and touched Rika's shoulder. "We understand how…how it is to miss the war. Things were simpler then. We had our orders, we had our missions; we did what we had to. Afterward…the rules didn't make sense anymore. It's why we signed up for the Marauders."

Rika nodded. She knew that all too well. As she stared down at the armor, she wondered if perhaps finding herself with this mercenary team was a good thing. Even so, a few questions burned in her mind.

"Do the Marauders often employ slaves?" she asked without equivocation.

Leslie shook her head. "No. You're the only one…in your situation that I know of—but you're not the only mech. There are a few others."

Rika's head snapped up. "Silva?"

Leslie frowned. "No. No one by that name. The ones I know the names of are Herman, Grace, Liv, and Freddie. Herman is a K1R, and the others are AM-2s and 3s. Know them?"

Rika shook her head. "No, the names don't ring any bells."

Leslie shrugged. "Didn't think so. Want any help with the armor?"

"No, I got it."

"Alright, then. We're going to go over the mission brief with you after we eat. Based on the speed at which Jerry is burning the food, that'll be in about fifteen minutes.

"Hey!" Jerry called out from the hot plate he was standing over.

Leslie met Rika's eyes and smiled. "It's going to be OK. The Old Man is a good guy. I bet that if you do a few missions, he'll sort you out properly."

Rika wasn't so sure. The sort of person that bought other people wasn't usually the type to 'sort things out properly'."

Leslie walked away, and Rika looked down at the armor. It was a newer model than what she had been equipped with back in the war; though the helmet was an older model.

First, she set the two pieces of armor that wrapped around her waist in place—what the women of Team Hammerfall had always referred to as the 'corset'—and sucked in.

She had gained a bit of weight since the war, and the armor was made for someone a size or two smaller than her—but once the two sides met, they hooked onto her mount points and ratcheted into place.

Rika pulled out the chest plate and set it into place, carefully ensuring that each of her breasts was seated properly before pushing the armor down into the mounts set in her sternum and shoulders.

That was one advantage of being an SMI-2 mech; every meat the GAF had put into her model was a thin, lithe woman.

It was the whole point: small women with lots of hardware, who could still function as highly mobile scouts.

The rest of the armor only took five minutes to put in place, and Rika smiled as she examined her arms—no longer seeing the raw understructure, but something that looked a bit more like a real arm, with layered plating giving it form.

She stretched up, and then side to side, lifting one knee to her chest, then the other, ensuring the fit was good. She reached down and touched her toes, and then pivoted, pushing one leg straight up into the air while grasping both her calves.

"Nice view," Barne said, and Rika glanced over at the mercenaries, realizing that they were all staring at her.

"Fuck you," Rika replied as she lowered her leg and stood up straight.

Just as she was now cocooned in physical armor, Rika wrapped herself in the mental armor of quick comebacks and coarse language. She was in a pack of wolves, and there was no way she was going to reveal weakness and be torn apart.

"Food's ready," Leslie said, gesturing to a plate of reheated MRE's sided with a few slices of buttered bread that sat on a crate.

"You eat food?" Barne asked, as he pulled himself onto another crate and rested his plate on his lap. "I thought you mechs all took that nutricrap."

"Yeah, I eat food," Rika replied. "NutriPaste tastes a lot like I imagine your balls do, except it actually has substance. But I spent a decent amount of credit to get a face again, and I didn't go through that so I can pump crap into my stomach—not like the hookers that suck you off."

"Whatever," Barne grunted, flushing as Jerry and Leslie laughed.

"Oh, you're in for it," Leslie said. "She seemed meek at first, but it looks like our Rika's got some teeth after all."

"We'll see about that when we hit the shit," Barne said. "Anyone can talk a good game. How many kills you have, Rika?"

"Beats me," Rika said. "I never counted."

"You may not have, but the GAF did," Jerry said around a mouthful of the meat-substance from the MRE. "What was your confirmed count?"

"Just over seventy thousand," Rika shrugged. "But there were a lot more unconfirmed. Like I said, I never really kept track."

Leslie made a choking sound, and Rika glanced at her to see a look of awe on the woman's face.

"How…how did you…"

"Kill so many people?" Rika asked. "Simple. We never got days off, never got any leave. I was in for four and a half years; most days, I killed thirty Nietzscheans. You do the math."

"Thirty a day…" Even Barne sounded impressed.

"Doesn't work out to seventy thousand," Jerry said. "You're still short twenty thousand."

Rika nodded as she took a bite of bread and chewed it slowly, savoring the fresh taste. She swallowed and said, "There were a few above average days in there. I nuked a regiment, once. That upped the count a lot."

"Shit," Barne whispered.

"Think she can do the job, now?" Jerry asked.

"Now I think she's too much for the job," Barne laughed, his deep bass voice resonating in the crates around them.

"So, what is the job?" Rika asked Jerry. "And does it get me my freedom at some point?"

"The orders didn't say anything about your freedom, but there was a note about some sort of packet with your enlistment details. The packet wasn't in the crates, though— could have something about working off your debt. After this job, we'll hook back up with the regiment where you'll get to meet the Old Man, and we'll see."

Rika nodded slowly. That would have to do for now. So long as Jerry had the codes to her compliance chip, it was in her best interests to take him at his word and be agreeable.

"The mission," Jerry said, "is simple. We're here to kill the Theban President, and as many Theban top brass and politicians as we can.

Rika almost spat out her mouthful of bread. "What?!" she asked.

"Septhians hired us—or so we think. They want to shake things up, and this job will give them their in," Barne said.

"The four of us are effectively going to topple a government?" Rika asked.

"No," Jerry smiled. "There are thirty Marauder teams in the city now. We all have specific targets, and we're to strike simultaneously four days from now."

"And who's *our* target?" Rika asked, dreading the answer.

Barne gave her a predatory smile and leaned in close. "Like he said; the Theban president."

THE CHASE

STELLAR DATE: 10.25.8948 (Adjusted Years)
LOCATION: Starview Lounge, *Noon's Glory*
REGION: Approaching Maui, Ontario System, Septhian Alliance

It hadn't been easy, but Chase eventually learned the name of the hooded figure that had purchased Rika at Pierce's auction—Gregor. He worked for the Marauders, a mercenary outfit comprised mostly of Genevian veterans from the war with the Nietzschean Empire.

By the time Chase had been able to track him down, the man was long gone from Dekar. Not that Chase had any idea what he would have done had he caught up with Gregor.

The more he looked into the Marauders, the more dead ends he found. With the Genevian systems now a part of the Nietzschean Empire, the Marauders didn't operate openly within their borders. From what Chase could tell, their headquarters was somewhere in Septhia; at least that's where most of their public recruitment centers were.

Septhia—one of the many interstellar nations within the Praesepe Cluster. Once an ally of Genevia, they had not gone so far as to openly join the war with the Nietzscheans, or offer them any real assistance.

Nevertheless, Chase knew that's where his best chance of finding Rika lay.

The memory of that night with Rika was still crystal clear in his mind. The soft skin of her face, and where it met the coarse grey skin at her neck; the soft hints of her breasts. She was a beautiful woman, but he found her striking blue eyes to be her most captivating feature; they could convey so much, and held so much strength.

Chase knew that those eyes had seen things he could only imagine—yet they were still kind, and had shown him that there was a gentleness inside Rika. One she kept buried deep below the hard shell that she presented to the outside world.

He let out a long breath and signaled the bartender for another round, then turned on his stool to gaze out the window on the far side of the bar. It wasn't a real window. The bar was somewhere in the middle of the *Noon's Glory,* but the holodisplay perfectly rendered the external view with a three-dimensional effect that made it appear as though open space began just after the last table.

Ahead, slowly resolving into more than just an indistinct blob was Maui—a massive orbital habitat on the outskirts of the Ontario System. Ontario was one of the systems near the rimward edge of the Septhian Alliance, close to its border with Thebes.

"What's your business on Maui?" a woman asked as she settled onto the stool next to him. Chase glanced at her out of the corner of his eye, seeing enough to note that she had dark hair, and wore a loose grey suit.

"Looking for someone," he replied, not really interested in having a conversation—though still glad for a little human contact at the end of the three-month journey. Septhia wasn't far from the Parsons System as the photon flew, but the *Noon's Glory* had made several stops along the way. Enough that Chase was starting to feel like he should have tried to book private passage—though that would have completely depleted his savings.

"Aren't we all?" the woman said with a laugh. "Anyone in particular?"

"A friend," Chase replied. "We got separated by... unfortunate circumstances."

"A lot of that going around lately," The woman responded. "I hear that the Parisians just attacked the Roman Republic."

Chase shook his head in dismay. "Galaxy is going to shit lately. It's like the FTL wars all over again."

The woman nodded. "All thanks to that stupid old colony ship showing up—no one's even seen it since it left Bollam's World, yet they're all still fighting out of fear and distrust."

"I think people just needed an excuse. Mind you, not everywhere is a mess," Chase said. "Praesepe still seems unscathed; no wars to speak of in the cluster."

The woman nodded. "Yeah, we need places like this. Have to have somewhere safe to build new ships and weapons. Good business in that."

"That's not what I meant," Chase replied.

"I know, but that's my business, so it's how I look at it."

"Oh?" Chase asked. "I didn't get your name, by the way. I'm Chase."

The woman offered her hand. "I'm Sally. Nice to meet someone willing to chat; been a long, dull trip."

Chase chuckled. "Yeah, I've caught up on all the sims, vids, and even did some reading on the trip."

"I have to ask, this person you're trying to find…is he or she a romantic interest?"

"She," Chase confirmed.

"How do you know she's on Maui?" Sally asked.

Chase gave a long sigh and reached for his drink. He took a sip before answering.

"She's probably not, but I'm just chasing leads right now. I might have to take work for a bit on Maui. I can't afford to go chasing her all across the stars on my savings."

"What's the lead that brought you here?" Sally asked.

"Well, she got pi—she joined the Marauders; they're a merc outfit. They have a recruitment place on Maui. I have no idea what I'll do once I get there—I'm not sure if I can convince them to tell me where she is."

Sally laughed, and then took a sip of her drink, her eyes twinkling above the glass. "You're probably right. You could enlist, though."

"That crossed my mind—which is nuts. I've had my fill of fighting."

"Have you?" Sally asked. "Chase, formerly of Hal's Hell on Dekar Station in the Parsons System. Before that, squad sergeant in the second platoon of Charlie Company, 4326th Regiment, 23rd Battalion, 19th Division, Genevian Armed Forces. Have you had your fill?"

"What the hell is this?" Chase scowled. "That information isn't in any shipboard database."

"You're right about that. But I knew it before I boarded back at Hintin. Gregor sent me; he was curious who was looking into him. From what I can tell, there's nothing to worry about, though—just a lovesick boy, chasing after a girl."

Chase slammed his drink down on the bar, spilling its contents as he stood, and took a step back. "You're a Marauder? You fucking slaver! Where's Rika?"

"Hey, easy now," Sally raised her hands defensively. "I don't know where she is, but she's listed as active duty on the roster."

"Active duty...so she's fighting in a war somewhere," Chase said, his tone accusatory.

"To my knowledge, the Marauders are not currently fighting in any wars. But she's probably fighting somewhere."

"You know she's a slave, right?" Chase asked. "She was sold at auction."

"I saw that in her record. The way we see it, the Marauders saved a Genevian war hero from a horrible future somewhere. She'll have to work off the money we paid for her, but she's no slave."

Chase gave a cynical laugh. "Most people don't make a huge distinction between slavery and indenture, you know."

"Yeah, well, we're not a charity," Sally shrugged, and took another sip of her drink.

"It'll take her *years* to pay that off!"

Sally nodded. "But it's a small price to pay for freedom."

"If she survives," Chase spat. "I know how you mercs operate. Chew people up and spit them out."

"Hey! Check your attitude, Sergeant. I was enlisted in the GAF, too. Staff sergeant. Did my share of time in the shit. I'll tell you one thing for certain: we treat our own a lot fucking better than we got in the war. If Rika survived that, then she'll do fine with the Marauders."

Several of the bar's other patrons had turned to stare. Sally pointed at Chase's stool. "Now sit the fuck back down and finish your drink. What you didn't spill all over the bar, at least."

Chase was at a loss for words, but followed Sally's instruction and retook his seat on the stool. He picked up his glass, took a long look at it, and then downed the remains in one swallow.

"Another one for my friend, here," Sally said to the bartender before giving Chase a conspiratorial smile. "It's on the company dime, anyway."

Chase felt like an ass for losing his temper. It wasn't going to get him any further with Sally, and he was glad that she didn't just tell him to shove off and leave. Still, it took him a few sips of his next drink to ask the question burning a hole in his tongue.

"So, can I see her?"

Sally smiled. "You really have it bad, don't you?"

Chase chuckled softly. "Rika's an amazing woman; you'd understand if you knew her. She's…she's so strong inside, like a diamond."

"Forged in the war's crucible," Sally said.

"Breaks the metaphor, but yeah. She thinks that what they did to her broke her…ruined her. But she's wrong; they made her better."

"You into mod girls?" Sally asked with a raised eyebrow.

"No…well, yeah, a bit. But that's not what's special about her. Shit, I can't believe I'm telling all this to you."

Sally winked. "It's one of my specialties."

"Huh…I can tell."

"Look, Chase, you're a good guy. Your heart is in the right place, and you're not afraid to call a broom a broom. I was serious about you enlisting—the Marauders could use a man like you."

Chase had been mid-drink, and he coughed, getting more than a little on Sally.

"Sorry," he said, and handed her a napkin.

"Don't worry, I get that a lot," Sally said with a grim smile. "So, should I pass you a contract?"

Chase knew that if he said no, his chances of seeing Rika again in the next decade were slim to none. He wiped his mouth, took a deep breath, and nodded.

"Yeah, send me the contract."

NIGHT

STELLAR DATE: 12.15.8948 (Adjusted Years)
LOCATION: Warehouse on the northeast edge of Berlin
REGION: Pyra, Albany System, Theban Alliance

The rest of the team had gone to sleep; though not before Barne gave Rika a stern admonishment not to 'try any sneaky shit' during the night.

She had to admit that she'd considered it. Jerry had not given her any specific orders to remain in the warehouse, and so long as she could maintain a mental belief that leaving the warehouse was in the best interests of the team, she could fool the compliance chip and not be disciplined.

But she had nowhere to go, and she suspected that somewhere in the armor she now wore was a tracking system that would bring the Marauders right to her.

There was also a part of her that liked being part of a team again. No one here was responsible for buying her, and Leslie and Jerry didn't seem to have any issue with her being a mech. Barne wasn't happy about her, but she suspected that was because he was used to being the biggest muscle; but he hadn't called her 'meat', so that was a plus.

For now, she'd play along and see where things went.

*Well, you do **know** where this is going; you're going to assassinate a president.*

Rika knew that a younger version of herself would have been horrified, or perhaps morbidly curious about doing something so crazy. But she'd spent a lot of time on the streets. 'Kill or be killed' was something she had embraced long before the military had carved her up and made death her full-time job.

As a scout mech, she had relied on her GNR-41B sniper rifle to take out more than a few thousand enemies. She didn't feel any special remorse at the thought of actual assassination—a realization that worried her more than a little.

All her work to become a normal person since the war had ended—as much as was possible—seemed to have been nothing more than a veneer over what still lay beneath.

The killer.

She pushed those thoughts down and brought Team Basilisk's intel on Pyra and their target location up on her HUD.

Pyra was the second planet from Howe, which was the name of the primary star in the Albany System. It was strange that the system's star and the system itself didn't share the same name; it was also odd that no planet or star in the five-system Theban Alliance bore the name 'Thebes'.

Not that any of that mattered.

Pyra was a well-settled world, boasting a population of five billion. Most of that number was concentrated in mega-cities, leaving the majority of the planet's seven hundred million square kilometers of land open for farming and recreation.

The world had continents at both its north and south poles, making for a colder climate in the temperate zones than was common on terraformed planets. However, from what Rika could see, the locals had a real affinity for winter sports. She wondered if that was cause or effect.

She focused in on the location of the capital city, on the outskirts of which lay the warehouse the Marauder team was occupying.

The city, named Berlin, was nestled in a wide bay on the east coast of one of the world's continents; just a few degrees below the northern tropic line. Unlike the mega-cities elsewhere on Pyra, Berlin had an older more cultured feel. Local laws restricted building heights so that none could come close to the height of the capitol buildings. Rika noted that long-range urban shots would likely be out of the question.

She brought up the dossier on her target. President Ariana appeared to be popular with her people, having been recently voted in for a seventh consecutive ten-year term.

That was too long for anyone to hold power, by Rika's estimation. Maybe the Marauders were doing Thebes a favor by ushering in a change of the guard.

As Rika reviewed the president's daily schedule, as well as the briefs and dossiers of her guards and staff, the local time slipped past midnight. She noted that it was now the twelfth day of the third month on the local calendar. Strangely, a month named Julius.

She set a countdown: eight hundred hours on the morning of the fifteenth. That gave her just over one hundred and eight local hours until she pulled the trigger.

It was going to be a long wait.

She straightened and stretched her arms overhead. The feeling of being armored was still comforting, though the change in balance was taking some getting used to.

Rika turned and looked behind her at the sleeping forms of the other three members of Team Basilisk. *'Other'? Does that imply that I am one of them?*

She walked quietly to the crate containing civilian clothing and grabbed a long robe. At first, she had wondered why the team had equipped her with full armor—it wasn't ideal for blending into an urban population—but when she saw that the local fashion tended toward long flowing robes, it made more sense.

The robe they had supplied her with was more than simple cloth. It contained impressive EM-masking technology, and would even flow around her body in a fashion that masked her double-kneed legs.

She carefully pulled it over her head. The robe was made of tan cloth, with intricate white whorls across its surface. She left the cowl down and crept to a staircase that led to the warehouse's roof.

Her augmented vision revealed the steps least likely to creak and groan under her considerable weight, and she made it to the top without waking anyone below—she hoped.

The door on the roof was unlocked, but she saw a sensor on it and punched in the code to deactivate it—that much the team had trusted her with; then she pushed open the door.

Rika drew in a deep breath, relishing the scent of the clear night air as she leaned her head back and gazed at the stars above.

"Wow," she whispered, taking in the stellar beauty above her. The Theban Alliance lay on the rimward edge of the Praesepe Cluster, which consisted of a thousand stars, all within one hundred light years. Pyra was in the stage of its local year where the night sky was dominated by the display, illuminating the city and forests surrounding it with far more light than even most moons reflected.

Rika walked by the light of that brilliant display to the edge of the warehouse's roof, taking care to follow a route that would not pass over the team below, and leaned against the decorative cornice lining the top of the building.

Genevia—now a part of the Nietzschean stars—was not visible in the night sky at this time of year. She wished it were; Parsons would be visible from Pyra. She could have gazed at its light and wondered about Chase: where he was, what he was doing.

For her, it had been less than a day since they had been in each other's arms; for him, it had been well over a hundred. Did he think of her? Was he even still on Dekar? Rika doubted that she'd ever know.

She pushed the melancholy thoughts from her mind and gazed around her.

The warehouse was situated on the northeast side of the city, near a long string of wharfs mostly filled with recreational craft—though a few commercial fishing vessels were visible.

Rika wondered about a planet with so many inhabitants using human fishing fleets. Perhaps it was some sort of recreational activity.

To the southwest, seventeen kilometers distant, rose the capitol buildings. Rika gauged the building's spires to be no more than five hundred meters tall, but no other building in the city crested one hundred. Five kilometers north of the capitol and sixteen kilometers from the warehouse, lay the presidential estate.

The intel the Marauders had gathered showed that the presidential palace's grounds bordered a national forest, and that the president often went for a run in the morning on its twisting paths.

That would be their primary strike point, close to the palace grounds—Rika didn't want to be too deep in the woods if the president's schedule changed that day.

The sound of footsteps on the stairs and the soft swish of the door opening a moment later reached her ears, and Rika turned to see Jerry approaching.

"Quite the view up here, isn't it?" he asked as he carefully walked across the rooftop toward her.

"Checking on me?" Rika asked.

Jerry shrugged as he reached he side. "Maybe a little bit."

Rika gave a soft laugh. "I would have, too. Sorry I woke you; I just wanted to take a look at the city with my own eyes. There's always something missing from the intel. Everyone sees things differently."

"It's OK," Jerry said as he ran a hand through his messy tangle of hair. "I wasn't really sleeping well, anyway. I'm surprised you're not, though; I always find that cryo takes a lot out of me."

"I soaked up a lot of calories today. Took in some NutriPaste after the meal," Rika said. "I can make it a few days without sleep if I'm well fed."

"Yeah, that's fine for the body, but what about the mind?"

Rika turned to Jerry, meeting his dark eyes. "Seriously? You care about my mental state?"

Jerry gave a self-deprecating laugh. "Well, it's not entirely altruistic. I'm not excited about the thought of an overstressed, exhausted mech within arm's reach."

"And here I thought you cared," Rika said, turning back to the view of Berlin and the distant lights of intermittent air and ground traffic, flitting about under the starlight.

"Hey, I'm not exactly excited about having you here against your will," Jerry said. "But orders are orders."

"By 'against my will', you mean as a slave," Rika said.

"Hey, you're not a—" Jerry began, but stopped when Rika shot him a quelling glare.

"Am I getting paid for this job? Can I leave?"

"Uhh…well…"

"Slave," Rika said in a tone that brooked no further discussion on the subject.

Jerry didn't speak for a minute, and then he let out a long breath.

"Look, I admit that I didn't want you here—and before you go and get all pissed off at me, I don't mean *you* specifically. I mean anyone who's not Jenny—she was our last sniper. Got killed a few months ago on another op. We knew they'd send someone to fill her shoes, but we weren't expecting…"

"A slave," Rika finished for him.

"You think you're the only one that knows what that's like?" Jerry asked, anger seeping into his voice. "I was drafted, just like you. I didn't want to be in the GAF, but I couldn't leave, either."

A sour laugh escaped Rika's throat as she turned to face him. "Are you serious? You got *drafted*? I was *coerced*. Hell, I don't even know if there is a word that combines 'entrapment', 'coercion', and 'blackmail' into one. I stole food. *Food!* And for that, I was given the option of enlistment or execution!"

Jerry's face fell, and he swallowed. "Shit, Rika. I had no idea. They always told us you mechs were mostly volunteers; that the compliance chips were just to keep any that went nuts from killing the rest of us."

"Yeah, well now you know. So maybe what happened to me was a *bit* worse than when you were drafted."

"Our government was really just a bunch of fucking shitheads, wasn't it?" Jerry asked quietly. "Ever wonder if we're better off since the Nietzscheans won?"

"Fucked if I know," Rika said. "Now instead of our government flushing us all down the drain, we're doing it to ourselves—all while the Nietzscheans watch and make a profit off our backs."

Jerry nodded. "Yeah, it's pretty rough in some places. But you see that a lot after a war. I've been around a bit since then, and some of the other Marauders even longer. Things are shit almost everywhere. Everyone is attacking everyone."

"Seems nice enough here," Rika said as she looked over the city. "Well, 'til we kill off their leaders, at least."

"Kill or be killed, Rika. That's the way of it. Twelve thousand years of civilization, and that's what we humans do best. I'd rather be one of the killers."

Rika had no response for that. She agreed, but she didn't want him to think that she was OK with what they were going to make her do.

"Well, now that I know you're not going to jump off the roof and leave the premises, I'm going to go see if sleep will visit me tonight," Jerry said as he straightened.

"'Night," Rika replied.

Jerry tentatively laid a hand on Rika's shoulder, and she did her best not to flinch. Human contact was not something she'd had much of, other than the evening with Chase, which was beginning to feel like it was in her distant past—or like a dream.

"I meant what I said before," Jerry said. "The Old Man's a good guy. He'll reward you for a job well done. I know it."

Rika turned her head and met Jerry's eyes. He appeared sincere; his heart rate was slow and his blood pressure low.

"Thanks. I hope so."

Jerry turned and left, and Rika resumed gazing out over the city.

Berlin.

Where she would assassinate a president.

THE GENERAL

STELLAR DATE: 12.14.8948 (Adjusted Years)
LOCATION: Combat Information Center, MSS *Foe Hammer*
REGION: Interstellar Space, near the Praesepe Cluster

General Mill closed the report from Gregor on the situation with the mech girl, Rika. She had been successfully delivered to the team on Pyra assigned with the assassination of President Ariana. However, there had been no time to brief her or Basilisk before her arrival.

Even worse, the packet explaining that she only had to work off half her debt to the Marauders didn't make it into the shipment; just the information for Lieutenant Jerry on how to use her compliance chip to control her if there was an issue.

Still, the coordination officer on Pyra hadn't picked up any distress signals from Basilisk, so General Mill had to assume that all was as it should be—difficult as that was.

Operation Phoenix was still a go.

Mill rose from his desk and walked to the window in his ready room. It didn't look out over the stars, but instead down into the main shuttle bay of his flagship, the *Foe Hammer*.

He watched as two B'Muths were loaded under a drop ship, ready to hit the dirt. The massive, four legged walkers were well suited to different types of ground combat, both urban and rural. They were one of his favorite weapons platforms.

The Septhian Government hadn't contracted the Marauders to launch a ground assault on Pyra, but he suspected they would. The Thebans may look like a soft target, but Mill knew it would take more than a series of assassinations to take them down.

When Septhia came calling for troops, the Marauders would be ready.

Near the assault craft, a dozen fast exfiltration ships were loading supplies, getting ready for departure within the hour.

<General?> the voice of the regimental administration AI entered his mind.

<What is it, Laura?>

<The Romany and the Djinn have just jumped in. They're maneuvering into position now.>

<Very good. Thank you, Laura. Have they brought any updates from Pyra?>

<Just that the coordination officer on the ground still has a green light on all missions,> Laura replied.

<Excellent,> Mill replied.

Mill returned to his chair and sat down, spreading the mission briefs out once more. He had never planned a covert operation this large before, though it was not his first regime-toppling action—just his first as a mercenary.

There were forty teams on Pyra; thirty in the capital city alone. Another three-dozen teams were spread out in the Albany System, ready to take out targets on the other worlds, and key stations.

His contact in the Septhian government had assured him that different outfits had the four other Theban star systems well in hand. He suspected that the Septhians meant the news to comfort him—but it didn't. Instead, it kept him up at night. If any one of those other mercenary companies messed up and got caught, it would put his people in jeopardy.

Which was another reason why fast exfiltration teams were preparing their crafts for departure in the bay below.

Mill pulled up the holodisplay of his fleet relative to the Albany system. He was taking a risk, assembling his ships within the Theban alliance; but with his vessels seven light-months away from the Albany System's primary—a main sequence G-spectrum star named Howe—there was little chance that they would be spotted.

It also made a jump into the Albany System a nine-hour trip, which was far better than jumping all the way from Septhia; it was unfortunately still far enough out that any rescue ops could take a day or more with the final insystem flights.

General Mill rose and paced across his office, the myriad things that could go wrong flooding his mind. A small voice was telling him that Phoenix was a crazy op; that there had to be a better way to secure the Praesepe Cluster against the Nietzscheans.

There probably was, but he couldn't think of it at the moment.

TRUST

STELLAR DATE: 12.16.8948 (Adjusted Years)
LOCATION: Warehouse on the northeast edge of Berlin
REGION: Pyra, Albany System, Theban Alliance

"Well that's just great," Barne said. "They send us a tin soldier and all her toys, but they forget the fucking ammo for her rifle!"

"I can use the electron beam," Rika suggested.

"Maybe," Jerry said. "But if they have magnetic deflectors, it won't work. The kinetic power behind your rifle's uranium rods is a lot more reliable for this sort of kill shot."

"Any chances we can get some rounds?" Leslie asked. "Maybe from some of the other teams?"

"We don't even know where the other teams are," Barne said. "Fat chance of getting ammo from them—though it wouldn't fit anyway. No one else has anything close to that caliber of weapon."

Jerry stroked his chin as his eyes flicked up—his Link tell. "I know a gal; she operates a site from Pyra these days."

Leslie raised her hands. "Whoa, Jerry. I know who you're thinking of. We're not going through Cheri—that bitch is nuts. Didn't she try to kill you during the war?"

Jerry shrugged. "Yeah, but she tried to kill everyone at least once. It was a sort of rite of passage for our 'toon."

"No wonder we lost." Rika shook her head. "What are the chances she has the right ammo for my girl?"

Barne laughed. "*Your* girl already, is it?"

Rika shrugged. "When your weapon is a part of you, you tend to get attached to it."

"No pun intended," Leslie chuckled.

"Focus, people," Jerry said. "And yeah, she has some. Five rounds."

"What?!" Leslie yelled, then lowered her voice. "You reached out to her already?"

"Yeah. I routed it carefully. Look, she's a long way from here; it's going to be off the locals' radar. We jet up there, get the ammo, and then come back. One day. We have plenty of time."

"I didn't mean that," Leslie replied. "I mean that we can't trust her. Rika's gun doesn't shoot marshmallows. The reasons you need those rods are few, and there aren't any legal ones on Pyra."

"She has a point," Rika said. "I read the orders. We're to have no contact with anyone outside of the mission parameters. Risk of exposure is too high."

"*Corporal* Rika, it's my call. We're going to meet with Cheri, get your ammo, and be back by morning." Jerry said with finality.

The reprimand stung, but Rika was pleased that he used her rank to keep her in line, rather than Discipline.

"Who's 'we'?" Barne asked.

"Leslie and I," Jerry replied.

"I should come, too," Rika added. "I can make sure they're the right spec."

"No," Jerry said with a slow shake of his head. "You're our ace in the hole. Besides, it's a bit hard to get you on a cloud hopper or a maglev across the world. Your cloak is good, but I don't want to test it against a hundred scanners and keen-eyed security guards."

Rika nodded silently. She knew he was right, but the thought of getting out and about was too enticing to not have tried.

"Just going to leave me here with her all day?" Barne asked. "What if she goes nuts and kills me?"

"She won't; right, Rika?" Jerry asked. "Rika won't harm any one of us. Correct?"

Discipline tingled in the back of her mind. The compliance chip recognizing a direct order that required confirmation. *It's like he's read the manual or something since last night,* she thought.

"No, Jerry, I won't harm you three, or any other Marauder." She hadn't needed to add the last part, but she wanted them to be at ease.

"See?" Jerry smiled. "Safe as houses."

"However, I'd like to scout the primary location," Rika said.

"Oh, yeah?" Barne asked. "Something wrong with our recon?"

"There's always something wrong with someone else's recon," Rika replied. "Plus, my eyes are better than any of yours. I see things you can't."

Jerry gave her a long look before nodding. Barne snorted, and even Leslie looked surprised.

"You'll scout the site, and be back by night, right?" Jerry asked.

"Understood," Rika replied. "And 'night' is…?" The last thing she needed was an ambiguous order with a compliance chip in her head.

"Uhhh, twenty-two hundred, local time," Jerry replied.

"Plenty of time," Rika said. "Thanks."

Jerry and Leslie wasted no time dressing in their long, flowing robes, and they left the warehouse while Rika was still trying on different gloves, looking for ones with a good fit.

"Think that gloves are gonna hide the fact that you only have three fingers on each hand?" Barne asked with a smirk.

"They may cover themselves head to toe here, but they still have mods," Rika replied. "Three fingers shouldn't raise too many eyebrows."

"Just make sure you keep your neck covered," Barne said, pointing out that Rika's armor encased her neck right up to her chin.

Rika grabbed a shawl, wrapping it around her neck and over her head. "There, look good?" she asked.

Barne walked around her and nodded. "Yeah. If I didn't know better, I'd be fooled into thinking you're human."

Asshole, Rika thought, though she only nodded in response.

"Better get going. Long walk," Barne commented.

"Thirty five klicks round trip," Rika replied as she slipped pads over the toes on her feet to cover her metallic footfalls. "I walk at just under four an hour; won't even take nine hours to get there and back. I'll still have time to smell the roses."

"You do that," Barne said with a grunt. After a pause, he said, "Well, fuck off already. I could use some time alone."

Yeah, like forever, Rika wanted to say.

She turned and walked to the warehouse's north entrance; a different one than Jerry and Leslie had used. She reached up and set the alarm on the door to pause for thirty seconds, and then stepped through, out into the bright morning sun.

She pulled her robe's cowl up to shade her eyes, not wanting to use their filters to dim her vision. After spending months on Dekar station—which wasn't brightly lit *anywhere*—feeling the warmth of Howe's bright yellow light on her face was pure joy.

It occurred to Rika that this was the first time the light of a yellow star had struck her skin since the day she was caught stealing food.

Nine years between exposures to real sunlight. *Nine years.*

She walked across the loading dock, then hopped down and crossed a stretch of dull grey pavement to reach the back road. According to the map she had pulled down, the road connected the warehouse to a larger street half a kilometer away, and saw little traffic.

She had to admit she was impressed by the location Basilisk had chosen. The warehouse was one amongst several in a small cluster. None appeared to be in heavy use, but there was some traffic in and out that would serve to mask their arrivals and departures.

It was also far enough away from the city center to avoid any heavy surveillance, but still close enough for an efficient strike.

As Rika walked, she took in the local foliage, which was thick and lush—though she didn't recognize most of it as anything other than types of ferns and palm trees. Maybe there would be coconuts; she had enjoyed climbing coconut trees in her youth, and getting a drink of that sweet milk within.

Before long, the road she was walking alongside of reached the larger thoroughfare, and she turned left, heading west into the city.

Ground cars flitted by, most hovering above the road on magnetic systems. Some a-grav cars moved through the air further above, though still staying above the roads. Rika took a deep breath, savoring the light scent of ozone and charged electrons.

"Gotta love planets," she said to herself with a smile.

She strolled down the sidewalk at a leisurely pace, enjoying being outside in the sunlight with no one around who wanted to hurt or kill her. She had a full charge—on new batts, too, thanks to the Marauders—and was in no hurry to return early and spend the evening with Barne.

I think I'll wait outside till twenty-two hundred on the nose.

The feeling was exhilarating. She had food, charge, and nowhere to be for the better part of a day. The feeling was so foreign she barely recognized it.

She wondered if it was possible to be relaxed and excited at the same time.

Rika passed through the commercial area around the docks, and into a residential district. She smiled at other pedestrians as they passed—some walking alone, like her, and others in groups or with children.

They all wore robes like her, though many had their heads exposed. From her research, Rika hadn't seen any religious reason why everyone on Pyra wore robes out in the hot sun; it just seemed to be the fashion.

Strange as it was, the custom suited her fine. If everyone on the street was wearying skin-tight polymers, she doubted that Jerry would have let her roam about for the day—unless it had been a world of heavy modders. Then she'd fit in perfectly.

The residential district gave way to rows of small shops along the street, and Rika laid eyes on a coffee shop that had a holosign displaying a rotating array of drinks that made her mouth water.

Each of the Marauders had fake idents, and was masquerading as a Theban visiting Pyra. Rika's used her real name, though it cited her birthplace as Lils—an orbital habitat further out in the Albany System. She had credit, too; physical, and online in a planetary bank.

When she'd checked the balance, it had blown her away. She may not be getting 'paid' for the job, but she had more disposable credit available than she had seen in years.

She decided there was no reason not to treat herself to the local delights—a perfectly reasonable thing to do for a tourist. Rika approached the shop, and as she pushed the door open, the scent of freshly ground coffee beans hit her nostrils. She drew in a deep breath with a broad smile on her lips.

"Has that effect, doesn't it?" a man said with a grin as he walked past, holding a steaming cup of coffee with an intricate pattern in the frothed milk floating on top.

"Sure seems to," Rika replied.

She looked over the menu and opted for a caramel latte. She had never tasted caramel before—not outside of a sim, at least—and wasn't about to pass up on this chance.

As she ordered the drink from a woman with a kind smile behind the counter, she felt a pang of guilt for the turmoil the Marauders would cause on Pyra in just a few day's time.

Unbidden, the memory of Chase being beaten once again dominated her thoughts. *Is he still there? Still slaving away in Hal's Hell while I go for sunny morning strolls, and drink my latte while planning the death of a president?*

That was months ago for him, she reminded herself. *He's recovered; he's forgotten about you, for now. Probably chasing some other girl.*

She wasn't so sure, though. He had asked her out for drinks every day for months. Chase didn't seem like the sort to give up so easily.

But where would he go to find me if he had the means to do so, which he doesn't? Even if he found out I've been bought by the Marauders, what would he do? Visit their HQ?

She didn't even know where that was. For all she knew, it was on a ship, or on some rock, floating in the interstellar void. That's the sort of place she'd always heard that mercenary outfits operated out of.

"Rika," a sweet voice said, and she turned to see the woman behind the counter holding out her drink.

"Thanks," Rika answered, and took the cup, touching it to her lips and savoring the scent before taking a taste. "Stars!" she exclaimed. "Oh, wow, that's so good."

The woman giggled. "Glad to make your day. Next, please?"

Rika realized she was holding up the line and stepped aside, taking another sip of the coffee as she walked out of the shop and back into the late morning light; all her worries about past and future already forgotten.

"Oh, stars," she whispered. "Can't this just last forever?"

* * * * *

Rika strolled down the paths in the forest to the north of the presidential palace, taking in the sights with an innocent joy that was barely an act.

Even though she was surveilling the protections the president's security had placed along President Ariana's running path, the high volume of cameras, automated turrets, and sensor systems didn't diminish the joy she felt.

Shit, if this is slavery, I'll take more of it, she thought; but then a frown creased her brow.

No, a gilded cage is still a cage.

She knew agony awaited her if she didn't get back to the warehouse by the proscribed time. That was not freedom.

The chain may be long, but it was still present.

She refocused on the task at hand. Rika knew from the intel that Team Basilisk had gathered already that the president took only one of three routes through the forest for her early morning run. However, all the routes converged at a specific point; a dozen meters beyond that point, the trail passed into a wide glen.

Rika walked through the glen, looking at the large trees that bordered it, eyeing each in turn, looking for one with the right branches in the right place.

As she reached the far side of the clearing, she spotted the perfect tree. It had a cluster of trunks that stayed close together for almost twenty meters before branching out. She could hug one of the trunks, and rest her rifle along a branch. The cloak she wore could double as camouflage, and there was mesh back in the warehouse with which to cover her GNR-41C.

She would be invisible.

Rika kept walking further down the trail, noting fallback positions and places where Jerry and Leslie could hide.

Their job would be to keep on the lookout for anyone who may compromise Rika's position—but also to finish the job, should Rika's shots not prove fatal.

That wasn't an outcome that worried Rika. She would kill President Ariana; it was a foregone conclusion.

Barne's job was the getaway. He would park a truck holding several hoverbikes nearby, and would also pay off a local bike gang to drive by the palace and throw rotten fruit at it.

Two kilometers away, there would be other transportation for them to switch to, and access to three possible safe fallbacks. She hadn't been given the location of the fallbacks yet, but Jerry had assured her that she would know about them in due time.

Rika nodded to a young couple as she walked past, giving them a warm smile. The gesture wasn't entirely disingenuous, but enough to make her feel guilty for enjoying this peaceful place, knowing that she would forever mark it as a place of mourning.

Instead of admiring the beauty of the glade, passersby would remember their beloved leader and revile her killer.

Better her than me, she thought, pushing the concern from her mind once more.

Eventually Rika left the park and took a different route back toward the warehouse, walking at the slowest pace she could manage while still giving herself a buffer, in case she ran into any trouble.

Rika hadn't bothered to mention to Jerry that receiving discipline while out in public would most certainly reveal her—and their operation. If he'd known, he probably wouldn't have let her go on her own; now that she had spent this day in paradise, she was all the more glad that she had omitted the information.

Or maybe he knew; maybe he was trusting her, allowing her to prove that she was part of the team.

Quite the risk to take.

Dusk was beginning to fall as she neared the warehouse. Everything appeared to be as it was when she left, save the positions of transport vehicles around some of the other buildings.

As Rika walked down the road, something caught her eye: a light was on in one of the warehouse's windows. Not an overhead light, but a small one, close to the glass. Rika focused on it, picking up slight pulses in its intensity.

They contained a message, which she decoded: *Intruders. Seven.*

Rika slowed her approach and casually stepped into the ferns lining the road, activating her robe's camouflage. Once hidden from sight, she ducked down behind the greenery and switched her vision to IR, followed by UV, as she scanned the perimeter for sentries.

She picked up two—one rounding a corner on the far side of the building, and another one closer, walking past the road she had been strolling down a minute earlier.

Rika remained still, praying that her robe's camouflage would fool whatever sensors the closest sentry possessed. He paused a moment and then resumed his route, heading south around the warehouse.

The robe that had hidden her form would now be a hindrance. Rika pulled it off and bundled it up before stuffing it beneath a fallen branch. The scarf and pads on her feet followed.

Thirty meters of open space lay between the warehouse and the trees. Rika considered her options. She could run across, hoping that no one spotted her—but if whoever these people were had half a brain between them, there would be motion sensors that would pick up her movements.

She eyed the roofline, looking for a good landing spot—something that wouldn't make too much noise, or transfer vibration into the building's wooden structure.

Walking east, keeping well within the tree line, she saw a loading crane that sat ten meters from the building. That put it only twenty from cover; an easy jump even without much of a start.

Rika checked the ground and moved a few branches out of the way. Then she backed up several meters and took off at full speed. As she left the trees, she pushed off, soaring through the air and catching the crane with her still-gloved hands before swinging underneath and arcing through the air to the cornice around the roof of the warehouse.

She caught it with her clawed feet and crouched low, scanning the rooftop. No sentries were visible; though several air conditioning units blocked her vision. Rika carefully crept across the crushed rock on the roof to a staircase, which led down into the warehouse below.

It wasn't the one she'd used the night before—that one let off almost on top of where Team Basilisk had set up their base. This one would bring her down on the far side of the warehouse, a few dozen meters away.

As her hand stretched toward the door, she prayed that whoever had taken the warehouse had disabled the alarms, or her element of surprise would be gone in the next few seconds.

The door was unlocked, and as she eased it open, Rika saw that the sensors were indeed off. Analyzing the stairs leading down to the warehouse's wooden floor, she took slow, careful steps—the wooden stairs only giving two soft creaks as she went.

Given how much the old building moved and sighed as the sun set and the air cooled, she hoped it wouldn't be noticeable.

Once down the stairs, Rika ducked behind several dusty old crates and looked for movement and heat sources. Though she had spotted two sentries outside, Rika had to assume that there were at least seven within. Maybe more. Barne may not have seen the whole team when he set up the light.

An IR bloom appeared to her right, and Rika saw a woman prowling past, her eyes on the doors and windows, not looking within the warehouse. She walked within four meters of Rika and then kept going.

Rika considered taking the woman down and seizing her weapon, but she didn't want to alert the other intruders without getting a better grasp on what was happening.

Carefully moving from cover to cover, Rika crept through the warehouse, spotting two more sentries before reaching a stack of crates with a small gap between them. She peered through and saw Barne with five other figures.

Two of the intruders held Barne against a stack of crates while one of the others paced in front of him.

"You said she'd be back by now! Where is she?" the pacing one asked—a woman, though rather husky sounding. Rika wondered if she had always been a woman, or if she was in the midst of a gender change.

Barne gave his deep chuckle. "How would I know? She's just the meat. I don't talk to meat."

So much for no one calling me 'meat' yet, Rika thought.

"Well, ping her again," the woman said.

"Just did," Barne said with a shrug. "She's not answering. Maybe she ran off."

A smile formed on Rika's lips. She had received no message; maybe Barne wasn't a complete ass after all.

"Cheri got it out of Jerry that your mech girl has a compliance chip. She's not running off, and she wouldn't miss her return deadline."

Barne laughed again, leaning back against a crate. "Back in the war, I saw a mech lose its shit. AM model. It killed seventeen men and women in my regiment. The LT was hitting it with more Discipline than he ever had before, and it just kept coming. That shit is a rope, not a chain."

Rika wondered about that. She had never heard of any mechs successfully resisting Discipline; granted, she had only met a few hundred, and there had been over a hundred thousand of her kind in the war. It was probably safe to assume that tales of mechs resisting Discipline were kept hushed.

The woman continued to press Barne, and Rika took the time to examine the intruders.

Like the sentries she saw before, they wore robes—though theirs were not as advanced as the one Rika had spent her day in. Her enhanced vision traced the outlines of light armor as they moved, but the speaker's was heavier and powered to some extent.

Their weapons were multifunction rifles, capable of firing pulse rounds and projectiles. None of the intruders appeared to be carrying beam or plasma guns.

She turned and looked behind her, catching sight of one of the sentries twenty meters away. That would be her first target.

Rika crept back through the warehouse, angling toward where that sentry would be in a minute's time. She waited behind a crate, and when the sentry's boot came into view, she rose to her full height, clamped her hands around the person's head—a man, younger by the looks of him—and broke his neck in one swift twist.

She grabbed his rifle as it slipped from his lifeless fingers and looked it over. It was the same model as the ones the others carried. Rika also saw that it was biolocked.

Without an unlock kit, it would be death to grab the weapon's grip—for a human. Even so, Rika wasn't keen on the idea of shorting out her hand. Looking around, she saw some metal strapping nearby and quietly wrapped it around the weapon's grip. Holding the gun by the stock in her left hand, she took a deep breath and slipped her right hand onto the grip.

Nothing happened. She wondered if the weapon's biolock was enabled. Then sparks flew from the metal strapping wrapped around the grip, and it grew hot in her hand—not that Rika cared. Then the sparks ceased, and she carefully pulled off the strapping.

It was easier said than done, as some of the pieces had been welded together by the electrical current. Once she had them free, Rika checked the weapon's readout and realized that the pulse functionality had been fried.

No matter, she thought. *I wasn't planning on using that, anyway.*

The weapon had a mechanical firing system for the projectiles, and she checked its action, making sure that it was still functional—which it was.

Time to kick some ass.

Rika circled around to come in behind Basilisk's staging area, where the intruders were holding Barne. During her first kill and the time it had taken to make the weapon usable, the woman yelling at Barne had moved on to hitting him.

That was good news for Rika. It meant that three of them would be distracted. The remaining two—a man and a woman—were standing near the cases that her armor and weapons had been in. Rika crouched low, getting right behind them before leaping up onto the cases and stooping down.

She gave a wild scream as she grabbed the intruder on her right by the hair and pulled him off the ground, while firing three rounds into the back of the female intruder's head.

The woman fell to the ground, dead, while the man writhed in Rika's grip, his hands wrapped around her wrist.

Rika flung him straight up into the ceiling, but by some miracle he managed to hold onto her wrist. She swung her arm back down, slamming him into the ground as she jumped off the cases and landed on his chest, smashing his ribs like they were twigs.

The two guards holding Barne had seen the whole thing, and for the five seconds it had taken for two of their comrades to die, had simply stared with mouths open.

"Oh, there she is," Barne said with a laugh, as he pulled his right arm free and grabbed one of the men by the neck. Barne grunted and swung his arms together, and his two former captors slammed into one another; then one of them—Rika wasn't sure which—got a boot to the chest.

Rika had only been watching Barne with half an eye because she was busy emptying her weapon's magazine into the large woman who had been driving her fists into Barne's gut a moment before.

The rounds ricocheted off the woman's armor, and she gave a grim smile. "Gonna take a lot more than that to kill me, meat."

Rika threw the weapon aside and charged at the woman, driving both fists into her torso, and the satisfying crack of shattering armor plates reverberated up her arms.

The woman, for her part, staggered back, but didn't go down. She set her teeth, grabbed Rika's forearms, and delivered a powered kick to Rika's gut.

The blow pushed Rika back, but she was on the woman a moment later, grabbing both of her arms. Rika rotated her wrists, twisting them nearly all the way around—one of the benefits of being less than human—until she heard two loud cracks, and the woman began screaming.

The sounds were like music to Rika as she planted a foot on the woman's chest—her three claws digging into the cracks that her initial blows had caused. Her heel claw drove through the cracked plate and the under-layer, sinking into the woman's gut.

Rika took a deep breath, straightened her leg, and pulled the woman's arms off. Her enemy fell to the ground, and Rika planted her other foot on the woman's chest, tearing her chest plate off.

"I. Am. Not. Fucking. *MEAT!*" Rika screamed, and slammed her foot into the woman's chest while tearing the other free, pulling a string of intestines out into the air.

"Holy shit," Barne whispered from behind her.

Rika turned to see Barne standing over the two men who had been holding him back, his eyes locked on the pair of arms she still held.

"What?" Rika asked, her voice still filled with rage. "Don't like your rescue?"

"Uh...no..." Barne stammered. "I just haven't seen anything like that since..."

"The war," Rika said with a nod. "Guess the war's not over yet, is it?"

"I don't know what that means, but could you put those arms down? They're creeping me out."

Shots rang out and ricocheted off Rika's armor. Barne ducked down behind a crate, but Rika turned, catching sight of three more enemies closing in. Her IR and UV blend also picked up the two sentries from outside entering through the north and south doors.

The closest attacker was twenty meters away, and Rika rushed toward him brandishing the arms she still held, as the assailant fired before ducking behind a crate for cover.

It didn't help.

Rika slammed into the crate at full speed and pushed it back against another stack, crushing the man in between. She strode around to see him struggling to get up, his right arm hanging limp at his side.

Wordlessly, she swung one of the severed arms, striking him in the head, before grabbing him by the throat with her foot and tearing him free from the crates. At the apex of her swing, she let go, and he flew headfirst into a nearby support pole.

She wasn't certain if he died before or after he hit the pole, but as his twitching body landed on the floor, she knew it didn't matter.

Gunfire sounded from Barne's position, and responses came from two locations.

<*Thanks for the rifle,*> Barne said.

<*You're welcome. Let me know if you need me to come and rescue you again.*>

<*Fuck off.*>

<*That's more like it,*> Rika replied.

Rika selected her next target—the sentry entering through the south door—and ran toward her. The woman didn't fare any better than the rest had.

Rika circled around the enemies in the warehouse, getting behind the one furthest from Barne, who was trying to move into a flanking position.

She smashed the farthest sentry's head. Barne opened fire once more, and then stopped and called out that he was clear.

Rika returned to Barne's position. "You got two?" she asked.

"Yeah," Barne said with a nod, as he dropped the rifle and walked over to one of their supply crates.

"So Cheri sent them, did she?" Rika asked.

"Yup," Barne said with a grunt, and pulled out a tank of light brown liquid. "Bring all the bodies over here; we have to clean up."

"'Clean up'?" Rika asked.

"Yeah, we have to get out of here, and we can't leave it like this."

<*Get out of here to go rescue Jerry and Leslie, right?*> Rika asked as she stalked off to grab bodies.

<Yeah, but first we dissolve these dickheads. Then we load up all our gear onto a truck, and burn this place to the ground.>

<Won't that look suspicious?>

She grabbed two of the closest bodies and carried them back to where Barne had pulled all the equipment out of a case and was pouring the liquid into it.

"Nope, the crates on the far side of this warehouse are fireworks. We'll just set something up so it looks like a spark from a truck started it, and then we'll watch, well, the fireworks."

"What are fireworks?" Rika asked, walking away once more.

<What…seriously? The things people shoot up into the sky that go boom and then rain sparks down everywhere.>

<Sounds like you're describing AA guns or something.>

<Kinda. They're old school, but these Thebans seem to like old-school.>

<I've noticed.>

Rika gathered all the bodies and then walked to the east side of the warehouse where she had spotted a cleaning closet. Inside, there was a hose and some cleaning supplies. Rika spent the next twenty minutes getting the bits of bone, blood, and hair out of her armor.

<Be back in a minute. Just need to go get my robe,> she informed Barne.

<Get a truck while you're at it,> he replied.

<Do you have the codes for it?> Rika asked.

*<No, I said get **a** truck, not get **the** truck; Jerry and Leslie took ours. Steal another one.>*

Rika sighed. *Have a nice stroll through the city, enjoy a latte and a walk through the woods…check. Kill a bunch of people, dissolve their bodies, and steal a truck…double check.*

She grabbed a hack unit from the staging area before walking outside, and carefully surveyed their surroundings.

By some miracle, the commotion within the warehouse didn't appear to have drawn any attention. Rika didn't see another person as she retrieved her robe and pulled it on, wrapping the shawl around her head once more.

The cluster of warehouses had no shortage of trucks, though most were too big for their needs. Something with a box only eight meters long was preferable.

Rika was walking around the fourth building when she spotted the perfect candidate: a white box truck with no markings on it whatsoever. She pulled the lock off the back and lifted the rear roller door. A bench ran along each side of the interior, and duffels filled the space in between.

<I think I found our visitors' truck. It'll do perfectly.>

<Great. Bring it around to the dock and start loading our stuff up. I'm about half done, but we'll have to take their armor with us. Stuff won't melt down.>

Rika walked around the truck and opened the driver's door. She pulled out the hack unit and then slapped it on the truck's control panel. The Marauders' tech was good. Thirty seconds later, the truck started, and Rika climbed in and drove the truck to their warehouse's loading docks.

It occurred to Rika, as she pulled the truck up to the building, that this was the first time she'd ever driven anything with wheels.

It was strange to feel it bounce and jostle over the uneven pavement, but it also gave her a sense of power. It took her two tries to back it up to the dock, and then just fifteen minutes to load all of Basilisk's gear.

"You're pretty damn fast at that," Barne said as she approached where he was carefully pushing the last body into his makeshift vat of acid.

"I have a lot of experience," Rika replied. "Why do you use acid for that? Can't you get nano to do it better?"

Barne nodded. "Yeah, but it's hard enough getting what we need planetside for missions like this—like your rifle's rounds. Acid, we can source locally and make out of stuff that no one will wonder about."

Rika nodded silently, watching one of the attacker's faces dissolve. She knew that she should feel something—be sad, angry, something.

Mostly she just felt disappointed. Disappointed that she had killed so viciously, disappointed that her perfect day had ended like this.

She had noticed, however, that Barne hadn't said a single insulting thing to her since the fight. It seemed like he couldn't decide to be wary of her, or grateful that she had saved him.

"Can you help me with this?" he asked as he closed the case. "There's a drain over where you cleaned off. We can pour this down, and rinse it out."

"Sure," Rika said, and lifted the case, carrying it over to where Barne had directed.

"I gotta ask," Barne said from behind her. "Why did you save me? I didn't order you to."

Rika set the case down next to the drain and shrugged. "I don't know…it never occurred to me to do anything but help you. I know you don't really want me here, but I'm on the team." She gave him a slight smile. "Even if it's like how your rifle's on the team."

Barne's face reddened as he opened the crate and carefully drained its contents.

"I'm sorry about that. I can be a bit of an ass sometimes."

"A bit?" Rika asked with an arched eyebrow.

Barne laughed, "OK, a lot. And probably more often than 'sometimes'."

"How bad do you think they're hurt?" Rika asked, changing the subject. No point in making Barne feel like she was going to forgive him just yet.

Barne grabbed the hose and began spraying out the case. "Hopefully not too bad. Jerry's sweet on Leslie, and if Cheri's worth her salt, she probably picked up on it. A few good bruises and cuts on Leslie, and Jerry probably spilled it."

"Shit, I thought he'd let her take a bit more punishment before he ratted us out."

It was Barne's turn to give her a raised brow. "He wanted to make sure they hit me here before you came back. That way *you* would have the element of surprise, not them. He knew I could take whatever that woman had to dish out."

"So you don't think he ratted us out?"

"No," Barne replied. "He wanted us to live so we could come save them. Which is why I'm so glad you decided not to make a run for it. Looks like his trust in you wasn't misplaced."

"I guess I have a trustworthy face," Rika said with a smile.

"Or something. Just don't shriek again, like you did when you tore that woman's arms off. Scared the shit out of me."

Rika laughed and clapped Barne on the shoulder. "Good, I think you could use a little less shit in you."

THE ROMANY

STELLAR DATE: 12.16.8948 (Adjusted Years)
LOCATION: Enlisted Commissary, MSS *Romany*
REGION: Interstellar Space, near the Praesepe Cluster

Chase settled into his seat in the *Romany*'s commissary and eyed what the cooks were trying to trick him into eating. It looked like steak and eggs, but he doubted that the Marauder ship had enough steak to feed their entire crew such a meal.

"Wondering what the mystery is with the meat?" a voice said from across the table, and Chase looked up to see Ralph— one of the squad sergeants from Chase's new platoon—settle into the seat across from him.

"Aren't you?" Chase asked.

"Nah, we're just out of port; it'll be the real thing. Once we're a week in, then you can start to worry about what the protein really came from."

Chase stabbed a fork into one of the steak tips and gave it a tentative bite. "Damn! This *is* real meat…or such a good fake that I don't care."

"Oh, you'll know when they start faking it," Sergeant Casey said as she sat next to Ralph. "We've got good cooks, but they're not that good."

Chase took another bite and shook his head. He'd never expected to be sitting on a warship, talking about how shitty— or how good, in this case—the chow was with his 'toon-mates again, but here he was.

For a woman, he thought to himself.

But he knew that was oversimplifying things. Rika wasn't just any woman; she was *the* woman. He was going to find her, and then…and then they'd figure something out.

"What do you know about where we jumped to?" Chase asked.

Ralph shrugged, but Casey gave a conspiratorial smile. "Command's not talking, but I can recognize the stars out there, easy. We're still in the Praesepe Cluster."

"That's not saying much," Chase replied.

"Well, what if I said that we're on the rimward edge of the cluster…and that we jumped very close to a system?"

"Still not following," Chase said with a shake of his head, but Ralph exclaimed, "Thebes!"

"Got it in one!" Casey grinned at Ralph. "Thebes is key. Powerful, small; some might say it's ripe."

"We're attacking a sovereign nation?" Chase asked, his eyes wide. From what he knew of mercenary outfits, they disrupted trade routes, harassed settlements, or operated as hired security. But he had never really thought about them being part of an invasion force.

He wasn't sure that it sat well with him. Still, he supposed it was better than oppressing civilians on some backwater world. An invasion force would at least be fighting a military.

"What's wrong, Chase?" Ralph asked. "You look like you just ate something that didn't agree with you."

"Just thinking about what the action might involve."

Casey shrugged. "Hard to say. For all intents and purposes, the Marauders are pretty new—even though we have a large force. The Old Man has been selective in what jobs he's taken, but it's usually stuff that will piss off the Niets in some way or another."

"Plus a few jobs for the Septhians here and there," Ralph added.

"Yeah," Chase said with a nod. "They covered some of that in orientation. "But they didn't say anything about taking on something like the Theban Alliance. I kinda thought we'd be going after bad guys."

Casey shook her head. "Seriously, Chase. You were in the Genevian Armed Forces. Can you really say that there were 'bad guys' in that last war? Sure, the Nietzscheans were—and are—raging assholes, but our government wasn't exactly sunshine and roses, either."

Chase didn't reply—his thoughts were on Rika and what his own government had done to her. She had never told him any stories from the war, but he knew what the mechs were made to do. Any mech that made it to the end of the war had a lot of blood on their souls.

"Not to mention that our fleet admirals were built from buckets full of stupid," Ralph added.

"I'm curious," Chase said, pulling his thoughts away from what Rika might be doing at that moment. "How did the Old Man get so many ships, anyway? He wasn't in Fleet Command. He was ground assault, right?"

"Right-o," Ralph said. "I was in his division back in the war. We kicked a lot of Nietzschean ass, but we kept losing because we had no space-support. Slowly, as dumbass fleet commanders got blown into space-dust, the General drew more and more ships under his direct control. Even though he wasn't fleet command, he was the senior officer after a lot of losses.

"He was good; could do more with twenty ships than some admirals could manage with a thousand. So, the top brass let him keep them. Gotta say, it was nice knowing that if you needed to call down starfire, it would hit."

"There were a lot more than twenty ships outside when we jumped here," Chase said.

"A lot of people didn't just lay down arms when the government surrendered," Casey said. "Some joined the Marauders. Plus, there are two other outfits I know of that are made up of Genevian ships and soldiers."

"I heard a lot went pirate, too," Chase said. "Mind you, I was inside the Nietzschean Empire. They're not subtle with the propaganda, and I didn't buy most of it, but I still didn't expect so much organization. I just figured that most defectors were solo operations, hitting soft targets for supplies and credit."

Ralph nodded. "Yeah, there are a lot of solo ships out there; people who think that they can make a difference on their own. Every few months, a handful come to the Marauders with their tails between their legs. Old Man takes 'em in, but he breaks their crews up to integrate them. At the beginning, a few took advantage of his refit and resupply and then took off again."

"Bastards," Chase said. "I may be new here, but I can appreciate what the Old Man is building. Maybe if he'd been in charge of the Genevian Space Force, we'd still have a nation."

Ralph raised his glass of milk. "I'll drink to that. Maybe someday we'll kick the shit out of the Niets and get it back, too."

The three touched their plastic cups, though Casey shook her head. "I don't want Genevia back, but if the Old Man were to set up a little corner of space under himself, I would settle down there."

"So," Ralph said after he downed his milk. "What is it that got you to enlist? Got tired of living in Niet-land?"

"You could say that," Chase said. "I wasn't like you two; when the orders came down to surrender, we just had our asses handed to us. The ship's captain turned off the shields, and allowed us to be boarded. I was pissed—more than pissed. I'd just watched half my platoon die, and he was just giving up. Some of the crew fought when the Niets boarded us; I would have, if I could have gotten to a weapon in time…."

"Heard a lot of stories like that," Casey said. "What happened?"

"They tossed the whole lot of us onto Mortlach. Took me half a year to get off that shithole."

"Damn! You got off Mortlach?" Ralph asked, his eyes wide. "Half our freaking people are still down there."

"Yeah, how'd you swing that?" Casey asked.

Chase shrugged. He knew, but he wasn't ready to share it yet, so he related his customary story.

"They were letting people off for a while. Since I didn't fight the boarding, I was on the 'good' list. I'll be honest…it made me sick to leave. So many left behind."

Ralph and Casey nodded in agreement.

"Maybe someday…" Ralph said again.

Casey snorted. "Don't get your hopes up, Ralph. It would take the overthrow of the Nietzschean Empire to get our people off Mortlach."

"A guy can dream, can't he?" Ralph asked.

From the faraway look in his eyes, Chase wondered if there was someone down on Mortlach that Ralph was holding onto hope for. Not that there was much hope to be had, with a place like that.

"So, Chase…nice little bit of evasion there, but you were dicking around out there for years. Coulda joined the Marauders long ago. Why now?"

Chase figured it would slip out some time. "Looking for someone."

"Oh, yeah?" Ralph's eyes lit up, and the eagerness in his voice solidified Chase's earlier suspicion. "Who's the lucky girl?"

"What makes you think it's a girl…or even romantic?" Chase asked, not entirely comfortable discussing his search for Rika with people he had just met a day prior.

Casey chuckled. "It's a girl because you've glanced at a couple of the prettier Marauders to pass us by, and may have let your eyes linger on my tits; though I'll give you a pass since I spilled gravy on them when you did it—"

"You got nice tits," Ralph interjected with a grin. "I glance at 'em all the time."

"Yeah, Ralph, you have the subtlety of a supernova; I kinda notice. Plus, I have to keep a napkin handy for the drool."

Ralph took on a wounded look while Casey leveled a stare at Chase.

"It's good to know your teammate's motivations. Helps them bond," Casey said. "OK, we know it's a girl, and suspect your interest is romantic. Where is this girl, that you'd join up with the Marauders to find her?"

As Casey spoke, a look of understanding dawned on Ralph. "Casey! Chase's girl is *in* the Marauders!"

Casey snapped her fingers. "By the Old Man's wrinkly ass, I think you're right! Look at Chase, red as a tomato!"

"Don't talk about tomatoes," Ralph said with a shudder. "I fought on Boston where they have those freakish tomato forests. Fucking juice off the stems could peel the camo layer off your armor. And house-sized tomatoes? Are you fucking kidding me? Some things just can't be unseen."

"Seriously, Ralph? They were just plants. I fought on Boston, too," Chase said.

"Don't change the subject again," Ralph shot back. "The girl. Who is she? Is she on the *Romany*?"

Chase sighed and shook his head. "Not that I've seen. She's not on the roster, and no one knows anything about her; before I enlisted, though…well, let's just say that I have it on very good authority that she's in the Marauders."

"Name," Ralph said.

"Yeah, tell him," Casey said around a mouthful of eggs. "Ralph knows everyone, and if he doesn't know 'em, he knows someone who does."

"Rika," Chase said. "Her name's Rika."

"What's her specialization—if she has one?" Ralph asked.

"She's a mech," Chase replied, his tone guarded.

"Really?" Casey sat up.

"What model?" Ralph asked with a look of concentration on his face as he reached out across the Link.

Chase hated that people thought of mechs—well, Rika mostly—as models. Even if it was a good way to identify them.

"She's an SMI-2," Chase replied.

"Ohhh yeah," Ralph grinned. "SMI-2s were all chicks; they were some hot meat."

Chase felt the blood rise in his face once more. "Ralph, you seem like a good guy, but if you call Rika 'meat' one more time, I'll cave your teeth in, got it?"

"Dude—" Ralph began to say, but Casey put a hand on his shoulder.

"Cool it. Both of you. Ralph, apologize. Chase, ease up on the macho reactions, 'kay?" Casey said.

Ralph sank back in his chair and stared at Chase—who returned the expression. Suddenly Ralph smiled and nodded.

"Sorry, man. You're right. I picked up a lot of bad habits in the war. We were all meat to the brass. Mechs saved my life more than once, too. You'll never hear that word pass my lips again, unless I'm talking about our delicious victuals, here."

Chase was surprised by Ralph's words—the man's recognition of his misstep shaming Chase for having such a visceral reaction.

"Me too. I just really want to find her. I'm worried we're going to get into some crazy action here and one of us won't make it out."

"No chance," Casey said. "Marauders do the fucking-up of shit, not the other way around."

Ralph let out a sound that was half snort, half laugh. "Casey, that has to be the worst metaphor I've ever heard."

"We turn the enemy into shit fuckers?" Casey asked.

"I vote that we abandon all analogies combining fucking and shit," Chase said. "How's about 'we rub their faces in shit'?"

"For fuck's sake!" a woman said from a few seats down. "People are trying to eat, here!"

"Sorry," Chase muttered.

"Either way," Casey said. "Now that Ralph's on the case, he'll ferret her out. Not a lot of mechs in the Marauders. People will have seen her."

Ralph grinned and nodded. "Sergeant Ralph is on the case. I'll find your smecksy mech girl in no time! I might have to extract payment with some leering, and maybe a bit of drooling, mind you."

"Way to own your misogyny, Ralph," Casey said.

Chase couldn't help but smile at Ralph's enthusiastic grin. "You're a class act, Ralph. Seriously, though, I appreciate it. Finding Rika is…well…I just have to do it."

RESCUE

STELLAR DATE: 12.16.8948 (Adjusted Years)
LOCATION: Northeast Berlin
REGION: Pyra, Albany System, Theban Alliance

The fireworks had been amazing. Rika had stared out the truck's window at them for a full five minutes before fire drones finally arrived and began putting them out.

She imagined that they must be even more impressive in the sky than on the ground.

News feeds on the local nets had been abuzz about the fire, but there was no mention of anything suspicious about it—though it was far too soon to tell. Rika doubted that inspectors would be able to start crawling through the mess until the next day.

Barne drove the truck several kilometers and then parked it in a garage next to another, equally nondescript truck—though this one was black. Together, he and Rika swapped all their cargo over and swept the truck clean. Barne had informed her that it was long-term storage parking, and that he'd rented the space till the end of the month.

They would be long gone by then.

The drive to the next location was short, just ten minutes, and they pulled into another warehouse area before reaching a self-storage lot.

"We going to set up shop here?" Rika asked.

"No," Barne replied as he opened the storage unit's door, revealing a smaller car.

By the time he had driven the car out, and she had parked the truck in the storage unit—which it just barely fit into—Howe was beginning to rise in the eastern sky.

"I haven't asked, because I assumed you had a plan, but how are we going to get to wherever Cheri is?" Rika asked. "Jerry said it was halfway around the world."

"He was exaggerating," Barne replied as he leaned against the car. "It's near Jersey City—about seventeen hundred klicks up the coast. They have high-speed highways here, and this baby can do four hundred an hour. We'll be there by lunchtime."

Rika nodded and opened the back of the truck, and then she jumped up and opened a crate. She tossed two rifles down to Barne, followed by a duffel bag full of ammunition. She turned to another case and opened it up, pulling out her gun-arm and helmet.

"You think you'll need that?" Barne asked as she jumped out and pulled down the truck's overhead door.

"Maybe. I'd like to keep them close."

"Sounds reasonable," Barne replied with a shrug.

Five minutes later, they were pulling onto the highway, the car sliding onto a high-speed maglev ridge and accelerating to top speed.

Rika opened up a panel on her leg and pulled out her charge cord, sliding it into one of the power sockets in the car.

"Glad it has that," she said. "Wouldn't want to go into our big rescue with only half a charge."

Barne gave a soft laugh. "I know what you mean...I don't have to plug in—not modded enough for that—but I do need to eat a ton to keep going."

"Speaking of which," Rika reached into the back and grabbed a fistful of protein bars, dumping half in Barne's lap.

"Thanks..." he said, a pregnant pause hanging between them.

Rika didn't want to spend the next four hours in an uncomfortable silence, so she asked, "What is it?"

"Well," Barne began. "What's it like? I mean, I'll be honest—you were kinda sour and mopey at first. But in a fight…I've never seen anything like it. You just charged them like their guns were shooting spitwads."

"Well, in my defense, I woke up in that warehouse only minutes after being sold at auction—by my reckoning," Rika replied. "I was feeling just a bit down. Shit…that was still just over two days ago for me."

"At auction?" Barne shook his head. "I had no idea…"

"Is one form of selling a slave somehow more dignified than another?" Rika asked, her tone acidic.

"I guess not," Barne said. "But I hadn't really thought about how the regiment got you. I figured they had you in a warehouse at HQ or something."

"Yeah, back to miniscule differentiations of humiliation."

"Sorry…you don't have to be such a bitch to me about it. *I* didn't chop you up and sell you off after the war." Barne's face took on a pouty frown, and Rika realized that she was punishing Barne for what others had done to her.

"Gah. I'm not good at this, Barne. Personal interaction and I are not close friends."

"You too, eh?" Barne said, and then laughed. "Look at the two of us—both shithead messes after the war, barely able to talk to anyone, and stuck together in here."

Barne continued laughing, and Rika joined in, letting the cathartic release calm her down. Eventually, when they were silent once more, Barne glanced over at her.

"You didn't really answer the question."

"Which question?" Rika asked, knowing full well what he was referring to.

"About what it's like. What they did to you."

Rika looked down at herself, at her steel limbs, at her three-fingered hands.

"I won't lie," she said. "There are times when it's wonderful. The power, the speed—they're intoxicating."

"You like killing," Barne said quietly. "I saw it in your eyes. Don't try to bullshit me. I know the look; it stares back at me in the mirror every day."

Rika didn't respond for a minute. Then two. Then five. She wondered if Barne was going to let it drop, but knew he wouldn't. She knew she shouldn't.

"There are two Rikas," she said at last. "There's a Rika who just *stopped* that night when they took me, when they made me into this…machine. That Rika would give anything to go back to how things were—hell, she's still just a nineteen-year-old girl. I can't stop her from wanting to go back to before—she craves it constantly. But there's this other Rika. The one that came out on the battlefield, the one that survived the war, when so many others didn't…"

Rika closed her eyes, and the vision of Kelly—her friend laying before her on the deck of the shuttle with a hole blown clear through her torso—came back to her.

"I know that guilt," Barne said.

"Yeah, all the psych programs go on about survivor's guilt," Rika said. "But they don't tell you what to do with the other feeling…"

"The joy you get from killing," Barne said.

"Is it joy?" Rika asked. "For me it's just rage; I want to make them all pay for what they did to me—for what they took. But maybe…maybe you're right, Barne." Rika let out a long sigh. "Maybe there is joy mixed with that rage."

Barne nodded, silent for a minute. "I don't know if it's wrong or not, Rika. But it's what we are now. We're killers, you and me. Why don't you rest a bit? We'll be killing again soon enough."

Rika closed her eyes and leaned her head back. A killer. That's all Barne saw when he looked at her; it was all he had ever seen. The only difference was that now, she had killed to save him.

Maybe he was right. She was on Pyra to kill. Though she had spent her day enjoying a lovely walk, its purpose had been to help her kill more effectively. Even the rescue they were about to undertake—even if it was bloodless—was just so they could kill once more.

Killer….

* * * * *

The sun was beginning to set as she and Barne settled behind a rock to survey Cheri's 'hideout'. Though it only took a few hours to reach Jersey City, it had taken several more to get deep into the nearby mountains and make their way up the steep valley without being seen.

"How come this Cheri person gets a nice villa at the foot of a mountain, and we had to hang out in a dusty warehouse?" Rika asked.

"Covert mission," Barne said. "Cheri doesn't seem to be doing the 'covert' thing, here."

"Barne, I was kidding," Rika said.

"Huh, musta been your robot voice."

Rika opened her mouth to give Barne a tongue-lashing he would never forget, when she saw the twinkle in his eye.

"Asshole," she said, and gave him a mock punch on the arm.

"Ow! Shit, Rika, even your pretend punches hurt like balls. Ease up, OK?"

"Sorry-not-sorry," Rika replied in a robotic voice.

Barne chuckled. "Now who's the asshole?"

Rika shook her head and allowed a small smile to grace her lips. If someone had told her that two days after being sold at auction she would be smiling—with the people who had bought her, no less—she would have slapped them upside the head. And not in a nice way.

Is this Stockholm Syndrome? she wondered. *I never felt this way about the GAF...I hated them. Well, most of them.*

She made a note to have her internal psych-eval program check for Stockholm the next time she ran it. For now, getting Jerry and Leslie out of that rather nice-looking villa was all that mattered.

The question Barne had asked echoed in her mind once more. Why *had* she saved him? Sure, there were all the issues with getting offworld, and where she would go without the help of Basilisk. That was all logical and fine; but Rika knew she hadn't thought of any of that when she saw his warning in the window.

She'd had a teammate in trouble, and she had to rescue that teammate. Was that some sort of leftover conditioning from the military, or was she just so desperate to belong somewhere that she'd side with her owners?

"Hey, Rika, you with me?" Barne asked.

"Yeah, sorry."

"Enough dicking around. Time to get frosty. I can see seven sentries, what's your count?"

"I see eleven—make that twelve."

Barne and Rika had parked the car further down the valley, and hiked the last few kilometers to the villa. Since it was rather secluded, they decided to go in packing. Rika had spent the last two hours of the car ride adjusting the socket and mount on her gun-arm, so that she was able to place it on her right arm. It felt good to have it there. Even better, since it was the GNR-41C, and not the old B she used to have.

A JE78 multifunction rifle was on her back, and two pistols were slid into the clips on her thighs.

But the icing on the cake was her helmet. It was an older model, the one used by SMI-1 mechs. It only had two-seventy vision; not the three-sixty of her SMI-2 helmet from the war, but it fit. That helmet had only fit so long as the wearer didn't possess a nose or ears.

Given the fact that she had spent a lot of credit getting those features back, she was glad not to have to sacrifice them again.

Her hair, however, had been a different matter. It had taken several tries to get the helmet on and sealed without blonde strands sticking out around her neck, causing the seal-leak warning to flash.

In the end, she had lain down on a log with her head hanging off, while Barne carefully placed her hair in the helmet, and then raised it up to her head.

That was, of course, after joking that they should just shave it all off. He had almost called her 'mech-meat' at the time, but stopped himself, a look of apology on his face.

She hadn't made a big deal about it. He wasn't swearing at her, and calling her military hardware anymore, so she'd take what progress she could get.

Now as she watched the sentries through her helmet's enhanced sensors, she remembered how good it felt to have the extra senses it provided. She could hear animals in the brush two hundred paces away, see through haze and fog clear to the edge of the horizon, and even see through some of the walls in the villa.

"What's our plan, then?" Rika asked.

"Not sure," Barne replied. "I estimate we could take out five or six of those sentries before they figured out what was going on. But then they'll be on high alert. I bet there are at least forty or fifty of them in there, and they probably have no small number of automated defense systems, as well."

"Want to do something crazy?" Rika asked with a sly grin.

"How crazy?' Barne asked.

* * * * *

An hour later, Rika stood with Barne on the mountain slope, a kilometer above the villa.

"Let me get this straight, you want me to get on your back?" Barne asked.

"Yeah. You get on, and I'll run down the mountain. There's an escarpment sixty meters from the villa. Running downhill, I can probably hit one-fifty before we get there. Then I jump, we sail over everything, and—if I aim well—we smash right through that glass ceiling in the back."

"So your plan is to run down the mountain and jump into the villa," Barne said. "That's crazy."

Rika nodded. "Yes, I said that before we climbed up here. What did you think we were going to do?"

"I don't know, I figured you saw a secret door with your fancy helmet."

"Wouldn't that be nice," Rika laughed. "OK, climb on."

"This is the dumbest thing I've ever done," Barne complained, as he clambered up onto her back and wrapped his arms around her neck.

"I *really* doubt that this is the dumbest thing *you've* done," Rika said.

"At least you're sexy," he said morosely. "If you were a guy mech, I'd never live this down."

Rika wanted to tell Barne to shove his backhanded compliments up his asshole, but he might like that too much, so she let it drop.

"Hold on tight!" Rika said instead, and began her run down the mountain. She wove around rocks and trees, careful not to jostle Barne overmuch. Her speed crossed over a hundred, and then a hundred and fifty kilometers per hour. The edge of the escarpment rushed toward her, and Rika leapt off it at nearly one hundred and seventy kilometers per hour.

She gauged her trajectory and saw that her aim was true. The glass ceiling on a rear room of the villa's main structure rushed up to meet them, and they smashed through it and slammed into the room's floor.

Barne leapt off her the instant they broke through the glass and landed nearby, rolling to his feet, the medium armor he wore helping to absorb the shock.

The sensors in Rika's helmet, coupled with her neural augments, gave her a full layout of the room by the time she landed—and smashed a rather expensive-looking table.

Two men were standing near one of the doors, both looking surprised, though still raising their rifles.

Rika shot one with a ballistic round from her GNR-41C, while Barne took out the other.

<Which way?> Barne asked over the tightband they had established. So long as they were close or in line of sight, the signal would be very difficult to pick up, and they would run little risk of detection.

Rika swept her active scan across the room and saw a cluster of people sixty meters to their right.

<A big group that way,> she said, gesturing to a door that led in the general direction they needed to go.

Barne ran to the door, flattened himself against the wall, and then reached out and turned the knob. Rika leapt through into the hall beyond, her GNR pointed right, and her JE78 covering the left.

<Clear,> she announced and turned to her left, walking quietly down the hall toward an intersection. She reached it and scanned the area again, picking up movement in the corridor to their right—the direction they needed to go.

She nodded to Barne and he moved to the other side of the hall, holding his rifle ready.

He had visual before she did and opened fire, taking out two enemies in seconds.

<They're not armored. She must really trust her perimeter security,> Rika said.

<Or she's just cheap. Why give your goons good armor when you can sell it?>

<The more you tighten your grip, the more slips through your fingers.>

<Sounds about right,> Barne replied as he peered down the left hall.

Rika moved down the right, and Barne followed after, covering their six. Behind them, the sound of raised voices came from the room they had crashed into, and Rika picked up the pace, not wanting to be caught in a crossfire.

Ahead, a door opened and three guards rushed out. None had their weapons ready, and Rika made short work of them.

At two more intersections, Rika paused to listen and scan, each time leading them further into the south wing of the villa.

<Just ahead,> Rika said, gesturing to a set of double doors at the end of the hall.

<Behind us!> Barne replied, and fired a trio of rounds at a pair of guards that had darted across the hall behind them. <Looks like reinforcements are catching up.>

Rika flipped her GNR to its electron beam mode. The next time one of the guards leaned out to take a shot, she fired.

A straight line of blue lightning streaked down the hall—a nimbus glow of blue cherenkov radiation further emblazoning its passage. It hit the guard square in the chest and burned a hole right through him. Lightning arced all around his body, blowing out the overhead lighting and setting a wall on fire.

<Showoff,> Barne said as he kept an eye out for more pursuers.

Rika turned back to the doors at the end of the hall. She could pick up five figures on the other side of them. Two seemed to be seated, with another one nearby. Another pair was on either side of the doors.

She took aim at the figure on the left side of the door and fired her electron beam again. The force of the electrons travelling a hair under the speed of light blew a hole right through the wall and the person beyond. Rika smiled as the wall splintered, and the left-side door groaned before the top hinge came free and fell to the ground. Rika peered around the door to see Leslie and Jerry strapped to a pair of steel chairs in the center of the room.

Behind them stood a tall woman with mousy brown hair. She wore a cozy-looking red sweater, navy leggings, and fuzzy white slippers. If she was the nefarious Cheri, her wardrobe did not mirror the reputation.

The guard on the right side of the door moved into view, and Rika fired a ballistic round from her GNR, taking the top of his head off.

"Rika! No!" Leslie cried out as Rika stepped into the room. Barne was close behind, taking up position behind the remaining door, watching the hall to their rear.

The woman punched Leslie in the back of the head—a blow that was well delivered, and Leslie's eyes grew unfocused.

"So, you're the great Rika," the woman said. "These two have told me a lot about you."

Rika looked at Leslie and Jerry. Jerry's mouth was covered by a gag, but other than that, he looked OK. Leslie had a few bruises and a chunk of her hair was missing, but she didn't appear to have any broken bones that Rika's quick scan could see.

"And you must be Cheri," Rika said cautiously. "I have to admit, I'm a bit underwhelmed here."

The woman didn't even have a weapon. Rika raised her GNR but Leslie pulled her head up straight and cried out. "Rika, run! She has the Discipline codes."

Cold dread washed over her. The moment the GNR pointed at Cheri, a spike of Discipline hit Rika, and she lowered the weapon.

"That's better," Cheri said. "Getting your location was easy; too easy, if I know Jerry, here—which I do. Still, I sent Gamine in with a team to see if they could pull it off. I suspected that Gamine couldn't manage, but then I'd still get what I wanted: you. Except you'd deliver yourself, all nice and tidy. Gamine was getting a bit too big for her britches, so it was really a win-win for me."

Rika took a step back. "How?"

"How did I get the Discipline codes from Jerry?" Cheri asked as she stroked Jerry's head. "Oh, I just used a nifty little tool I got a while ago. It breached his neural security and extracted the code from his mind. It was easy to find; people always try not to think about the thing they want to hide the most, but in reality, it's all they think about."

Rika shook her head in denial. "No, there's just no way…"

Cheri's eyes narrowed. "Rika. Kill Barne."

The words flowed into her mind like ice water, and the tingle of Discipline grew stronger. She turned to Barne and saw true fear on his face as he stepped away from her.

"Rika, no, please," he said, raising his rifle.

She darted forward, swatted the gun out of his hand, and reached for his throat. But she couldn't bring herself to hurt this ass of a man. He was her friend—she hoped he was, at least.

Rika pulled her hand back, gritted her teeth, and lowered her head. She remembered what Barne had said, about mechs that somehow fought Discipline.

She turned to Cheri.

"No."

This time it was Cheri who looked concerned. Though it was just for a moment; then a wicked smile crossed her lips. "Rika, Kill Barne now. That's an order."

Even before Cheri had spoken, the Discipline sent searing pain into her mind. But not just her mind—it made her entire body feel like it was on fire. Like her skin was melting off, and the only way to put it out was with Barne's blood.

Blood she would not spill.

The pain brought her to her knees and she gasped for air, fighting against the searing agony. Still, she managed to raise her head, and she stared into Cheri's grey eyes.

"No!"

The Discipline hit her harder this time, tearing at her mind, bringing unimaginable agony. It was as though white-hot knives were in her brain, slicing away every part her, cutting her to pieces.

The pain subsided for a moment and she gasped for air, realizing that she was now sprawled on the ground with her JE78 a meter away. She wondered when she had dropped it.

"Rika!" Cheri yelled. "Kill Barne *now!*"

Rika glanced to her right. Barne still stood weaponless, and she wondered why he hadn't made a move to grab his rifle and kill Cheri. She was unarmed; it would only take a second.

Maybe he wanted to see if she had the strength. Or maybe he worried that killing Cheri wouldn't erase her last standing order—which it probably wouldn't.

Crippling waves of pain wracked Rika's body, but somehow she managed to get back up to her knees.

She whispered, "No."

Then she got her feet under her, and managed a crouch. "*No!*"

Cheri kept screaming at Rika to kill Barne, to kill Leslie, Jerry, all three; but Rika barely heard it at all. What she did hear was Barne give a soft laugh behind her.

"I knew you had it in you, girl. Go get her."

Something snapped in Rika's mind. The compliance chip was still functioning, still delivering its debilitating waves of pain, but somehow it didn't hurt anymore. Instead, the pain had become power; a rage that had been building ever since that dickhead technician named Jack had gleefully assembled her, and used the compliance chip and its Discipline to control her.

Years of *real* pain and anger gave her strength to fight against the artificial agony.

Rika sprang forward, flying over Jerry and Leslie to land behind the woman who was now the focus of all her rage. Rika stretched out her arm, the motion feeling slow in her pain-fueled rage, and snapped Cheri's neck.

She expected the pain to stop, but it didn't. It seemed to get worse—something she had not thought possible. Rika realized that her heart rate and blood pressure were both dangerously high. She fell to her knees, looking up to see Barne rushing forward to tear the gag from Jerry's mouth.

"Compliance systems off!" Jerry shouted.

The pain was gone in an instant. All that remained was the pounding of her heart in her ears. Rika pulled herself to her feet and scanned the room. The guards that had been closing in behind them were almost at the door.

Rika raised her GNR and fired three bolts of lightning, blowing a hole in the door with the first, and then tearing holes in four guards with the next two.

She saw three other guards run down the hall, two of them tossing aside their weapons as they went.

Barne had already cut the straps holding Jerry, and the LT stood on shaky legs, giving Rika a grateful smile.

"Holy shit, Rika. You are one hardcore woman."

Rika smiled and rapped her fist on her chest. "No way, LT. In here, I'm a squishie, just like you."

FLIGHT

STELLAR DATE: 12.16.8948 (Adjusted Years)
LOCATION: Northeast Berlin
REGION: Pyra, Albany System, Theban Alliance

Jerry and Leslie were embracing and taking deep breaths, while Barne checked the corridor to ensure that no more of Cheri's guards were interested in becoming statistics.

"Did you get eyes on the ammo?" Rika asked, remembering their need to find ammunition for her GNR-41C.

Jerry pulled himself away from Leslie and nodded. "She showed the rounds to us." He turned and led them through a door in the back of the room to a well-appointed office.

"I'm really sorry about this, everyone," Leslie said. "This is all my fault. Cheri asked what we needed the rounds for, if we'd retrofitted a GNR onto a mount of some sort—stars knows none of us could fire that thing without it tearing our arms off."

"No, it's not your fault," Jerry replied as he approached a cabinet on the wall. "You just slipped up."

"Slipped up in the den of the lion, and let her know that we had an SMI-2 with us," Leslie replied. "Sorry, Rika; looks like you're a hot commodity."

Rika nodded absently. She was still processing the fact that she had beaten Discipline—that she had weathered the torture and come through the other side. Even so, the rage she had tapped into scared her. It was worse than what she had felt during the war, worse than what she felt when she killed the woman who attacked Barne at the warehouse.

It was raw, and primal, and not something she thought she could control.

"Hey, mission control to Rika," Barne said, snapping his fingers in front of her face. "You OK? I gotta say, I think that counts as the second time you saved my ass in as many days."

Rika focused her eyes and smiled. "You got a big ass, Barne; it needs a lot of saving."

Rika looked to Leslie, realizing what the woman had been saying, and gently placed a hand on her shoulder. "It's OK, Leslie. For all we know, Cheri would have done this out of suspicion alone. Never trust someone who combines fuzzy slippers and sweaters."

"Uh…I frequently wear fuzzy slippers and sweaters," Leslie replied with a grin.

"Well…maybe you should stop," Rika replied, her voice dead serious.

Leslie's face fell and she took a half step back.

"Leslie, seriously! Who doesn't like comfy sweaters and slippers? I was kidding."

"Rika! Don't do that! I just watched you snap a woman's neck like you were twisting the cap off a bottle. You're a bit scary, you know that?"

I've noticed, she thought, her eyes turning downward.

"Hey! Leslie, be nice to Rika," Barne said as he gave Rika's arm a light punch.

Leslie's eyebrows were nearly at her hairline. "What happened with you two, anyway? I thought you hated her, Barne."

"Rika?" Barne asked. "I'd never hate her. She's a Marauder. She's Basilisk."

Rika gave Barne a smile, and as her gaze swept across the room, she noticed Jerry was sagging against the cabinet he had been trying to open.

"LT, you OK?" she asked.

"Yeah. Cheri wasn't gentle when she pulled the compliance codes out of my mind. I thought I was doing better, but...I seem to have developed one clusterfuck of a headache."

Leslie rushed to his side and half carried him to a chair.

"I think...she might have the ammo in there," Jerry said, pointing to the cabinet.

Barne looked it over. "Locked."

Rika approached the cabinet, placed a hand on the left door, and prised her fingers into the small gap between the top of the cabinet and its right-side door.

It was solid, but Rika gave a quick jerk and the door tore off its hinges. She pulled the left one open and spotted a slim black case. Her rad counter crept up, and she flipped the latch, opening it.

Inside lay the dull grey forms of five depleted uranium sabot rounds in mint condition. Just what her GNR-41C wanted to fire.

"Stars, you're handy to have around," Leslie said. "Who needs bolt cutters when we have Rika?"

"That's me, your one-stop utility tool," Rika chuckled, surprised that Leslie's statement didn't sting—and that her own response wasn't caustic.

"Can we keep her, LT?" Barne asked.

Jerry pulled himself up straight in the chair. "Of course we can, Sergeant. Like you said—Rika's Basilisk."

Rika felt a lump form in her throat, and redirected the conversation before she had to find a cloth to wipe tears from her eyes.

"We have a car a ways down the valley," Rika said. "But I don't think you can make it that far, Lieutenant. We can steal one here, or I can carry you."

"I don't think my head would appreciate being slung over your shoulder for a run through the forest," Jerry replied.

"Let's steal one of Cheri's cars. Bitch won't be using them anymore, anyway."

"Want me to carry you through the villa, at least?" Rika asked.

"No. We need you ready for a fight," Jerry said as he rose. "I might use Leslie as a crutch for a bit, though."

Barne had been watching the entrance to the office and now moved out into the foyer beyond, which was still clear of any hostiles. Careful not to get too far ahead, he led the way down the corridor to the intersection.

"This way," he said, and turned right.

Rika posted herself at the intersection until Jerry and Leslie were past; then she moved in behind them, walking sideways so that her two-seventy vision could see both ends of the hall.

They were nearing the end when someone stepped out from an intersection behind them. Rika fired and then caught sight of a telltale insignia on the figure's chest.

<Shit, I just shot a cop,> she said to the team, zooming in her vision to see if the person—a woman—was still alive. Rika let out a long breath as she watched the officer touch her armor and then scurry out of sight.

<It's OK, she's alive,> Rika relayed.

<Yeah, but what are they doing here?> Leslie asked. *<It's not like Cheri was the sort to be on good terms with the local constabulary.>*

<On the take?> Barne asked, as he reached another intersection and checked down the halls. *<Clear.>*

<Who knows,> Jerry replied. *<Good or bad, dead cops can put a serious wrinkle in our mission.>*

Rika ran an active scan, looking through the walls as far as she could.

<Yeah, we have company for sure. There are two groundcars out front, and an air-cav overhead. No, make that four cars out front.>

<So probably eight cops…and after Rika just fired on one of them, they'll come in ready for bear. They don't run around without armor, like the shitheads Cheri had,> Jerry said.

<Whoops,> Rika replied, a sheepish tone to her voice.

<This is a bit bigger than 'whoops', girl. Garage is down here to the right,> Barne said.

<Cops' cruisers are all pulled up out front. From where we are, they're about forty meters to our left,> Rika added.

Jerry peered back over his shoulder. <Rika, we need a diversion—but don't kill any of them. We don't need a cop-killer manhunt before the operation goes down.>

<On it, LT,> Rika said, and tossed the ammunition case to Barne. <Hold these for me, will you?>

<Oh, yay, I get to hold the radioactive ammo,> Barne groused.

<It's not **that** radioactive…anymore,> Rika said as she turned down the left corridor. She checked her magazines and saw that her GNR still had twenty-two ballistic rounds and enough charge for six more electron beam shots before she would start tapping into her reserves.

All Rika had to do was disable the cruisers and take down the air-cav—which may be human-piloted—without killing anyone.

She considered her options. *Not* killing anyone wasn't really her specialty. Perhaps there was a side-window she could get to that would give her a good angle on the four cruisers.

Rika spotted a staircase and took it up to the second level. At the top of the stairs, she rounded one corner, then another, and almost collided with two of Cheri's guards.

Terror filled their eyes and Rika grinned. These two, she could kill. She punched one in the face, caving in his nose and cheekbone, while the other fired his rifle into her side from only two meters away. The rounds ricocheted off and one struck him in the chest. Rika felt a twinge of pain and realized that a bullet had slipped through a point in her armor where two of the plates overlapped. She fished it out and noted that it was clean. No blood. Score one for her carbon-poly skin.

"Stop!" A male voice called out, and she turned to see a cop down the hall, leveling a rifle at her.

"Uh...no?" Rika responded, and dove into a room to her left as the policeman fired.

Are they supposed to do that? she wondered. Details of police procedure—when they could fire on suspects and all that—was not something she had ever needed to know in the past.

She stood inside the entrance to the room, waiting for the cop to step through. Five seconds ticked past, then ten, then twenty.

Shit, he must be waiting for backup. Smart man.

A moment later, weapons fire sounded and a barrage of projectiles tore through the wall where she was standing.

I guess they have IR, Rika thought. She considered her options and then did the exact opposite of what the police expected: She broke through the wall and rushed them.

There were two of them, and neither even had time to register surprise before Rika tore the rifle from the first cop's hands and smashed it into the head of the second—as gently as she could manage.

Then she hit the first cop on the side of the head with the barrel of her GNR and watched him fall.

"Damn squishies," she muttered, examining their vitals. "You'll live."

She returned to the room she had just burst out of, which had an excellent view of the four cruisers parked below—pulled up right in front of the broad stairs leading into the villa. Rika scanned them for occupants. Her luck, such as it was, had held; they were empty.

Rika took aim and fired an electron beam at the first cruiser, blowing a hole through it and shattering its battery.

She fired on the second, and was lining up on the third when an all too familiar sound met her ears.

Gatling guns always take an instant to spin up before they fire, and that telltale whine was all it took for Rika to dive out of the window as the room above and behind her was cut to shreds from the high-velocity rounds.

If those dumbasses kill their own people back in the hall, I'll kill 'em, Rika thought angrily.

She looked up and saw the air-cav only twenty meters above the cruisers. It had stopped firing, but was repositioning to shoot at her new location.

Rika didn't give it time to take aim. She ran across the open space in front of the villa's main doors and leapt off the ruins of one cruiser onto the villa's wall, her feet grasping a windowsill. She crouched, and a second jump propelled her to the villa's roof.

The air-cav was turning, and its gatling gun was winding up once more when Rika leapt from the roof, sailed through the air, and landed on the air-cav.

She looked inside and saw that there was indeed a human pilot in the cockpit. Rika leveled her rifle at him and screamed *"Land"*, loud enough that they probably could have heard her halfway down the valley.

<*Nice distraction,*> Barne said as he raced by in a car, down the twisting road leading into the valley.

<*Took you guys long enough,*> Rika replied as the air-cav touched down, and she gestured for the pilot to get out. He jumped out and ran into the villa. Rika saw that the air-cav's controls were still initialized and hopped into the cockpit. She brought the craft a few meters off the ground and unloaded its gatling gun into the other two cruisers.

Once they were suitably disabled, she brought the air-cav up over the villa and pushed the manual control stick forward.

The air-cav pitched, and Rika jumped out, landing again on the villa's roof.

The air-cav sped forward and slammed into the escarpment behind the villa before falling to the ground in a twisted heap of metal.

Rika turned and scanned the road, easily spotting the car her team had stolen from Cheri's garage. She leapt off the villa's roof and chased after. A few shots came from the villa as Rika disappeared into the night. Most missed, and those that didn't were unable to penetrate her armor.

She rolled her head back and laughed as she ran down the mountainside, not bothering with following the road. She reviewed her sensory capture of the battle. As far as she could tell, she hadn't killed any of the police. Maybe she wasn't *just* a killer after all.

Rika neared the location where the other car was hidden and scanned the area to make sure it was clear. As she looked up, a flash of light appeared in the skies, and a scan showed that there was another air-cav closing in. IR indicated another human pilot—this time approaching at a much higher altitude.

Rika raced to the road, reaching it just as the air-cav opened fire on Basilisk's escape vehicle. Her electron beam wouldn't be effective against the air-cav at its current range, so Rika sped up, racing toward it. Ahead she could see Leslie leaning out of the car, firing on the air-cav. Her shots were hitting the craft, but appeared to make no impact.

Barne swerved the car wildly, avoiding the air-cav's spray of bullets. It pulled around, coming in for a strafing run behind the car. Rika knew it wouldn't miss this time, and scanned the trees for a good candidate to climb. They were all young and spindly; then her eyes locked on a thirty-meter pine close by.

Without a moment's hesitation, Rika leapt into the tree's branches and clambered up its trunk. When she reached the top, Rika leapt toward the air-cav, closing the distance enough—she hoped—and fired her electron beam.

The straight line of lightning streaked out and hit the air-cav on its left side, taking out one of its a-grav units and sending the craft into a tailspin.

The pilot, either purposefully or by accident, opened up with the gatling gun, and fifty-caliber rounds filled the air in a broad circle around the falling air-cav.

Rika saw that the car with Team Basilisk in it was past the falling air-cav, but she was not. In fact, her trajectory still had her approaching it.

A round struck her thigh, then another hit her in the chest, and two more slammed into her left arm.

Rika hit the ground hard and rolled to her feet, her HUD registering severe damage to her left arm. She looked down and saw that an armor plate had been shattered below her elbow. She tried to flex her fingers, but they didn't move.

She glanced over the rest of herself and saw that her chest plate had a microfracture; she was otherwise all right. Ahead, the air-cav's damaged a-grav unit burst into flames, and Rika rushed forward to save the cop inside.

Within, she saw a woman slumped over the controls. Rika reached down to tear off the craft's canopy, when she remembered that her hand wasn't working.

Thank the stars for clawed feet, she thought with a smile, and smashed her foot through the canopy's clear plas, and then pushed the eject button next to the woman's chair.

An instant later, the chair flew from the downed craft, and deployed a parachute. It settled down to the ground one hundred meters up the road.

"You'll thank me later," Rika said, running from the burning air-cav and ducking into the trees a second before it exploded.

Four minutes later she arrived at the cars. Leslie was helping Jerry into the backseat of the vehicle she and Barne had brought. He looked a bit better but was still holding his head with one hand.

Barne had the trunk open and pulled out a small package. "Hopefully we didn't leave too much DNA in the villa, but we'd best scrub what we can."

He held up the package and then tossed it into the car they had stolen from Cheri. Small silver filaments spread from the kit, sweeping over every surface in the vehicle in a matter of seconds before retracting into the box.

"Like we were never here," Barne said with a smile.

He closed the trunk and got in the driver's seat while Rika collapsed in the passenger's side.

"You OK?" Leslie asked. "Your arm looks funny."

"Yeah, mostly," Rika replied. "Took some shots to my left arm—not the organic part. Not sure how messed up it is yet, but my hand's offline."

Barne backed the car out of the copse of trees it was hidden in and gave Rika a smile. "You know, being a mech must not be so bad sometimes. No pain, and you can swap that arm out in minutes."

Rika closed her eyes and sighed. *Maybe it isn't so bad. Maybe not always, at least.*

DELIBERATION

STELLAR DATE: 12.17.8948 (Adjusted Years)
LOCATION: Enlisted Commissary, MSS *Foe Hammer*
REGION: Interstellar Space, near the Praesepe Cluster

David sat in the *Foe Hammer's* enlisted commissary taking a meal at a table with Aaron and Genevieve, two other specialists who worked in the fleet's CIC on the ship.

"Something's not right," David said, and he reached into his pocket, pulled out a dampener, and set it on the table. It wasn't uncommon for the CIC teams to discuss their work at lunch, and because it got more work from them at the same pay, their superiors allowed it—so long as they took precautions not to be overheard.

<*What's that?*> Aaron asked as he plugged a packet of nutri-paste into the socket in his stomach. <*Seeing things out of the corner of your eye again?*>

David smiled at Aaron's pet term for his abilities. Aaron wasn't a P-Cog. His augmentations had been focused on heavy mathematics for close-quarters fleet engagements; the alterations he had undergone at the hands of the GAF were even more extreme than what the mechs had undergone.

Where David's alterations had been focused on enhancing the interconnectivity in his brain, Aaron's had been centered on adding raw computational power. In the war, the official term for people like him was 'Non-AI Sentient Computer'. Just like the mechs and the others who were heavily modded, the military had both treated and labeled NAISCs as objects.

Unlike with David, they hadn't bothered with saving any visual aspect of Aaron's humanity. His head was a half-meter-tall grey ovoid with two bulbous lenses where his eyes should be—though no organic eyes lay beneath. His face was also devoid of nose or mouth; his air coming through two breathing ports on his upper torso, and his food through the NutriPaste socket on the surface of his stomach.

David admitted that 'torso' wasn't quite the right word for Aaron's body. Because the Genevian Space Force had treated NAISCs like mobile organic AIs, they had removed all of Aaron's limbs and set what remained of his body inside a hard shell.

Though David had never said it aloud, Aaron looked much like a snowman that just needed the bottom ball.

Luckily for Aaron, the Old Man had taken him in right at the end of the war, and had a mobile stand of sorts constructed for him. It had a cup that his body sat in and six legs—any of which could also double as hands, as needed—stemming from the stand upon which the cup sat.

The level of technology to undo what had been done to Aaron was outside of what the Marauders possessed, and David had been impressed with the level of self-acceptance Aaron managed. David was sure that he'd lose his mind if he were in his friend's place.

One thing was for certain; it made Aaron one mean Snark player. He could simultaneously play six games against separate opponents, and typically win five out of the six.

Teams on the *Foe Hammer* continually tried to beat him—many of their players were heavily augmented as well—but the best contenders had still only managed two wins to his four.

<Hey-O. Mission control to David,> Aaron said. <You were saying something about something not being right?>

David shook his head. "Sorry, not enough coffee today."

"A P-Cog's favorite stabilizer," Genevieve said as she held hers out to David. "Need my packet?"

"No, I'm OK, just had one—it'll kick in shortly," David replied.

"Suit yourself," Genevieve replied.

David nodded his thanks. Genevieve was the most normal-looking of their little group. After the war she was able to access her savings, and she'd had enough money to get her shark fins replaced. She now sported a head covered in thick hairs that served the same purpose as his steel ridges.

Not that anyone would mistake the gleaming, white, one-centimeter-thick strands for real hair, but it certainly beat metal fins.

Genevieve was the backbone of their unit. Nothing fazed her; she never became upset, worried, or even agitated. She was an endless sea of calm. David had relied on her more than once to help him through hard times.

She always held herself perfectly erect, and her high, sloped forehead spoke of an origin in New Sweden—though her family had lived for generations in Genevia, on one of the terraformed planets close to a G-spectrum star.

As a result, Genevieve had naturally dark skin that contrasted with her white 'hair', giving her an otherworldly look.

<You're staring,> Aaron said privately to David.

<Damn...glad she doesn't mind. I think I stare at her a lot.>

<Pretty sure she likes it,> Aaron replied.

David coughed and tried to get his mind back on track, pushing down the excess stimuli around him to focus on what he had discovered. Patterns, analyzing connections—that's where he found his peace.

"It's with Operation Phoenix, of course," he began. "I'm worried about its effects."

"You mean the change of hands for the Theban stars?" Genevieve asked.

"That's one way to put it, but yeah," David replied. "See, I don't think that this benefits the Septhians as much as everyone would like to think it does."

<Everyone wonders about that,> Aaron replied in a tone that let them know there was a detailed analysis coming. <The upheaval provides little advantage over a strong Thebes, should the Nietzscheans, or anyone else, attack. But the Old Man believes it's for the best; while I can see a lot of ways things can go wrong, properly handled it can work in the Septhians' favor. It's not as though there is no support in Thebes for a merger with Septhia. Portions of their congress have been arguing in favor of it for decades. It's been their president, Ariana, who has quashed it. Makes sense that the Septhians would want her out of the way—>

"David does have a point, though," Genevieve said, interrupting Aaron's spiel. "By that logic, there should just be one team hitting the president and nothing more—well, maybe her VP, too."

"OK, I know it's all just suspicion and conjecture and I can't go anywhere with that," David replied. "But it did start me digging. I began to look at all the logs for the Old Man's talks with his Septhian contacts who arranged Phoenix in the first place."

<Hey, whoa, what?> Aaron asked. <Dude, that is not OK. You can't spy on the Old Man.>

"I didn't look at the messages themselves, just the logs in the comm systems."

Genevieve frowned. "Marauders, the Old Man especially, talk to Septhians all the time. Septhia is where our main facilities are. How could you pick out the communication with the contact for this operation amidst all the noise?"

"Because it was different," David said. "It had a unique pattern."

<In what way?> Aaron asked, his curiosity apparently piqued.

"It was in the packet segmentation on the comms," David said. "Septhians don't use octal code in their comm systems."

"Yeah, they use that weird-ass base-9 setup. They folded their parity bit right into the data structure. It's always a pain in the ass to translate."

David nodded. "Yeah, and you can see the pattern it creates in the headers alone—you don't even need to look at the message content. But there was a subset of messages where the pattern was different, and they were all communications sent to the Old Man."

<So?> Aaron asked. <This is obviously being run by their black-ops folks, with no link to their prime minister—all the better to have plausible deniability if we fuck up. It's why they hired us in the first place, rather than doing the job themselves.>

"I thought about that, too," David said. "But I really wanted to know how to achieve that pattern. I got kinda obsessed with it. I converted messages from a hundred different source systems into base-9, and then back to base-8; everything from raw-binary to SAI analog code systems. A lot were close, real close, and within the margin of error. But there were three that were dead matches."

"Here goes," Genevieve said.

"The Tarurae high command's exalted network, the Trisilieds space force comms, and…the Nietzscheans."

<That's ridiculous,> Aaron said. <The comm NSAI would have spotted messages of Nietzschean origin, even if it had been passed through Septhian relays and converted to base-9 and back.>

"I don't think so," David said. "See, it wasn't that the whole message was a red flag—just the parity bits. And not all of them, either—it was a weird pattern that looked almost random. Well, it still does, but I know something's in there. It's a pattern I can almost make out, like a detail that, if I just squint at right, I'll see."

<I still don't like that you've been poking around in the Old Man's messages,> Aaron said.

David raised his hands and nodded. "Hey, Aaron. I appreciate what the Old Man's built for us here as much as anyone. But if I have a Nietzschean connection to Phoenix, I have to pursue it. Do you think you could take a look at what I have?"

Aaron didn't respond for a moment, and then his long head nodded. <Send it over.>

David passed his analysis over the Link to his friend.

<Well, you're right about an anomaly, but it seems too random; not caused by specific comm hardware. Maybe...>

"Maybe what?" Genevieve asked.

<Well...older Nietzschean comm systems used a processor that had a rounding error. It never really caused issues for them; in fact, they leveraged it as a part of their encryption...>

"Simulate it," David said.

<What do you think I'm—shit! It's a dead match now. I can create the pattern by running the base-9 translation through a processor with the rounding error.>

"That's it, then. There's a Nietzschean somewhere in the Septhian government!" David exclaimed.

Genevieve sat back and let out a long whistle while Aaron's ovoid head pivoted. <That's far from a smoking gun. Hardware ends up all over the place, especially old stuff. Gets sold as surplus in every system.>

"I think your findings are sound enough to take it to Commander Siemens," Genevieve said. "I would, at least. Let her decide if the intel should get pushed up the chain or not."

<Let's hope not,> Aaron said. <We're only twenty-eight Pyran hours from launching Operation Phoenix. Barely enough time to call the thing off, if it's true.>

RESITUATE
STELLAR DATE: 12.17.8948 (Adjusted Years)
LOCATION: Northern Berlin
REGION: Pyra, Albany System, Theban Alliance

It had taken the team five hours to return to Berlin, and then another three to get the truck and drive it to one of their fallback locations.

It was another warehouse, but this one was smaller and newer—and decidedly cleaner. Leslie laid Jerry down on a cot in a nearby storage room and walked out rubbing her eyes.

Barne was away, taking the car to another storage location. That left just the two women to finish setting up.

"Jerry gonna be OK?" Rika asked as she attempted another reroute to get her arm working.

"Yeah," Leslie nodded. "I gave him a brainfix. The kit should deal with the swelling Cheri's methods caused; that appears to be the worst of it. The kit didn't report any neural damage—thank the stars."

"What about you?" Leslie asked Rika as she approached. "You took some hits, there."

Rika shrugged from where she sat on a crate. "I've seen a lot worse. Except for the gatling guns on those air-cavs, nothing out there was high enough caliber to really hurt me."

Leslie gave Rika a smile. "Well, I guess we should unload the truck."

Rika grinned and held up her left hand. "I'm going to need a hand. Literally."

Leslie covered her mouth and laughed. "Oh, shit. I totally forgot—you can't get your gun-arm off to put on a good arm, because your other arm is shot."

At first Rika wasn't sure if Leslie was making light of her plight, but she decided to believe that Leslie was just laughing at the irony of it, and chuckled. "Yeah, like I said; I literally need a hand."

"Where is your other one?" Leslie asked.

"In the cab of the truck," Rika replied. "Tools are in the back."

"I'll have to pull your armor off first, won't I?" Leslie said as she examined Rika's arm.

"Yeah, a bit tricky otherwise," Rika replied.

Leslie met Rika's eyes, her own showing a look of worry. "Do you mind if I get the rack, Rika?" she asked. "I don't think I can manage this without it."

Rika nodded. "No, I don't mind. I'll help you get it out...I can at least shove things around, if you need me to."

Thirty minutes later Leslie had the rack set up, and Rika stepped back, settling her armor's hardpoints into the hooks.

Leslie slid a tool into Rika's armpit and gave a twist, loosening the armor on the shoulder.

"Is that weird for you, Rika?" she asked as she slotted in another tool and opened up the armor around Rika's bicep.

"What, having someone else take my armor off?" Rika asked. "Not really; happened a lot in the war, especially when I took damage."

"Well, I was referring specifically to me slotting a tool up into your armpit..."

"Oh, that? No, not really. It does kinda tickle, though."

Leslie looked up at Rika, their eyes meeting before Leslie snorted. "Rika, the unstoppable killing machine, is ticklish?"

Rika had begun to smile, but the expression faded. "Please don't call me that."

"Shit, sorry," Leslie shook her head. "I spend too much time around these guys. Lovable bundles of testosterone that they are, they get me acting like everything is up for being a joke..."

"It's OK," Rika said. "Some mechs like being killing machines. I...I don't really know what I like."

"Well," Leslie grunted as she unfastened the armor from Rika's forearm, pulling it free where the damaged plate had wedged into her arm. "I can tell you this: you're a sight to behold when you're at it. The way you leapt from the building and landed on that air-cav? That was one of the most badass things I've ever seen. And I've seen a lot of badass shit in my day."

Rika shook her head as Leslie pulled the last of her arm's armor off. "Last night was nothing. Shoulda seen the time that my team and I took out a nuke-flinging K1R. That thing was a nightmare."

"How big was the team?" Leslie asked absently as she looked over the damage in Rika's arm.

"Three," Rika replied. "Though just two of us were on the K1R. I pulled a move like the one with that air-cav."

"Just two of you took out a K1R?" Leslie shook her head in wonder. "You sure you need the rest of us on this mission?"

"Well," Rika said with a laugh. "Looks like I need a mechanic to keep me running."

"That you do," Leslie said. "Let me get your gun arm off, and give you your right hand back. I'm not sure what we should do about that left one. It's beyond my skill to fix, and we don't have a replacement."

"Maybe we could find you a big hook. Arrrrr," Barne said with a lopsided grin as he walked through a nearby door. "I bet that would scare the shit out of the enemy."

"Give me a hook, and I'll use it to give you those friendly punches on the arm," Rika replied.

"Huh," Barne said. "Maybe a pillow attachment would be better. Think of it; you could lay that pretty head of yours down whenever you wanted and take a nice snooze."

Pretty?

Leslie snorted. "Shut up, Barne. Go make yourself useful and unload the truck."

Barne shrugged and walked away. "I'll take a look at that arm you got shot up when I'm done unpacking. I might be able to get it working again."

As Leslie removed the armor on Rika's right arm, she chatted with Rika about the Marauders—describing some of the missions they'd been on lately, and what it was like to work in a mercenary company after being in the Genevian Armed Forces.

"It's a bit different, for sure," she said. "Everyone keeps their military rank—for the most part, anyway—but the structure is weird. I mean, Jerry's a lieutenant. LTs aren't usually in charge of four-person fireteams."

"How does it work when you do platoon or company-sized ops?" Rika asked.

"Well," Leslie smiled. "We're spec-ops, attached to Alpha Company in the second Battalion. There are forty battalions now in the Marauders—which the Old Man has split up into four regiments."

"So, about twenty-five thousand soldiers altogether?"

"Closer to twenty-eight," Leslie replied. "There are a lot of spec-op teams like ours that aren't part of the regular structure. We report right to Alpha Company's CO, Captain Ayer. She's a good woman; sometimes a bit soft on the guys when they need a sterner hand, but I like her."

"And who's the Old Man?" Rika asked.

"Oh, I guess we never call him by name, do we?" Leslie said with a grunt as she twisted off Rika's gun-arm and stumbled backward, nearly dropping it.

"Shit, this thing weighs a ton! How do you just wave your arm around like it's nothing?"

Rika shrugged as much as she could, hanging on the rack. "Seems light to me. I do have to adjust my balance when it's on, though. It's why I preferred it on my right arm…felt more natural there."

"Well," Leslie groaned as she set the arm and the attached GNR-41C down on a crate. "You may have to adjust it back and get used to its weight on your left."

Rika nodded. That was her expectation, as well—unless Barne could work a miracle with her left arm.

Leslie picked up Rika's right arm and slid it into place, giving it the required twist.

"Right, the Old Man. He's General Mill. Was in the Genevian army for almost seventy years. Hates the fact that the war is over; some of the Marauders think that he's building us up to eventually strike out at the Nietzscheans."

"That's nuts!" Rika exclaimed. "Even with a million soldiers, he wouldn't stand a chance. "He'd need a fleet, for starters."

"Hey," Leslie raised her hands defensively. "I said some. Not all; certainly not me." She slid the bolts into place and locked them down. "OK, you're good to go. Hold on while I reattach your right arm's armor."

Rika waited silently while Leslie finished the work. "OK, Rika. Right as rain on the right, right?"

"Wow," Rika laughed. "You're a regular comedian, Leslie."

Leslie grinned. "Yeah, I get that a lot."

"No, you don't," Barne said as he walked past.

"Shut up, Barne," Leslie said good-naturedly.

"How's the LT, by the way?" Barne asked as he stopped beside the two women.

"I think he'll be alright," Leslie replied.

"I hope so. Tomorrow's the big day."

Rika held her left arm up for Barne to see. "I doubt you'll be able to fix this. Looks like the control mechanism and one of the actuators are shot."

Barne grunted. "Yeah, you're right. I could probably source the parts, but it may arise suspicion—especially this close to the job."

"S'OK," Rika grinned. "I'll just get to relax here and watch you do the heavy lifting for once."

"Need me to swap out your left arm?" Leslie asked.

"That'd be nice. I don't think I could flip the mount back around on the gun-arm with one hand."

"Hey," Leslie said with a smile. "What are friends for?"

Rika and Leslie continued to chat as they reset Rika's gun-arm to mount on her left. They talked about the Marauders, Basilisk's past missions, and what the future might hold.

It felt nice—like maybe Rika had finally found a place in the universe, after all.

REPORT

STELLAR DATE: 12.17.8948 (Adjusted Years)
LOCATION: MSS *Foe Hammer*
REGION: Interstellar Space, near the Praesepe Cluster

Commander Siemens was off duty. By the time David had passed his findings through the CIC's Officer of the Watch, who wanted to crosscheck everything he and Aaron had uncovered—with a particular focus on the amount of unauthorized time spent on the task—before finally getting the Commander's attention, several hours had passed.

Siemens had entered the CIC with a furrowed brow and tousled hair, but paid close attention as David laid out the information, and grew more rapt as the P-Cog went on. When David showed the simulation Aaron had constructed, her eyebrows shifted from hanging low over her eyes to nearly disappearing into her hairline.

"Holy shit, specialist! If this is true, we have to call off the whole op!" Siemens exclaimed.

"That's the point I've been trying to make," David said, casting a hard look at the OOTW.

"Come with me," Commander Siemens said as she rose and left the CIC. "I'm calling Colonel Niels; the operation command team is assembled. When they see this…."

David followed Commander Siemens through the corridors surrounding the CIC, and then up a lift to the *Foe Hammer*'s mission management deck. The deck was a beehive of activity; people were rushing about, checking and crosschecking the status of drop ships and assault teams, and reviewing status updates from ground coordinators.

Siemens led David into a meeting room filled with officers being addressed by Colonel Niels.

"Sir!" Commander Siemens said as she rushed in. "I know you said to wait when I pinged you, but this can't wait. We have critical intel on Phoenix."

"What are you talking about?" Niels frowned. "We're running the intel on this op. What does fleet CIC have that could be relevant?"

"My specialist here, a P-Cog, has ferreted out a Nietzschean connection to Phoenix."

One of the officers sitting at the table, a major named Sarah, nearly spit out the water she was drinking. "Are you serious?"

"Unlikely," another said.

"Please!" Commander Siemens raised her voice. "This is serious! We believe that General Mill's contact in the Septhian government is actually a Nietzschean operative!"

"Show me what you have," a calm voice said from behind David, and he turned to see the Old Man himself standing at the entrance to the room.

"Yes, sir!" David said. He took control of the room's main holo projector, and nervously began to outline his findings. As he spoke, the General's face grew more and more red. David started to wonder if he would find himself on the wrong side of an airlock before he was done, but Siemens nodded whenever he faltered, so David pressed on.

When he was done and Aaron's simulation results were floating over the table, the General blew out a long breath.

"Laura," he said. "What do you think?"

<I can see no fault in the findings,> she said. <Specialist David's logic is sound. I believe we have been played.>

"Colonel Niels, Phoenix is shut down. Initiate Operation Ashes. We jump for Pyra in t-minus fifteen minutes."

"Sir! Yes, sir!" Colonel Niels said, and a moment later every person in the room was pulling up new displays, and the halls outside exploded with increased activity.

General Mill placed a hand on David's shoulder, and he was surprised to feel the Old Man's grip shaking slightly.

"P-Cog Specialist David, you may have just saved the Praesepe Cluster from the Nietzscheans…and my folly."

THE HIT
STELLAR DATE: 12.18.8948 (Adjusted Years)
LOCATION: National Forest, North of Presidential Palace, Berlin
REGION: Pyra, Albany System, Theban Alliance

Rika walked through the forest drawing in deep lungfuls of the moist, predawn air. Her robe—a new one, since her old one was somewhere in the valley below Cheri's villa—rustled quietly around her as she enjoyed what she knew to be the last few minutes of peace she would experience for some time.

She held her coffee lightly in her right hand and took another sip. Using that hand with fine control was taking a little work, but Rika was more concerned with using her GNR on her left.

In yesterday's combat, when her gun-arm had been in place, it had felt like her proper right hand. A gun—a multi-function weapons mount with a GNR-41C—felt more natural than a hand.

She took another sip of coffee, raising her third finger off the cup as she did. This appendage, with fingers and the ability to grip and hold, just felt strange. Maybe that had been one of the things that had bothered her so much after the war, and she hadn't been able to name it—or to admit it to herself.

She took a final long drink of the coffee, tossed the cup toward a trash bin, missed, and picked it up to deposit it more carefully. Even if she found herself with a gun-arm on her right side more often than not, she still needed to work on her fine motor skills. There was no telling when she'd need them, now that she was in the Marauders.

I'm in the Marauders.

Rika still wasn't certain what she thought of that. Basilisk was one thing. She had bonded deeply with the team over just a few short days—something that life-or-death situations seemed to facilitate. However, the Marauders were a different story. Somewhere within their structure were people who thought it was OK to buy and sell humans. Her, specifically, and that wasn't the sort of group she wanted to call family.

Rika was nearing the large glen with the tree that she had scouted out three days prior, and she turned off onto a smaller path that eventually faded away but took her close to the tree. She crouched behind a bush and activated her robe's camouflage systems and then crossed the final few meters to the tree, carefully scaling it.

Once in position, Rika stretched her left arm out and reached under her robe with her right, drawing out the GNR-41C that had been strapped to her back. She carefully wedged it between herself and the tree while pulling out the shroud that would cover it.

Rika slid a loop from the end of the shroud over the weapon's barrel, and then grasped the weapon and brought it up to her mount.

It took two tries to get it on, and at one point she almost dropped it; then the GNR-41C slotted into place, and her HUD updated with its readings and loadout.

Rika nodded with satisfaction as she saw the five uranium sabot rounds show up on the weapons loadout.

For the first time in years, Rika was fully functional.

With the weapon in place, Rika pulled her helmet from a pouch under her robe and wrapped it in the shawl before carefully placing it on her head. This time Leslie had helped her prepare by pinning her hair up, and Barne hadn't made any jokes about shaving her head.

The helmet registered a positive seal, and Rika pulled the cloak's cowl up over her head.

It was time to wait.

She knew that somewhere nearby, Leslie and Jerry were getting ready to take their positions. Not too soon, though;

their hiding spots were closer to the presidential palace and not as well hidden. The pair would take their positions at the last minute, ready to finish the job and give Rika covering fire if she needed it.

Rika hoped that Jerry would be all right. He seemed better today—though he said his head still felt like he'd gone a few rounds with a starship. Rika had kept a close eye on him, and the LT had only wobbled once while the team got ready.

If it were up to her, he would sit out the mission—but there was nothing she could do to stop him. He *was* the LT, after all.

Rika checked the local time: just a few minutes after 06:00 hours. The Theban president wouldn't be passing by until the end of her run at about 08:05. Rika couldn't use the Link or anything else that could give away her position, so she started practicing her breathing while touching her thumb to each of her fingers.

It was something to take her mind off what she was about to do. Killing Cheri and her goons had been one thing, but she was now lying in wait to assassinate a head of state.

To topple a government.

Rika had researched the Theban president in greater depth the night before. From what she could tell, Ariana was a good woman. She had several grown children, and they seemed to love and respect their mother.

There was no husband in her life, but that was normal in Thebes. Long-term spousal relationships were rare.

Rika swallowed, forcing down her uncertainty. She had just found a place where she fit in. Failing to complete this mission would put that in jeopardy.

It was distasteful, but it was her job. It was what she was.

* * * * *

The time slipped past 8:00, and Rika re-checked her GNR-41C, making sure the uranium sabot rounds were ready to fire and crosschecking her targeting reticules.

Several presidential guards had passed by fifteen minutes before without giving the tree she was in so much as a second glance—after that, no one else operating in an official capacity came by.

This surprised Rika. She had expected to see several more guards keeping ahead of the president; so far, she had only seen a woman and two kids run past.

Another minute slipped by, and then Jerry reached out to her.

<Rika, we have a problem.>

<How so?>

<Barne just got an update: the president's schedule has changed. She got pulled into some meeting at the capitol building,> Jerry replied.

<Crap, really? What's our fallback?> Rika asked.

<The president is the most important target. The other teams will already be in motion; that means we need to get to the capitol and take her out fast.>

<What, just waltz into the capitol and kill the president? Sorry LT, but that sounds a bit nuts.>

<Just wait till you see Barne's plan. Then you'll **really** think we're nuts. Meet us back at the rally point. Quickly.>

<Got it,> Rika said as she carefully descended the tree.

She wondered if Jerry remembered that he hadn't reactivated her compliance chip. Either way, it was nice to get an order and not feel the warning from Discipline in the back of her mind.

If he *had* remembered and left it off, she owed him one hell of a thank you.

Once on the ground, Rika pulled off the GNR-41C and slipped it back under her robe. She started moving through the brush, but then remembered her helmet. After quickly removing it, she rewrapped her head in her scarf before replacing her cowl.

She reached the path a minute later and jogged to the meet-up point where the rest of Basilisk was waiting.

The hoverbikes were out, set up beside the truck, and Jerry and Leslie were sitting on the back, chests heaving from their run.

"You guys out of shape or something?" Rika asked with a grin.

"Har har," Leslie replied between breaths.

<OK, so Barne's intel has the president in the east wing of the capitol building. She'll be in a room with windows, but we don't think that even your rifle can shoot through them,> Jerry began while Leslie spoke out loud about her run, bending over to stretch her calves.

Rika laughed aloud and said something in response to Leslie, while replying to Jerry over the Link.

<Stands to reason,> Rika said. <I imagine a couple of shots would make it through, but they'd have moved her by then.>

<Right,> Jerry replied. <Which means we need to get you into the capitol, and fast. The other hits are about to go down, and once they do, you can bet they'll get the president to a bunker as soon as they can.>

<So what's the big plan for getting me into the capitol?> Rika asked. <I seem to recall you saying it was 'nuts'.>

<Oh, it is,> Barne laughed as he stepped around a stack of cases in the truck holding several explosives. He jumped off the deck and walked to one of the hoverbikes, and then lifted the seat. <This one's yours, Rika. It's got a little something extra.>

* * * * *

Rika sped down the streets of Berlin at over three hundred kilometers per hour, with four police bikes and two air-cavs hot on her tail. Ahead, she periodically caught sight of Jerry and Leslie on their bikes, weaving in and out of the slower street traffic.

A car pulled out from the side of the road, and Rika boosted her hoverbike, jumping it into the air and over the car. She nearly hit another vehicle, and swerved sharply to avoid it. Behind her, a car also swerved, and slammed into another, obstructing the road.

Now that was more like it. *The harder the pursuit, the better.*

A map of the city streets floated over her vision, and she saw that after a right in three blocks, they would be just two blocks from the government parking garage.

She slowed the bike and dropped her foot, dragging it along the street to swing the bike around the corner, and then she jammed on the throttle again. Ahead, Jerry approached the parking garage and fired into the guard booth.

Instantaneously, stop posts jumped up and turrets dropped down, firing on Jerry as he sped off. Leslie was just a second behind him, and she tossed a detpack at the entrance to the garage. Barne was monitoring feeds, and blew the pack at just the right moment for maximum damage.

At least Rika hoped it was maximum damage. She scanned the entrance, trying to see if any of the stop posts had been taken out. Her vision cycled through several modes and picked up a gap wide enough for her bike.

Rika passed through it a second later. One of the turrets sputtered a few shots at her, but none did any noticeable damage.

She slammed on the bike's rear brakes and turned left up the ramp. Guns fired on her the whole way, but their tracking wasn't fast enough to deal with an overpowered hoverbike ridden by a mech who felt no fear—at least, no fear about this.

Six levels later, she was on the roof of the parking garage. Rika got her bearings and pushed the bike's throttle wide open. It bucked, rising up as it raced across the rooftop, and Rika hit the edge at exactly the three hundred and twenty-two kilometers per hour Barnes said she needed.

Except she didn't hit the *edge*. She ramped off a car and sailed through the air, waiting for the prescribed ten-count to pass.

Time seemed to slow, and she looked around, her view augmented by her two-seventy vision.

Ahead loomed the capitol building and the east wing where the president was having her meeting. Below her laid a few smaller buildings and a park. As Rika passed over the park, she pushed off the hoverbike, sending it down and her up.

Four missiles streaked out from hidden defense points, targeting the bike. Rika watched, soaring higher, as the four missiles reached the bike at almost the same moment.

Right before impact, the bike exploded.

The blast gave Rika the extra push she needed to make it up to the building's roof. Unfortunately, the force also sent her cartwheeling through the air, so when she landed, it was on a skylight.

A thousand kilograms of mech, steel, and high-density glass fell into the room below just as the remains of the bike smashed into one of the room's windows and fell to the ground.

Huh...the window did hold up. They should put that glass on their skylights.

Rika looked around, her locator systems finding her on the building layout she had saved that first night when she had reviewed Basilisk's intel on the operation.

This was the room; the president should be there.

<*It's empty! She's not here!*> Rika called out.

<Shit,> Barne responded. <They must have caught wind of one of the other ops. They'll take her to the bunker. It's under the west wing, middle of the bottom floor—marked 'mop room' on the layout.>

<Got it,> Rika replied.

One more look around the room now that the dust had settled revealed that something had been going on. Holosheets were still on the table, along with glasses of water, and some jackets were still draped over chairs.

The president had been here just moments before.

She plotted the most expeditious route through the Capitol and took off, smashing through the door and rushing down the corridor beyond. Several men and women were approaching, all armed and wearing medium armor. Rika pulled her JE78 rifle off her back and fired four rapid pulse shots, knocking two people over and pushing the others aside. One tried to grab at her as she ran past, but she slapped his arm out of the way; the crunch of his bones snapping reached her augmented ears even over the general din of her passage.

She turned left at the next intersection and kept running while firing pulse blasts at anyone who got in her way. Her plan didn't require a return trip; the squishies could chase after her as fast as they wanted, they weren't going to catch her.

Rika passed under a large archway and into the capitol's main atrium. She was running along a balcony toward a door at the far end when she saw a soldier in heavy armor step through a doorway across the atrium. She recognized the weapon in his hand and dove to the ground as a blue streak of lightning flashed overhead, blowing a hole in the wall beside her.

Debris fell on her, and Rika struggled to get free—fighting her robe as much as the wall. She tore the robe asunder and scurried free as a second electron beam hit where she had been a moment earlier.

Rika took off running, taking a moment to fire a return shot from her own electron beam before leaving the atrium.

Her rear vision revealed that her shot hit the soldier center mass. She wasn't certain if his armor could withstand the beam, but she wasn't going to stick around to find out.

Inside the next corridor, she pushed past several men and women in highly ornate robes. One called out, hurling insults that Rika barely heard as she raced on.

<I'm almost at their main meeting hall, or whatever they call it,> Rika announced, not worried about EM silence. <Any word on where their president is?>

<They call it the Assemblage,> Barne said. <I'm not picking up anything on Ariana's location, but I'm also not picking up their protocols for when she's in the bunker—if I have the right ones. I think I have the right ones.>

<OK, let me know if that changes.>

Rika continued her mad dash, wishing the Marauders had secured drones for her armor. She constantly had to slow at intersections to see if anyone was lying in wait, and one time almost got her head shot off as a group of soldiers opened fire on her.

She didn't bother engaging them; instead she raced back to a nearby lift, prised the doors open, and leapt down the shaft. The elevator car was on the main floor, and she crashed through the ceiling, narrowly missing a terrified woman who spilled coffee down her robe.

"Sorry 'bout that," Rika said as she took off once more.

Again the incongruity of what she was doing hit her. She had no issue with the Thebans. Aside from the possibly corrupt police up north at Cheri's villa, all her dealings with them had been pleasant and enjoyable.

And here she was, barreling through their capitol building, hell-bent on taking out their president.

She was close now to the 'mop closet' and as she rounded a corner, she caught sight of a group of people rushing down the hallway ahead.

Rika surged forward, banking up onto a wall, and came around the corner to see a woman—the president, her HUD confirmed—being ushered into a lift.

There were too many people around for Rika to take a shot. She'd have no way to know if she'd hit the president. No way to confirm the kill.

<I'm going down,> she sent, and then leapt over the crowd toward the lift. Someone must have spotted her, because the doors began to close. A hand reached up and grabbed at her leg, and she kicked to free herself.

The action caused her to lose forward momentum, and she dropped fast. The doors were half a meter apart, and Rika gave one final push to break free of the dozen hands on her and slipped through into the elevator.

She struggled to her feet and a pulse rifle fired into her torso. Rika reached out, grabbed the weapon, and pulled it free from the shooter. Four hostiles, as well as the president, lit up on her HUD. Two were without armor—one of which was the man she had just disarmed—and the other two were in heavy armor.

One of the heavily armored guards pushed the president into the back corner and protected her bodily while the other opened fire on Rika. She stepped in close, past the man's short rifle, and punched him in the throat.

His armor cracked but didn't break. Rika was about to hit him again when she felt her right arm pulled back. She saw that the other two guards had grabbed the barrel of her GNR and were trying to pull her away from the president.

In the close quarters of the lift, Rika could barely maneuver her left arm—but she was able to swing it enough to lift the two men into the air and slam them into the elevator's ceiling.

The armored guard took advantage of Rika's distraction to pull out a sidearm and unload a magazine into her helmet. Rika gasped in surprise as her visor cracked, but it held against the point-blank fire.

She lifted her left leg up and sank her claws into the elevator's wall, and then punched the man again, straightening her leg at the same time.

This time the man's gorget broke; so did his neck. As he fell, the two unarmored guards were rising. They scrambled to their feet just as the lift doors opened. Rika reached for the president as the armored guard rushed her out, but the two men pulled Ariana back.

"Enough!" Rika yelled. She unslung her JE78 rifle and unloaded a quartet of pulse shots into the two men, before spinning and chasing the president and her guard across a foyer and through a massive blast door that was slowly closing.

She slipped in with plenty of room to spare, only to come face-to-face with a pair of Assault Mechs. She had met some of these guys during the war. Mostly they were made from large men; like a tank version of a scout mech, but not large and clumsy like a K1R. Unless she missed her guess, these two were model threes.

Rika surveyed the room and saw that it was a large foyer with thick pillars, five-meter-high ceilings, and a number of desks and consoles along two walls. The fourth wall had a number of crates stacked against it.

The guard all but carried the president past the two mechs and through a door amidst the consoles. Rika wondered for a brief moment—during which the AM-3s raised their chainguns—if they were under compliance or were still making war with their freedom. Like she was.

"Guys…do you really want to do this? We were on the same side once," she said, smiling pleasantly—even though they couldn't see it behind her helmet.

"Stand down, SMI-2," one of the AM-3s said in a sharp tenor.

"Or don't," the other shrugged, his voice gravelly and deep.

Rika knew that if she backed down now, death would be the best possible outcome she could hope for.

"No can do," Rika said, and fired one of her uranium bolts at the AM-3 on her right. He saw her GNR rise and moved to the side—but not far enough.

The bolt hit his left arm where the chaingun was mounted and blew it clear off. The AM-3 models, unlike the SMI-2s, did not have any part of their organic limbs remaining, so the man only grimaced as the stump of twisted metal sticking out of his left shoulder twitched and sparked.

Rika knew that a fight against two of these mechs would be one of the most difficult she'd ever had, but a part of her reveled in the opportunity to test her mettle against them.

She closed with the one she had wounded, knowing that the best way to keep the other from bringing his formidable ordnance to bear was to have him run the risk of shooting his teammate.

Hopefully these two like one another.

She remembered hearing that the AM-2s had a weak spot on the edges of their chest plates where the armor connected to the hard mount on their bodies—hopefully it hadn't been fixed on the 3s. She toggled her JE78 rifle to kinetic slugs and fired a rapid burst of the two-centimeter rounds at the weak spot, spinning the already-wounded AM-3 to the side and driving him back.

Though Rika tried to keep the one-armed AM-3 between her and his gravelly voiced companion, she wasn't entirely successful, and he fired off a trio of blasts from his pulse rifle, pushing her back into the open.

The whine of the chaingun got her moving, and Rika dove behind a pillar as rounds chased after her. Two struck her in the side and one got her in the ass, but her armor registered no penetration—though the plate on the side of her butt was fractured.

Luckily the Marauders didn't believe in playing fair—Team Basilisk even less so—and Rika pulled a burn-stick from the pouch strapped to her left thigh and primed it for an impact ignition.

The burn sticks were thermite incendiaries modified to stick to their targets for maximum damage. One stick may not make it through an AM-3s armor, but it certainly would scare the shit out of them.

Rounds poured past the pillar, chipping away at its sides as the two AMs spread out, narrowing the cone of safety behind it. Rika considered her options and then leapt, twisting in the air so that her feet were up and her head was down.

She prayed her aim was true and almost shouted out in triumph when her feet clamped onto a decorative capital on the top of the pillar. She twisted around the pillar, threw the burn stick at the already-wounded AM-3, and then twisted around the other way, and aimed her GNR at the other AM-3.

He had anticipated her move and let loose with another barrage from his chaingun.

It would have hit, too, if the capital hadn't torn off the top of the pillar. Rika fired her round as she fell; the depleted uranium bolt struck the AM-3 in the head and snapped his neck back, but not enough to have broken it.

The front of the mech's helmet was a ruined mass, and he tore at it with his other hand, desperate to pull it off and regain sight.

Rika wasted no time and fired her electron beam at the struggling mech, burning a hole clear through his head.

She hadn't heard any screaming from the other AM-3 and assumed her burn stick had missed—but when she peered around the pillar, a pulse blast hit her square in the face and threw her backward, exposing her again.

As she struggled to her feet, she saw the second AM-3 was limping toward her, his right hip a mess of melted steel and blood.

"Gonna fuck you up," he said, his voice filled with rage. "Benny was a good friend. You're going to regret this."

Rika sprinted away as the AM-3 fired kinetic rounds from his rifle at her. Three bullets traced a line down her thigh and shattered the armor plating, then a fourth hit and tore through the front of her leg.

Rika fell to the ground once more, her gun-arm twisted under her body. The AM-3 held out his rifle and pulled the trigger.

CLICK!

In the time it took him to switch his rifle's firing mode, Rika rolled over, straightened her GNR, and fired her third uranium rod into his torso.

Her aim was good and the shot penetrated the armor where the burn stick had melted it away. The upper half of his body exploded outward, blood, bone, and armor spraying across the room.

Rika looked around, amazed that no other guards were present. Maybe these two had been the only ones down here when the president arrived.

Biofoam was filling her wound, and Rika noted that the med-readout on her HUD showed her femur as intact. She grabbed a shard of nearby armor—one of the AM-3s, by its color—and stuck it into the biofoam filling her wound.

It wouldn't offer any significant protection, but something was better than nothing.

She got her left leg under her, picked up her JE78 rifle, and rose up, leaning on her GNR's barrel as she tested her right leg's strength. Her armor and mods dulled the pain, but it still hurt like a fucker when she put weight on it.

Rika glanced back to see that the massive blast door at the foyer's entrance was sealed. Rika knew that it would not open easily, so any pursuit was a ways off. Still, there could be a rear exit, and she had to find the president before she and her remaining guard reached it.

Rika turned and limped in the direction the guard had taken the president. She passed through the door on the far side of the foyer and into a maze of hallways filled with offices and meeting rooms.

She scanned the ground and saw a trail of blood. She wondered if the president had been wounded at some point or if the blood was from the guard—or even someone else.

Still, it was all she needed.

Rika ignored the pain in her leg and began to lope through the halls, following the trail of blood. It passed through the nicer portion of the bunker and into a rear area filled with supply rooms and environmental systems.

The droplets were decreasing in frequency, but so were the available paths to take. After five minutes, Rika heard voices and she slowed her approach.

"Can you open it?" she heard a woman's voice say, and she recognized it as the president's. She sounded scared, terrified, and Rika felt a pang of guilt. The worry that she was doing something terribly wrong assaulted her once more.

She peered around a corner and saw President Ariana and her guard at the far end—twenty-three meters away. Before them was a large door. One that either led deeper into the bunker or out to an exit. Given that it was sealed, Rika suspected it was an exit that had closed at the same time as the main door by the lift.

"Nowhere left to run," Rika said as she stepped into the corridor, her GNR-41C extended and aimed at the president's head.

The guard spun, raised his rifle, and fired it full auto at Rika. She twitched her GNR to the side and fired an electron beam that melted his armor, followed by a trio of ballistic rounds that tore his right arm off.

The man screamed in pain and collapsed, and Rika pulled her JE78 off her back and shot a pulse blast, pushing him back and away from the rifle still held by his severed, twitching arm.

She kept the JE78 trained on him as he whimpered in pain, and she leveled the GNR at the president once more.

"Why are you doing this?!" the woman shrieked. "Who's paying you? We can double it! Please!"

Rika shook her head. "I guess it's easy to see I'm Genevian, which makes me a merc. Funny thing is I don't get paid for this. I'm a slave."

"A what?" the president asked. "You're doing this under compliance? We can help you, we can free you!"

"Those two AM-3s, were they under compliance?" Rika asked.

"No!" the president shook her head emphatically. "What your people did to you was barbaric. We would never do that to any living being."

Rika felt sick to her stomach. Though she was still technically a slave, she was no longer under compliance. She was about to murder this woman of her own free will.

"I'm sorry," Rika said. "I have to do this."

"You can fight it," the woman said. "Others have! Fight the Discipline, please!"

Rika felt tears on her cheeks. "I don't have to…. I'm not currently under Discipline. My compliance chip is offline."

"Then why are you doing this?!" Ariana shrieked. "You have no reason to kill me!"

"I have to belong somewhere…" Rika said, her voice cracking. "I need a home, I can't make it on my own. I tried, I really tried."

"I'll help you, Thebes can help you! Just *please* don't kill me!"

A sob tore through Rika's body and she lowered her GNR. She couldn't do it. She *wouldn't* do it. Basilisk team had been kind to her—more than they had to be—but she just couldn't kill this woman in cold blood as she pleaded for her life.

"I won't…" Rika said quietly. "I won't kill you. I'm done."

She fell to the ground as Ariana began to weep with relief.

"What happens now?" Rika asked—knowing that things were unlikely to play out well for her no matter what.

President Ariana wiped her cheeks dry and pushed her hair back out of her face. "I don't know…you just killed a lot of people."

Rika sighed. "I tried not to…as much as I could."

The guard beside Ariana shifted, and Rika suspected that he had passed out and was just coming to.

"Madam President!" he called out, turning his head toward her. "You're…you're OK?"

Ariana nodded solemnly, glancing up at Rika, "For no reason other than my would-be assassin's conscience striking at the last moment."

Rika could tell that the president had meant the words to be kind—at least to a degree—but they cut her to the core.

The president glanced back down at her guard. "Are you OK, John? Other than the arm…."

180

The guard—John—nodded. "Yeah, I'll live. You, there; if you really mean no further harm, put down your weapons...if you can."

Rika pulled herself back to her feet, wincing as pain lanced up her injured leg. John tried to rise as well, but fell back against the wall.

"I can't" Rika said as she placed her JE78 on her back. "I'm not going to rot in one of your prisons any more than I'm going to be a slave."

"You're not getting out of here," Ariana said. "There'll be an entire army above, waiting for you to emerge."

"Maybe," Rika said. "Depends on whether or not the other trigger pullers had more steel than I did."

"Other?" Ariana asked. "How many others?"

"I don't know," Rika shrugged. "Slave, remember? Though I don't even know if my team knew for sure. Enough to wipe out the upper echelon of your leadership—both civilian and military."

"Fuuuuhck," Ariana breathed. "John! We have to get out of here!"

John coughed. "No. No we shouldn't. If what she says is true, then this is where you need to stay."

"Do you have Link access?" Rika asked. "You could get out a warning, at least."

"Offline right now. It has to be initiated from down here," John said, coughing again. "Could...could someone help me get my helmet off? I'm coughing blood here, and it's getting nasty."

"Yeah, how do I do it?" Ariana asked.

John reached up with his remaining arm and unclipped a latch on each side. "Just twist counter clockwise, and then lift straight up."

Ariana nodded and complied as Rika looked on silently.

When John's face appeared, his mouth and chin were covered in blood.

"John!" Ariana gasped.

The man gave a macabre smile. "Madam President, my arm is missing, how is a little blood on my face compared to that?"

"John, really, I don't know, OK? Let me help you up."

"For what it's worth, I'm sorry," Rika said sheepishly.

"Why don't you pull off your helmet so we can see who you are?" President Ariana asked.

Rika shook her head. "No, ma'am. John there is sure to have another weapon on him, and I wouldn't blame him for taking a shot at me."

Ariana looked to John, who nodded grimly, "I certainly would."

"No, John, you won't. This woman is not a threat anymore. If she wanted to kill me, she would have already. You're not to harm her. That's an order."

John gritted his teeth but nodded.

"I need to hear it, John," Ariana said.

"Fine. I won't harm her."

Ariana turned back to Rika. "See? I'm showing my trust in you. Now I need something back. Remove your helmet."

Rika sighed and signaled her helmet to unlatch; then she pulled it off and hooked it on her hip.

"Huh," John said, while the President shook her head. "You're just a young woman."

"Not so young. Just a new face," Rika said. "War took the old one."

"It's in your eyes," Ariana said as she approached. "You're what, twenty-seven?"

"A bit older," Rika replied.

"What's your name?"

"Rika."

Ariana nodded. "Well, Rika; if you'd like, let's go to the command center and see if we can find out if I'm still president of this alliance or if we've been invaded."

Rika gestured silently for the president to precede her, and John barked a laugh as he scooped up his rifle. "Fat chance. You're in the lead, *Rika*."

"John," President Ariana said. "Seriously. She's no threat."

"Respectfully, Madam President, you're wrong. She is *absolutely* still a threat."

"It's OK," Rika said. "I can go in front. Just let me know if I make a wrong turn."

Rika began to walk back to where she suspected the command center to be—a room filled with holotanks and consoles that she had passed on the way to their present position.

Strange as it was, Rika felt that she could trust the president. The woman seemed honorable—of course, she was a politician, which also meant she was likely a demagogue capable of telling any tale to suit her. If Ariana became hostile and broke her word, Rika harbored no illusions that John would go along with it.

As Rika limped along—her injury still sending waves of pain up her thigh with each step—Ariana caught up with her.

"Do you know who hired you?" she asked. "What outfit are you with?"

"I'd rather not say," Rika replied.

"About which?"

"About either," Rika said.

"Do you even know who hired you?"

"I don't, but my team has suspicions."

"Nietzschean Empire, most likely," John said from behind them.

Rika had been walking with her head turned just enough to keep John in her peripheral vision. She saw the sneer on his face and wondered about the relationship between Thebes and the Empire.

"Wouldn't be Niets," Rika replied. "Too many Genevians in the—uh...our outfit to ever take work from them. Besides. Assassination isn't the Niets' style. They only do full frontal assault." Rika remembered a few ambushes from the war. "Well, mostly."

Ariana sighed. "Whoever it is...if the rest of your teams were half as successful as you were, we're in serious trouble. Our constitution has a very tricky transfer of power built in. If top military leaders are dead, too..."

"Depends on whether it's an internal coup or an external attack," John said.

"Let's hope it's a coup," Ariana replied.

"Why?" Rika asked.

Ariana glanced up at her. "Because even if whoever takes over is a horrible despot, it's probably better than an invasion."

The sick feeling in Rika's stomach intensified. Here she was worried about going to prison or how she'd escape, and the woman at her side was concerned with the fate of millions of her citizens.

Even so, Rika's desire to get free was undiminished. She was tired of being the pawn of others. It was high time that she took control of her own destiny—even if that meant using President Ariana as a hostage to secure her freedom.

Of course, if the rest of the Marauders had succeeded, it was Ariana whose days were numbered. When whoever had paid the Marauders arrived to take advantage of the chaos, the bunker would eventually be cracked, and she would be executed.

Rika had to admit that she hoped such an outcome would not be the case.

They walked in silence for the remainder of the distance to the command center—which Rika had correctly identified. It wasn't far from the entrance. One of the AM-3s bodies was visible through the door.

Ariana glanced at Rika, who, for all her augmentations was still under only two hundred and thirty centimeters tall, while the AM-3s had been over three hundred.

"I can't believe you killed them…and are barely hurt."

Rika shrugged. "There's a reason they made my model after theirs."

Ariana locked her eyes on Rika's.

"Is that all you are? A model? A woman decided not to kill me. Not a machine. Do you see yourself as a woman?"

Rika felt a tear form in her eye and didn't trust her voice. *How is Ariana able to disarm me so completely?* She had to believe that the Theban President was sincere; if not, she was playing Rika like a harp.

"I try," she finally managed to reply, though her voice betrayed her emotions.

Ariana gave her a sympathetic look before turning and walking into the command center. She approached a console and keyed in a command.

"I'm opening up a connection to the surface networks," Ariana said and glanced back at Rika. "Send me your codes. I'll give you access."

"Madam—" John began, but Ariana held up her hand.

"We've been over this, John."

Rika connected to the bunker's network and sent her public token to Ariana.

<Thanks,> Ariana replied. <And thank you for not killing me. I know you aren't sure if you can trust me…the feeling's mutual, but I would like to salvage whatever we can out of this.>

Rika sent an affirmative response but didn't speak. She was desperate to find out what had happened on the surface, but also terrified.

A moment later, Rika felt the surface networks become available and sought out the encrypted channel Basilisk had used for comms.

Her queue was flooded with messages. From Leslie and Barne (though none from Jerry), one from Captain Ayer, and another from someone named Specialist David.

She was about to check the first message when Leslie's voice barreled into her mind. <*Rika! Rika? Are you there? Stand down! Don't kill the president!*>

<*Leslie, I'm here, she's alive,*> Rika responded, shocked by the change in orders.

<*Alive? As in 'barely breathing' or 'standing up and happy'?*>

<*Well, I don't know how happy she is, but she's physically unharmed.*>

<*Whaa...You're going to have to tell me what happened soon, but for now the Marauders have sided with the Thebans—we were hired by the Niets!*>

<*The fuck?!*> Rika exclaimed as she refocused on Ariana, whose face bore a wan smile.

"Well, Rika. Looks like we're on the same side now."

FORGIVEN

STELLAR DATE: 12.18.8948 (Adjusted Years)
LOCATION: Capitol Bunker, Berlin
REGION: Pyra, Albany System, Theban Alliance

Thirty minutes later, Rika stood with President Ariana and a very pale John as the bunker's main door slowly opened. She had moved the two AM-3s to the side and covered their bodies—what was left of them—with a sheet from a supply closet.

Ariana's generals were torn. Some wished to get their president out of the bunker—and away from Rika—as quickly as possible. Others didn't want her to leave the bunker until things with the Marauders were sorted out.

Between Ariana's updates and intel Rika got from Leslie and Barne, they had pieced together the events of the previous hour.

As Rika had been rushing through the Capitol building, hundreds of Marauder comm drones had dumped out of the dark layer into the Albany system, broadcasting abort codes to all Marauder teams.

Leslie had informed her that the drone swarm was a last-ditch failsafe to abort an operation. Most of the drones were destroyed in the dark layer, but enough made it through to get the message out.

Then a Marauder fleet had jumped deep into the Albany system, only twenty AU from Pyra, which they were decelerating toward and would reach in two days. Although the Marauders only possessed one hundred and twenty capital ships, no system reacted kindly to a mercenary force of that size arriving without notice.

On top of that, another dozen rapid exfiltration ships had boosted out of hiding around various moons and planetary rings, scooping up Marauder teams across the system.

"My generals are certainly nervous," Ariana had said at one point. "Granted, your Marauders' small number of ships are no great threat; but given your close proximity to me down here, no one knows if we're really in a hostage situation or not—despite my reassurances."

"Understandable," Rika had replied. "This is a mess no matter which way you turn it. But to think that I almost killed you for the Niets.... I'm sorry, President Ariana. I—I'm just sorry."

Ariana had nodded and placed a hand on Rika's arm. "Trust me, no one is more glad than I that you had a change of heart."

Once Leslie and Barne had given her the details about the Niets hoax, she had asked the question that had been burning in her mind. *<Where's Jerry?>*

Leslie didn't reply, but Rika sensed a wave of anguish over the Link.

<He didn't make it,> Barne said quietly. *<A missile from the Capitol's defense systems took him out while you were infiltrating.>*

<Leslie...I'm so sorry,> Rika said.

<I can't, Rika. I can't think about it right now, OK? If I start, then....>

Rika respected that, and changed the subject.

<What are my orders?>

Barne fielded the answer. *<We have a major on the ground here who is coordinating a reconciliation. One thing that everyone can agree on is that the Niets weren't going to sit on their asses and wait for the Thebans to regroup; they'll have an invasion force on Pyra's doorstep in no time.>*

Those words echoed in Rika's mind as the bunker's wide door swung open. A Nietzschean invasion. She didn't know much about the Theban space force's strength, but she didn't see how a five-system alliance could field anything powerful enough to withstand an assault from the Nietzschean Empire.

The orders Rika received were simple: regroup with Basilisk and sync up with Alpha Company under Captain Ayer.

Rika had just one issue with that.

She wasn't a Marauder. She never signed up for this shit.

But her thoughts turned to Barne and Leslie. They were her team; even though she had failed in her duties, failed to take out President Ariana, they had shown no displeasure in her inaction.

Perhaps they didn't need to know exactly what had occurred—maybe a half-truth would have to be enough.

Rika glanced at President Ariana. She knew that there could be a place for her in Thebes—despite the lives she had taken—but Team Basilisk needed her. Barne and Leslie were just squishies. There was no way they could survive a Nietzschean invasion without mech support.

"FREEZE! Drop your weapons!" A voice yelled as the door swung open far enough for Rika to see an AM-2 mech on the other side.

"Lower your weapons," President Ariana called out. "I've issued a provisional pardon for Rika, here. She is not to be placed under arrest or to be restricted in any other way."

Rika relaxed a hair. Despite all of the president's assurances, there was a part of her that had worried it was a ruse to lull her into a false sense of security.

Of course she was still in arm's reach of Ariana. Things could change once they were separated.

"Ma'am," a man said as he pushed past several presidential guards in powered armor. "You cannot do this. She killed at least half a dozen people on her rampage."

Ariana turned her head toward Rika. "Sergey. I understand that, but she thought what she was doing was necessary. Rika stood down of her own accord. She may be a killer, but she is not a murderer. And on that basis, I have issued my pardon."

"This is going to be a disaster," Sergey replied, gripping his hands together.

"Sergey," Ariana said with a tired smile. "We have a war to fight. Rika is a warrior, and she is now fighting on our side. I'll take all the help we can get."

"Yeah, but on our side for how long?" one of the nearby soldiers muttered.

"Fucking mercs," said another.

Ariana did not acknowledge the utterances, but instead walked toward the lift. "Rika, you may ride up with me. John, you're on the first ride up, too. You need to see a medic yesterday."

"A bit late for that," John said as he followed after the president.

Rika slipped between the soldiers, feeling dozens of eyes on her, waiting for a bullet or a blow. But none came, and she reached the lift unmolested.

She noted that the bodies had been removed but the bloodstains remained. She wondered if the two unarmored guards had been part of the kill count or not. She thought she had been careful not to harm them—too much.

"Rika," President Ariana began as two other guards entered, and the lift began to rise. "I may not see you in the days to come; fate may pull us apart. I regret what your government did to you, and what lot has been left for you in life. I know it's not the same, but I have been called a monster in the past as well..." Ariana paused and met Rika's eyes. "I guess what I'm trying to say is that it was your *humanity* that saved me down there."

Ariana touched Rika's hand, gripping it like she would any flesh and blood hand, and squeezed gently. Their eyes met.

"I forgive you, Rika."

Rika felt a surge of emotion rise up in her, and tears sprang from the corners of her eyes. She nodded rapidly knowing that her voice would betray the wellspring of emotion within her.

Ariana continued to hold her hand as the lift rose and the doors opened. The guards in their powered armor exited first then turned and waited for the president. Ariana smiled at Rika and exited the lift.

Just as Rika whispered, "Thank you."

That was the last Rika ever saw of President Ariana. She was killed two days later when an orbital strike from a Nietzschean cruiser destroyed all of Berlin, including the capitol and the presidential palace.

MARAUDER

STELLAR DATE: 12.22.8948 (Adjusted Years)
LOCATION: Northern Districts of Jersey City
REGION: Pyra, Albany System, Theban Alliance

"Move! Move! *Move!*" Rika screamed at the platoon under her care as they clambered over the debris of a fallen building on the outskirts of Jersey City.

A sniper was out there firing on them, and Rika had to take it out before they lost any more Marauders.

<*I think I have triangulation,*> Barne said and passed the coordinates to Rika. She leveled her GNR and fired, trusting in Barne's analysis.

A dozen projectile rounds flew into a building three blocks away, and she changed positions, waiting for return fire. When none came, she breathed a deep sigh of relief.

<*Thanks, Barne.*>

<*Anytime, Rika.*>

Rika turned and surveyed the city around her, which was shrouded in long shadows as Howe set in the west. She shook her head, saddened by the current state of what had been a beautiful city, full of life just six days ago when she and Barne had passed through.

In the four days since the aborted assassination of the Theban leadership, all hell had broken loose.

The Nietzschean armada had not been far behind the Marauders' fleet, jumping in with over ten thousand capital ships all bearing down on Pyra. Their intent was to take out the Theban capital world in one swift strike.

One small benefit of the Theban response to the Marauders' arrival was that their ships were already mustered and in motion by the time the Niets appeared on Scan. This gave the Thebans enough of an edge that they were able to stave off a full bombardment of their world. However, it wasn't enough to stop several Nietzschean strafing runs on the planet that took out cities and dropped multiple ground assault teams.

It was textbook Nietzschean strategy: blitzkrieg a world. If they were unable to take it quickly, destroy and occupy large population centers. Dislodging their troops always resulted in heavy civilian casualties.

Rika was leading one such dislodging action at that very moment.

Leslie and Barne were with her, as well.

Technically a lieutenant named Clancy was in command of the platoon; somehow though, over the last day, everyone had begun to defer to Rika as they worked their way ever deeper into the ruins of Jersey City.

Rika clambered up a beam rising out of the rubble and watched the nearby buildings for signs of the enemy as the platoon spread out in the street below.

She spotted movement four blocks down and cycled her vision, confirming the presence of Nietzschean soldiers.

<Lieutenant Clancy,> Rika called over the combat net. <I see twenty Niets on E street, two blocks down. I thought we scouted that area.>

<We did, but that was six minutes ago. There were no life signs at the time,> Clancy replied.

Rika called back to the Marauders' surface-to-surface artillery teams, ten kilometers behind them. <I have hostiles at the following coordinates,> she said. <Requesting immediate fire support.>

<Acknowledged,> the comm officer at the platform replied. <I have fire solution authorization. Hold please.>

Less than a minute later, two grey streaks fell straight down from the sky, lobbed high into the air before they dove into their marks.

The street and the part of the building where the Niets were hiding in the shadows exploded in twin balls of fire. As the haze cleared, Rika called her thanks back to the artillery platform while also letting Lieutenant Clancy know that she didn't read any more hostiles from her vantage.

Below her the platoon split up, its four squads each taking a different street toward the center of Jersey City.

<I'm on the right flank, out past first squad,> Leslie reported. <Ranging ahead.>

<Copy that,> Barne replied from his place back with Clancy and the platoon sergeant. <Rika, Clancy says that second squad out on the left flank has a fireteam that performs scout duties for the 'toon. Why don't you take the center?>

<You got it,> Rika replied and dropped from the steel girder onto the street below.

She moved down the street being traversed by fourth squad—second from the right flank—and slipped past the soldiers.

Several of the Marauders nodded to her as she moved by. Some shook their heads, but most ignored her. Seeing their attitudes—not to mention their armor—brought a lot of old memories back.

Most of the armor and equipment in the Marauders was Genevian. Unfortunately so were the troops, and that meant many of the soldiers thought of her as nothing more than a tool.

Rika thanked her stars that Captain Ayer hadn't felt that way when attaching Rika to fourth platoon.

* * * * *

Two days prior...

"Basilisk," Captain Ayer had shaken her head slowly as the team entered the company's HQ—set up in the back offices of a water-storage and pumping plant. "You're some tough sons and daughters o' bitches. I'm sorry about Jerry; he was one of the best."

As she had spoken the captain rose from her desk, and the other two people in the room—a man and woman—had also turned their attention to Basilisk, their eyes solemn as they looked on.

Ayer walked around the desk and approached Leslie, clasping both of her hands. "I'm so sorry, Leslie. I truly am. I'm here if you need to talk."

Leslie nodded silently before taking a deep breath and wiping an eye.

Ayer then turned to Rika and shook her hand without hesitation. A gesture that spoke volumes about her opinion of mechs.

"Rika, I'm happy to finally meet you, but it saddens me that it's under these circumstances."

"Thank you, Captain Ayer," Rika replied.

Lastly, Ayer turned to Barne and clasped his hand. "Sergeant Barne, I see you survived your first mission with Rika. I'm glad to see the two of you are unscathed."

"Captain Ayer, of course I am. I've got Rika at my back. She's Basilisk."

Ayer glanced at the coiled snake carefully painted on Rika's chest. "So she is. I'm surprised that you feel that way."

"No reason not to, ma'am," Barne said, his tone crisp and unequivocal.

"Glad to hear it," Ayer replied.

"Rika, I'd like you to meet First Sergeant Meg, and Gunnery Sergeant Stewart."

"Nice to meet you, Rika," Gunnery Sergeant Stewart said with a smile, while First Sergeant Meg only nodded and said, "Rika."

"Glad you were able to make it up here to meet us," Ayer continued once the formalities were over.

"Was a slog up the coast," Barne said. "But we heard this was where they were dropping the beer, ma'am."

"No beer yet, Sergeant, but I do have some gifts for Rika and some real armor for the two of you."

Rika wondered what those gifts could be, but didn't voice her question as Ayer continued.

"The Niets may have done a drive-by on Berlin and toasted it something fierce, but Marauder ships aren't commanded by pusillanimous cowards like the GAF was, and it would seem the Thebans aren't either. For now they've managed to push the Nietzschean ships back from Pyra, and are engaging them near Fresna."

"Good news is that we don't have to worry about Niet birds in our skies. Bad news is that they dropped over a hundred-thousand of their dickhead commandos down here, and we'll have to clear them out the old-fashioned way."

"Do we have any orbital support?" Barne asked.

Ayer nodded. "We've got the *Brisbane* in orbit and an artillery platform set up a few klicks to the north. It's a bit of a Niet magnet, so first platoon is keeping it safe until the *Brisbane* gets the shield generator down here. The Thebies have a few ships up there, too. They've taken what shots they can, but now the Niets have a lot of civvies rounded up, and the Thebans don't want to blow away their own people."

"So it's time to send in the mercs," Leslie said.

"You need to sit this one out, Corporal?" Captain Ayer asked, a sharp edge entering her voice. "I feel for you, and I feel your pain, too, but you signed up for this gig. Last I checked, so did Jerry."

Leslie swallowed and glanced at Barne and then Rika. "No, ma'am. I go where Basilisk goes."

"Glad to hear it," Ayer said with a curt nod. "We're going to send you out with Lieutenant Clancy and fourth platoon. However, I first need to square away some housekeeping."

Ayer turned to Rika as she spoke, and Rika wondered what could be coming next.

"Back in the war, a mech saved my life. Another mech saved an entire platoon under me. I watched mechs do the war's hardest work with the least thanks. You never got medals, ribbons, or promotions; that's not how the Marauders operate. I have authorization from General Mill to give you a field promotion to Second Lieutenant."

Rika felt a surge of mixed emotions, but shook her head.

"No, ma'am. No disrespect to you, but I cannot accept that promotion."

Ayer's face clouded. "Why not, Rika?"

"Because I'm a slave, and slaves can't be officers."

"Shit, Rika, didn't you get the message? It should be in your queue on the Marauders' general—aw, fuck." Ayer sighed and gave Rika a wink. "We try to be more efficient than the Genevian Armed Forces were, but it's not always easy. You never got tokens to access the general net, did you?"

"No, ma'am," Rika shook her head.

"We'll square that away once we're done here, but let me be the first to inform you that you are *not* a slave. There was a data packet that got left out when you were sent to Pyra—it was a bit of a rush job, not our best work. You were only to have to work off half the cost that it took to buy you at that disgusting auction. However, when the Old Man learned about how you saved your team when you could have disappeared, he decided that you had gone above and beyond the call of duty—especially for someone who thought they were a slave.

"You're free and clear, Rika. You owe the Marauders nothing, and when we're done here, I'll have the company's technician remove that compliance chip and get proper enlistment paperwork drawn up for you."

Barne let out a whoop of joy while Leslie reached out and grabbed Rika's arm. "Rika," she said with a smile.

Rika couldn't find the words, but she felt a tear slide down her cheek. She drew herself up and wordlessly saluted Captain Ayer.

She had finally been set free. There was no hesitation in her mind now. She *was* a Marauder.

Captain Ayer smiled and returned the salute. "Now, Lieutenant Rika. I assume that you'll properly enlist?"

"Yes, ma'am." Rika said the words with a calm certainty.

"Excellent. The gifts, by the way, are right-mount GNR and a new left arm. Now let's get Clancy in here and go over how we're going to kill all these fucking Niets."

* * * * *

On the front...

Rika had worried that Clancy would have an issue with another officer attached to his platoon. As it turned out, he was a first lieutenant, and the pecking order was clear—for the most part. Though he was in charge, Rika had a lot more experience in the field, and he was to take her advice.

Barne had them all beat for time in the service—even more than Clancy's platoon sergeant—but that just meant he'd make sure the officers didn't screw things up too much.

The plan had been straightforward: move south into the city, secure the manufacturing district on its north side, and then cross the canal into the downtown area and flush the Niets out.

Except there'd been a lot more Niets on the north side of the canal than anyone had expected. Second and third platoons were still further back, but Captain Ayer had instructed fourth platoon to push forward and secure the north side of the canal—which was now only four kilometers distant.

As Rika slipped past squad four's lead fireteam and down E street, she scanned each building for heat signatures and movement while also monitoring feeds from the platoon's drones.

<All clear so far,> she reported back, then caught movement on one of the forward drone's feeds. <Scratch that. I have movement.>

The drone had picked up a shadow moving at the head of a nearby alley. Rika unslung her JE78, ready for close quarters combat. She pulled a drone's feed from high overhead but was unable to see into the alley with the refuse and overhangs from the buildings on either side.

She considered sending a drone into the alley but didn't want to give away her intentions. Rika glanced at the twelve-meter-high building and crouched before springing up over the protruding roof, landing as quietly as possible, and then dashing across the to the next street and dropping down at the other end of the alley.

<Checking alley at my position,> she reported to Barne, relaying the message through the drones to reduce her EM signature.

<Understood.>

Rika crept down the alley's narrow confines, staying in the deepening shadows and searching for whomever or whatever she had seen. She progressed five meters into the alley and then stopped, pressing herself against the northern side, as a dull scraping sound reached her ears.

Nothing showed up in her enhanced vision, and she was considering sweeping the darkness with an active scan when a shape darted out from between two large metal bins.

<Just a dog,> she reported to Barne as the large grey hound approached her.

"Got left behind, did you?" Rika asked as she reached her left hand out to stroke its head. The dog didn't shy away, and she smiled to herself, happy to see that someone accepted her without reservation.

Though she knew that thought wasn't entirely fair. Leslie had never once seemed disturbed that Rika was a mech; nor had Captain Ayer.

As Rika stood, she heard a sound from behind her and she snapped her knees straight, leaping into the air as an electron beam streaked through the space where she had been a moment before.

Rika arched over backward and saw four shimmering figures at the entrance to the alley.

Shit, that's good camo, she thought while firing two projectile rounds from her GNR-41C, followed by a full auto spray from her JE78. The large caliber rounds from the GNR took out the Niet with the electron beam, and the other rounds drove the rest of the enemy back around the corner.

<Three tangos, F street, my position,> Rika called out as she hit the ground and moved deeper into the alley. The dog was gone, and she was glad to see it hadn't been a casualty of the Niets' ambush.

<Want a hand?> Leslie asked. *<I'm on G street, not far ahead.>*

<How'd you get ahead?> Rika asked.

Barne chuckled in their minds. *<Leslie's like a ninja.>*

<I'm never one to say 'no' to help,> Rika replied.

She saw Leslie's location on the combat net and fired a few shots out of the alley's mouth to keep the Niets engaged with her. One ducked around the corner and fired a few rounds, which missed because Rika was halfway up the wall of a building and climbing.

Another Niet tossed an HE grenade into the alley, and Rika raced up the wall, tearing out bricks and mortar as she went. The explosion blew past her just as she reached the top.

Rika heard weapons fire on the street below and moved to the edge of the building to look down. Leslie was across the street, just emerging from cover, and squad one's lead fireteam was half a block to the north.

The Niets were all dead.

<Thanks, guys,> Rika said over the platoon's combat net.

<Anytime, LT,> Corporal Veers, leader of the fireteam, replied.

Rika stayed on the rooftops for the next kilometer, ranging further ahead and using her drones to scout the alleys and streets around her. She was now within two kilometers of the canal and the downtown district on its far side, and she scanned the gleaming towers that rose into the air.

The streets on the north side of the canal ran at a forty-five-degree angle to the waterway, which provided line-of-sight protection for the platoon as they advanced behind Rika. Unfortunately, the manufacturing district had given way to smaller commercial buildings, which were still tightly packed but were often only one story high. They wouldn't provide much cover if any significant fire came from the three-hundred-meter-high buildings across the canal.

Rika sent her drones further into the sky and overlaid their feed with the images delivered from the ships and satellites overhead.

The combined visual showed a lot of activity in the towers along the canal. There were also a lot more heat signatures than could be accounted for by the Niets alone. Marauder Intel and Analysis determined that the towers were occupied by at least a hundred thousand Theban citizens.

Artillery was out of the question.

Along the northern edge of the canal—on the side Rika was approaching—lay a wide, heavily wooded park. At first it appeared as though the park was empty; Rika sent her drones down into the trees. They passed through an EM shield and suddenly picked up dozens, then hundreds, of heat signatures in the trees.

The Niets were waiting for them.

Three of her drones went offline, and Rika assumed the enemy had deployed EMP countermeasures against them. Rika released another passel but kept them high and further back.

<Got a welcoming committee,> Rika said as she passed her observations back.

<Not surprising,> Clancy replied. <Any suggestions?>

<With those towers back there raining down beamfire, it'll take a whole regiment to get across that canal. What we need is a feint.>

Barne offered a suggestion. <We could pummel locations to the west and east with artillery fire, creating a clear path for an advance. The Niets will concentrate their troops along the area we clear out, then we'll come right up the center.>

<It won't take them long to realize what we're up to. Then they'll smash us from the towers,> Clancy replied.

<Then Rika and Leslie had better get over there and take out a tower or two first,> Barne replied.

Rika liked the plan. <Leslie. Meet me at my position. I have an idea.>

CRASH

STELLAR DATE: 12.22.8948 (Adjusted Years)
LOCATION: Northern Districts of Jersey City
REGION: Pyra, Albany System, Theban Alliance

<So what's the big plan?> Leslie asked on a private connection to Rika as she approached. Rika had a hard time seeing Leslie; the other woman's light armor continually shifted in color to match her surroundings as she moved through the evening shadows.

<I did this back in the Parsons System when we were trying to make evac,> Rika said. <Storm drains will dump into that canal; we go down into them, cross the canal underneath, and then get through a storm drain on the far side and make our way up.>

Leslie cocked her head as she crouched next to Rika, considering the idea.

<That was a pitched battle, if I recall the reports. They didn't have good Scan. Here they'll be staring at that canal with a lot of tech. They will see us cross. Not to mention they'll have monitors on the storm drains on the far side,> Leslie said.

<Yeah, but we have to cross somehow. The canal has a lot of sludge and stuff growing in it—it should mask us, if we stay down in the muck.>

<And the detection systems they'll certainly have placed on the storm drains on the far side?> Leslie asked.

Rika brought up the canal's far shore, looking for other options.

<What about that little decorative inlet and pool there?> she suggested, sharing the location with Leslie.

<That could work. It's right next to the Withermere Tower, which is where Intel and Analysis thinks a lot of their heavy weapons are set up.>

<How good is Marauder I&A?> Rika asked.

Leslie shrugged. <*Pretty good. Better than what we had in the war.*>

<*We're Genevians fighting Niets,*> Rika replied. <*Feels like the war is still on.*>

Leslie gave a rueful laugh. <*Yeah, just a new theater.*>

The pair backtracked and found a storm grate that they would fit through. Rika pulled it up as quietly as possible and, once in, lowered it over them.

There wasn't enough room to stand so the two women crawled on all fours—all threes in Rika's case, with her GNR draped over her back. Leslie was in the lead and she reached the spout into the canal first.

It sat halfway out of the water, and Leslie glanced back at Rika. <*Here goes nothing.*>

She slithered out of the spout and down into the dark waters with Rika right on her tail. They fell to the bottom of the canal, which was just over four meters deep at this point, and lay still in the mud.

No weapons fire came, and Rika wished she had a drone feed to be certain that a hundred Niets wouldn't be waiting for them on the far shore—but the EM signals would have given them away.

It took the pair over ten minutes to cross the canal, staying low, crawling across the muddy bottom and angling across to the inlet. When they finally reached their exit point, Rika sent a drone to the water's surface and passively scanned the area.

The drone picked up two Niets nearby and a motion sensor to their right. However nothing appeared to be covering the route they needed to take to get to the Withermere Tower, which rose up on the water's edge like a great glass reed only a dozen meters to the east.

Rika motioned for Leslie—who was also tapped into her drone feed—to follow. They slowly rose, taking care not to cause too much of a disturbance on the water's surface.

Leslie moved ahead, her armor's camo systems giving her the edge, and she signaled to Rika when the coast was clear.

Rika kept expecting weapons fire to rain down on them at any moment as they moved from cover to cover, but none came. Five minutes later, they finally reached the entrance to the Withermere Tower.

Rika peered through the glass doors and saw a dozen guards. Leslie saw them, too, and she glanced back at Rika.

Both women knew that if they breached the building and took out the guards, it would alert the enemy to the possibility of an attack down the center. However, if they waited for the Marauders' artillery to strike, they wouldn't get to the weapon emplacements in the tower fast enough.

Rika noted a small patio wrapping around the Withermere Tower and hanging over the water. Chances were that another entrance would be on the far end of the patio.

She signaled to Leslie, who gave a nod, and the two Marauders began to creep alongside the building and around the corner onto the patio. They had a clear view of the canal and the park beyond—which would still be teeming with Niets. If just one enemy soldier peered back across the canal, their little surprise would be over.

The far end of the patio was occupied by a dozen tables with umbrellas; many of which were still holding the remains of food. Rika spotted a door that led into a small café. Leslie checked the entrance for any active monitoring and, when none was revealed, opened the door and slipped inside with Rika trailing right behind her.

Within, more tables—most covered with discarded food and drinks—filled the space. Overturned chairs and a smashed interior window showed the signs of a struggle. The door leading into the interior of the tower was closed, so they stepped through the broken window and slowly walked down the hall to the bank of elevators.

The first door was open, with an elevator car within. The second was closed, and Rika prised her fingers into the gap and pulled the doors apart.

She peered inside and saw a ladder to the right. Rika stretched a leg out and clamped her clawed foot around the vertical rail on one side of the ladder, and then swung out into the shaft, clamping her other foot on the other side. She'd learned long ago not to trust her weight to ladder rungs—most weren't rated to hold her two hundred and thirty kilos.

Rika proceeded to walk up the ladder, her body perpendicular to the elevator shaft, while Leslie swung out behind her and pulled the door shut.

<That looks really weird,> Leslie commented on a tight comm. *<It's like you're walking up the side of the shaft.>*

Rika laughed. *<I kinda am. You're going to get exhausted, climbing sixty floors like that—plus you're slow. Hook onto this.>*

Leslie accepted the cable that Rika spooled out from her armor and clipped it onto a hook at her waist.

<Now let's just hope that this ladder doesn't peel off the wall,> Leslie said as Rika began to 'walk' up the shaft.

<We only have fifteen more minutes before the artillery lights up the park,> Rika advised.

<Better get a move on, then.>

Rika picked up the pace while still trying to climb as quietly as possible. As they passed the closed doors to many levels, muted voices could be heard. Most likely the Theban populace, being kept in the towers to make them less appealing targets.

Their destination, the sixtieth floor—where I&A had placed the first of the Niets' heavy weaponry—took three minutes to reach. When they arrived, Leslie unhooked from Rika, pulled herself over to the door, cracked it a centimeter, and passed out a drone.

<I'm clear,> Leslie reported. *<Good luck,>*

<You too,> Rika replied as she resumed her climb, heading to the roof of the building another ten stories above.

She reached the top of the shaft less than a minute later and pulled herself up to the a-grav emitter in the machine room that sat atop the building. There was a service hatch on one side, and Rika carefully maneuvered herself through it and onto the roof.

Rika surveyed her surroundings. There were no Niets on the south side of the roof, but she could see several on the tops of the nearby buildings, clustered around railguns that were set up a few meters back from the northern edges. She imagined the same setup was on the Withermere—the guns out of view but ready to slide forward and rain down punishing kinetic fire on any attackers across the canal.

Rika logged the locations of the guns. Once the assault began, she would relay the weapon coordinates to the artillery platform; perhaps they had airburst options that could at least blind the enemy weapons.

If not, she would take them out the hard way.

She passed a drone around the side of the elevator machine room to get a clear view of what she faced before the assault began. As the drone peeked around the corner, it caught sight of a pair of Niets walking around to the south side of the tower's roof.

"Shit!" Rika whispered. She considered her options. She could circle around to the west side of the machine room, but the two patrolling Niets would probably make a full circuit anyway. That would force her into full view of the rest of the Niets on the roof.

Her best bet was to take them out as quietly as possible when they reached the south side. Five nearby towers were as tall as the Withermere, and the Niets on their roofs would easily spot anything more than a quick takedown.

Of course, the enemy was wearing heavy powered armor, so taking them out quietly was going to be easier said than done.

Damn, I'm an idiot, Rika thought, realizing that she could just climb onto the machine room's roof and stay out of view. She clambered up to the top with only a second to spare and lay prone, hoping that the patrol hadn't spotted her.

The fact that the Niets didn't have drones covering every rooftop, elevator shaft, and stairwell was a testament to the losses their assault craft had suffered when dropping to the surface of Pyra.

With her drones withdrawn, Rika had little visibility onto the roof around her and she didn't dare move until she heard the footfalls of the patrol move away. Slowly they passed around to the east side of the roof, but something was wrong. There was just one set of steps.

A thud sounded behind her, and Rika flipped onto her back to see a Nietzschean soldier in heavy armor standing over her.

"Gotcha," he said aloud.

"Get this!" Rika said, and swung her gun-arm up and fired a high caliber projectile round into his groin. The man's armor dented and cracked, and he fell back with a shout.

<Fire! Fire! Fire!> Rika called out. The best cover for the fight she was about to have would be heavy artillery raining down onto the park across the canal.

A few seconds later the scream of incoming shells obliterated the silence of the early evening.

Explosions a kilometer along the canal to the east and west flared brightly, throwing entire trees and clouds of debris into the air. Rika rose up on the elevator house's roof and noted that the Nietzscheans on other towers were sliding their railguns forward, training them to the east and west, assuming assaults would come from those directions after the artillery ceased pounding the park.

All the Niets were occupied except the team on the Withermere; they were spinning their gun to fire on Rika. She dove off the top of the elevator's machine room as the railgun fired, blowing it to pieces, and sending the a-grav generator falling down through the shaft to the base of the building.

<Rika! What's going on up there?> Leslie sent.

<Oh, nothing, just dodging rail fire.>

<I've set explosives on three of their guns and am ready to take the fourth to fire on their own troops,> Leslie reported.

<How come you get the easy targets?> Rika asked as she raced across the rooftop, trying to get enough distance to fire a uranium bolt at the railgun.

She reached the far southwest corner just as the Niets locked onto her with the cumbersome weapon, and she fired her GNR.

The uranium bolt flew from her gun's muzzle, and she sighed with relief as it hit the railgun, tearing it in half and causing the weapon's energy coils to discharge into the soldiers nearby.

Rika unslung her JE78 and sent a series of pulse blasts into the Niets, pushing them back as she charged forward. One tripped after getting hit by a pulse and fell off the roof of the building; another nearly followed, but managed to hang onto the edge.

Airbursts from the artillery platform began to shower the adjacent buildings with EM and shrapnel, further lighting up the sky as Rika fired several high-caliber rounds into two more Niets. Then she kicked the hanging one off the roof.

<Stars, I've missed killing Nietzscheans,> she said over Basilisk's net, surprising even herself with the visceral satisfaction in her mental tone.

<It never gets old,> Leslie replied, and Rika saw beamfire lance out from the Withermere Tower into the park across the canal. It wasn't aimed at the far side where fourth platoon was advancing, but rather at the Nietzscheans. <Even better to do it with their own weapons.>

Leslie's words were punctuated by explosions several floors down; Rika smiled, knowing that the Withermere Tower no longer posed a threat to the Marauders.

As Rika emptied a magazine from her JE78 into the last Nietzschean on the roof, she looked around at the other towers.

The team on the tower to the west of the Withermere was in disarray, but the one to the east was braving the artillery fire and had slid one of their railguns to the edge of the roof.

It fired at the advancing Marauders in the park, getting off two shots before one of Rika's uranium rounds slammed into the weapon, tearing it in half and showering the gun's crew with shrapnel.

Rika glanced down as beamfire erupted from lower floors in the adjacent building, lancing out into the night. She gauged the distance to the next tower and backed up ten paces before taking off, running toward the edge of the building.

She pushed off with her right foot, moving at over one hundred kilometers per hour, and sailed between the buildings. The gleaming side of the adjacent building rushed toward her, and Rika fired four ballistic rounds, shattering the plas and a desk beyond.

Her arms folded before her, Rika landed, rolled, and was up and running across the floor toward the Niets who were firing electron beams out into the night.

The first Nietzschean soldier flew from the building before she knew what hit her, and the second followed suit shortly after. The next two were firing at Rika, and she dove to the side, firing her JE78's pulses on full power.

One of the remaining two flew out the window, but the other managed to grab onto the edge of the sill, hanging on for dear life as Rika approached.

"You guys need to learn when to quit," Rika said as she stepped on his hand, crushing it beneath her foot. The Nietzschean screamed in response, and Rika lifted her foot, not even watching as the man fell to his death.

She stooped down, grabbed his crew-served beam rifle, shouldered its battery pack, and walked to the east side of the floor.

Rika kicked the window and it shattered, giving her an unobstructed view of the next building. She steadied the beam weapon and took aim. Then she held the weapon's trigger down, firing a continuous beam into the next building—targeting the floors from which the Nietzscheans were firing on the advancing Marauders.

The offending building was set back a dozen meters from the one Rika was in, and she had a clear shot. She hit one of the enemy positions, then another. She was sweeping the beam across the building when an enemy beam fired back, catching the side of her building half a meter from where she stood.

Rika collapsed, her limbs convulsing as the electrical discharge overcame her motor controls. She couldn't get her legs to respond, so she pulled herself back with her left arm while her robotic limbs ran a full reset. Several primary controllers were shorted out, and she switched over to secondary systems.

<You OK?> Barne asked. <I see a crazy spike on your systems.>

<Yeah,> Rika said as her legs began to respond to commands. <Got a bit too close to a beam.>

<You operational?> Barne asked.

<Yeah. How we doing down there?>

<I'm mowing Niets down like it's going out of style,> Leslie announced.

Rika looked back at the Withermere Tower and saw beamfire raining down into the park.

<They'll probably get up the stairs soon,> Rika commented, knowing that no one would be taking the elevators since the railgun had destroyed the a-grav systems.

<Nah,> Leslie replied, her words punctuated by an explosion one floor down from her position. <Not my first day on the job.>

<We're closing with the canal,> Clancy said over the platoon's combat net. <Cover our flanks.>

Rika saw weapons fire lance out from the building that had fired on her, and she rose to her feet once more. She set off for the stairwell. She didn't bother with the stairs; she leapt from landing to landing until she reached the door at the top and burst out onto the roof.

Two Nietzscheans were still alive next to the railgun that Rika had shot previously. She fired her pulse rifle at them as she ran by and didn't even look back before jumping off the edge of the roof and into the next building.

Rika landed one floor too high and debated the best way to get to the floor below. She opted for speed and shot out a window before sliding over its edge and down to the next floor. She came down right on top of a pair of Niets and she pushed one of them, and the crew-served weapon, out the window. Then Rika turned her purloined weapon on the remaining Nietzscheans and incinerated them.

With the floor clear, Rika turned back to the windows and laid the platoon's combat net over her vision. The locations of Nietzschean troops in the park appeared, and she fired into them, her barrage joining in with Leslie's and creating a clear path for the platoon to reach the canal.

Eight minutes later, the entire platoon had made it across the water. The artillery platform flattened the rest of the park, clearing the way for third and fourth platoons, who were not far behind.

Fighting lit up the streets at the base of the towers at the water's edge as the Marauders engaged the Nietzscheans. Rika and Leslie brought their beams to bear in those conflicts, and, meter-by-meter, the Nietzscheans fell back under the Marauder assault.

DROP
STELLAR DATE: 12.23.8948 (Adjusted Years)
LOCATION: Pyran Space, Above Jersey City
REGION: Pyra, Albany System, Theban Alliance

Chase clamped down on his bite-guard as the drop ship fell through Pyra's atmosphere toward Jersey City. He looked around at the other members of his platoon, noting that many had their eyes closed while others were staring at the overhead. A small number were chatting with their squadmates.

The Old Man hadn't been able to take his pick of drop ships, and some, like the one the second platoon rode down in, had seen their share of abuse. Luckily the pilot seemed competent, and they were still in one piece—which was the most any soldier could hope for in a drop.

He looked at the fourteen soldiers in his squad—squad four in the platoon. They were organized into three fireteams. He was short a few troops, so his two extras were assigned to the first and second fireteams.

He would stick with his third fireteam to give the squad three teams of five. A bit large for his liking, but he didn't think it was wise to reorganize the teams too much. They were still getting used to him, and he to them.

<Remember, we're gonna hit the ground hard and fast. I want the perimeter established within our first minute,> Lieutenant Sedis reminded the team in her no-nonsense tone—the only way Chase had ever heard her speak. <Our orders are to establish a beachhead for the B'Muths that are coming down behind us. Those things are already on their way, so we need to clear any nearby structures inside of ten minutes.>

Chase noted that everyone's eyes were open now, and glued to Sedis as she spoke.

<This is a theater of war, people. I know there are civilians out there, but don't get mamby-pamby on me. You see something you think is a threat, you put it down. Marauders come first. Are you solid?!>

<Yes ma'am!> a chorus of voices resounded over the Link.

<Good, now let's get ready to fuck some shit up!>

Chase chuckled and looked across the aisle at Casey who mouthed 'shit fuckers'. Ten seats down, Ralph just shook his head slowly.

<I told—> Ralph began to say on the squad leader's net, when Chase was nearly torn from his harness as something struck the drop ship.

A klaxon blared, and Chase was pressed back in his seat as the ship began to spin through the air.

Thick smoke filled the cabin, and Chase switched to his armor's internal air supply, trying not to look at how rapidly his HUD said they were falling.

The drop ship had emergency thrusters that should keep them from creating a new crater in the city below, but they weren't firing.

Then he heard someone cry out on the combat net that the pilot was dead.

Chase had flown drop ships before when things were dire, so he tapped into the ship's navigation systems. They were a mess; one engine was gone, and the other was on full bore. He switched it off and fired control thrusters to slow the drop ship's spin.

The ship passed below a thousand meters, and the emergency landing systems signaled that they were ready to deploy—but the braking jets were still offline.

Someone was screaming on the combat net, and Chase yelled, *<Shut the fuck up!>* as he tried to route control of the jets through the attitude thruster controls.

As the ship passed five hundred meters, Chase hit the jets, praying they'd fire.

Five of the eight jets lit and slowed the ship, but then two shut down and the remainder kicked the ship over into a crazy spin. Chase killed them all, and the emergency foam deployed both inside and outside the ship.

Then they hit.

The foam that filled the inside of the drop ship dissolved almost as quickly as it had appeared, and over the combat net, he could hear Casey shrieking <Out! Out! Out!>

Chase fumbled with his harness, trying to find the buckle around his right leg. Then he realized that the strap had been torn off and there was nothing holding him down anymore. He rose from his seat and rushed out the back of the drop ship.

Outside, Ralph was directing first squad to cover the north of the drop ship, while Henry, fourth squad's sergeant, was moving to the south.

<Third squad! Get around the ship and secure our east perimeter,> Chase called out as he watched Casey exit the drop ship and send her squad west.

<Casey, is the ship clear?> Chase asked.

Casey nodded. <LT's dead, Chase; so is Sergeant Inman.>

<Then who's in charge?>

<You're senior.>

Chase took a step back and surveyed the ruin of the courtyard the ship had crashed in. He suspected that it was a school of some sort—which he confirmed a moment later when he cross-referenced their location with his map of Jersey City.

<Henry, Ralph, you two clear the dormitories. Work clockwise. Casey, you establish a perimeter to the west, cover the roofs of the dorms and any approaches. My folks'll do the east right after we see what we can pull from the ship.>

A string of confirmations reached his ears, and Chase turned back to the drop ship. Losing the LT and the platoon sergeant in the first moments of a drop was bad, but every other soldier had survived, and the ship was mostly intact.

<Fireteams two and three, set up at the nose of the ship. Anything moves to the east, you put holes in it. One, get in there and pull out everything that's not bolted down. We need to be ready to move out in five.>

<Clear so far,> Ralph said, as Chase walked around to the front of the drop ship and noticed the nose was shot off. The pilot wasn't dead—well, she probably was—she was just gone.

He sent a passel of drones out, and they rose into the sky around the courtyard. There was no movement in the streets or the walkways around the dormitories his squads were clearing. He pulled up the map of Jersey City on his HUD, examining his platoon's options.

They were seven kilometers northeast of their designated landing zone. Through the drones' feeds, he could see the other drop ships coming down in the correct location, disgorging their troops and taking to the skies again.

As he watched, a ship exploded in midair—this one not so lucky as it fell from the sky in a ball of fire.

His drones made a comm uplink, and a voice came into his mind. <Say again, Platoon 89-423-1, do you read?>

<Gunny? This is Sergeant Chase. Sending our coordinates.>

<Shit, Chase, what are you guys doing over there? Where's Inman?>

<LT and Inman bit it, Gunny. I'm top, now.>

<Fuck!>

Gunnery Sergeant Dawson's statement was punctuated by starfire flaring bright in the noon sky as it rained down on several locations in the city.

Streams of plasma burned through buildings and, hopefully, no small number of Niets. With any luck, those shots would end the enemy's anti-air capabilities—but Chase wasn't holding his breath.

<Look, Sergeant,> Dawson growled. <Major Weston says we can't come pull your asses out of the fire. You're to advance from your position to the coordinates I just passed. Be there by eleven hundred; we'll meet for the final push. We'll have an artillery platform down on the ground in fifteen, so if you need support, you call for it.>

<Understood,> Chase replied.

<Hey. You keep those kids safe, you hear me?>

<Count on it.>

Dawson killed the connection. Chase returned to the back of the drop ship to see first squad stuffing a pile of magazines into duffels, along with four heavy beams, three surface-to-air missiles, and one launcher.

<OK, folks, just had a chat with Gunny. We're to meet them on this side of the city's main park—the one just south of their downtown. We have two hours to do it.>

<Better get moving, then,> Casey said.

<Sweep's done on our side,> Henry reported.

<Always have to be first,> Ralph said. <We're clear here, too. A lot of dead kids in one room; looks like they tried to put up a fight and the Niets killed 'em.>

<Fuckers,> Casey swore.

<Send a pair of runners to grab supplies for your squad,> Chase said. <Then you're in the lead, Casey.>

<Of course I am,> Casey retorted.

RESCUE

STELLAR DATE: 12.23.8948 (Adjusted Years)
LOCATION: Kenmore Building, Jersey City
REGION: Pyra, Albany System, Theban Alliance

The fighting had lasted through the night. It was arduous, brutal, and no small number of Marauders lost their lives in Jersey City. By morning, Alpha Company held the first three blocks of towers along the canal and was moving closer to the city's core.

Rika was sprawled on a sofa across from Leslie, who was asleep in a chair. They were in the lobby of one of the towers.

She didn't even know its name until Barne walked up with a smile and said, "Enjoying the Kernmore's hospitality, are you?" He was pointing at Rika's charge cable, which was plugged into a power socket in the floor.

She smiled before responding, "Yeah, they've got the best cocktails here. This juice is just my flavor."

"Weak metaphor, Rika," Barne smiled. "You better top off fast. Ayer is sending us to give Fifth Battalion a hand."

"Fifth? What for?"

"They're pinned down on the far side of the city center; didn't make it in as far as we did. The artillery platform is repositioning to soften up the Niets over there, but it'll take them over an hour."

"Just us, or all of fourth platoon?" Leslie asked, cracking an eye open.

"Just us," Barne shook his head. "Fourth is going to keep pushing toward the city center with the rest of Alpha Company. We've got a Theban regiment pushing in from the west, as well. They're going to focus on the building-by-building clear-outs.

219

"Welcome to it," Rika said. "That's brutal work. Have there been a lot of civilian casualties?"

Barne nodded. "More than a lot. The Niets didn't really play nice. They killed some in retaliation but from what we can see, a lot were already dead. I guess they didn't feel like taking care of them."

"Or getting attacked by the occupied populace," Leslie added.

"How we getting there?" Rika asked. "Can't really go through the city center."

"And I'm not crawling through kilometers of sewer," Leslie added.

"I'm wounded that you two ladies would doubt me," Barne said, drawing a hand to his chest. "I've secured a boat. It's in the canal, waiting."

"A gunboat?" Rika asked with a smile.

"Uh…no…just a boat boat."

Leslie chuckled as she pulled herself up. "Well, let's go take a look at your boaty boat. You topped off, Rika?"

Rika nodded as she pulled her charge cord from the floor. "Good enough. But I'm starved. Any food around here?"

* * * * *

Five minutes later they were at the canal. Rika carefully lowered herself into the boat while Barne and Leslie stood on the far side to keep the small craft balanced. Once in, Rika sat on the deck in the middle of the vessel while Leslie released the moorings and tossed the ropes onto the dock.

Once they were free, Barne gunned the engine, moving the vessel out into the water, but staying close to the south shore where the tall buildings would obscure their passage.

Rika closed her eyes and leaned back, enjoying the feel of the boat surging through the water. It occurred to her that she had never been aboard a civilian watercraft. It was strange to be in a vessel made for pleasure. Even after the war, she had only been aboard freighters and other utilitarian spacecraft.

As they passed more pleasure boats tied up along the docks, Rika tried to imagine what the canal looked like before half the boats had been smashed by fallen windows or falling debris from the park across the canal.

It must have been heavenly.

A part of her felt responsible for the destruction wrought on Jersey City, but she knew the blame was ultimately to be laid at the feet of the Nietzscheans.

She had stopped herself from killing the Theban president. And even though Ariana was dead now, Rika reminded herself that in the end she had done the right thing. Ariana's parting words still rang in her mind.

'I forgive you.'

Rika would treasure that utterance all of her days—even though she would never see Ariana again to thank her.

The boat passed into Jersey City's harbor, and Rika watched the pleasure craft that had dominated the canal give way to commercial vessels and larger cruise ships.

At one point a shot hit the boat, fired from a building near the water. Rika calculated the origin and returned fire with a ballistic round. She didn't know if she had hit anyone, but no further fire came their way.

The ride was almost surreal in its calming silence; though every now and then, the sounds of artillery or the burning glare of starfire falling on the city reminded them that they would soon be in the thick of it once more.

Rika watched a series of drop ships fall toward the city and wondered about the soldiers within. They tagged as Marauder craft on her HUD, and she suspected that some day she might fight alongside the occupants—maybe even this day.

A barrage of SAMs launched from one of the buildings in the downtown core, sending dozens of missiles streaking toward the drop ships.

The ships fired chaff and flew wildly to lose the missiles. Point defense systems activated. One ship took an airburst and dipped for a moment. Then another was struck and one of its engines exploded. The ship began to spin wildly, but somehow stopped; no small feat with the ship's nose missing.

"C'mon," Leslie whispered. "Get those jets going. Slow that fall!"

Rika didn't speak as the drop ship plummeted toward the city, its velocity continuing to increase. Then, just below five hundred meters, the emergency jets fired—not all of them, but the ship slowed and began to barrel roll.

"They'd better hope their foam deploys," Barne said. "They've slowed, but they'll still dig a hole."

The ship passed below the buildings, and the three members of team Basilisk didn't see if the foam systems deployed or not—though there was no visible fireball or debris cloud.

"Might have made it," Barne allowed.

"They're close to our route," Rika said. "We could take a look."

"I'd like to," Leslie said. "Marauders don't leave one another on the field."

"No objection here," Barne said. "We're here to help their push into the city. Seeing if we can help out a platoon fits the bill."

<Captain Ayer, we're going to check out the site of a crashed bird. It's just a few blocks off our route,> Rika proposed.

<Acknowledged,> Ayer responded. <Report your findings to Major Weston; that's his platoon that was just dropping.>

<Will do,> she replied.

Her response was punctuated by another drop ship exploding midair, and she watched as starfire rained down on four locations in the city.

No more SAMs streaked out from the ground, and the remainder of the Marauder ships touched down.

Four minutes later, Barne pulled the boat up against a pier and Leslie leapt onto the dock, tying off a mooring, and Barne leaned out on the port side of the vessel to balance it as Rika stepped off.

He snorted as he jumped onto the pier. "Gonna need to get you some lighter limbs if we ever take you to Innoa for some water sports. They have these crazy caverns under the ocean that get huge waves you can surf on underground. Fun times down there."

"It's beautiful," Leslie nodded. "All the lighting is bioluminescent. I—" She didn't complete the statement and instead began moving down the pier.

<The team went there a few times, she and Jerry made some memories,> Barne said. <I'm an idiot for bringing it up.>

<Sadness is how we cope. We can't hide from our memories,> Rika replied.

<Maybe not, but we sure can try.>

The trio spread out with Leslie in the lead, Rika in the center, and Barne bringing up the rear. Twice, Leslie spotted Nietzscheans, and both times, Basilisk made short work of them.

As they walked, Rika approached Leslie and gently touched her arm.

<We haven't had time to talk—well, we have, but I didn't know what to say. I'm really sorry,> Rika said. <Somehow I feel like it's my fault.>

Leslie sighed. <It's no one's fault. It just is.... I'll tell you what's nuts, though. Jerry killed Thebans, and they killed him; but

now we're fighting together against the Nietzscheans. How fucked up is all that?>

<Seriously fucked up,> Rika replied. *<Like what happened with the president.>*

Leslie glanced at Rika. *<You haven't shared that yet—well, other than the sentence you wrote for the mission brief. How was it that you didn't kill their president? From what I could tell, she let you onto their net—that means you had already decided not to kill her before our orders changed.>*

Rika nodded. *<I couldn't do it, Leslie. She was begging for her life, and I wondered what in the stars I was doing. I may be a killer, but I'm not a murderer. I know it's a nonexistent distinction to some, but it's a big one for me.>*

<You know…> Leslie said after a moment. *<Even though that means you defied an order…it sure makes me like you a lot more. I don't know if you know this, but you're scary, girl—damn scary. Knowing that you couldn't kill in cold blood? Well, that makes you a lot more than human in my book.>*

<Umm…thanks…I think?> Rika replied with a chuckle. *<She forgave me before the end.>*

<The president?> Leslie asked.

<Yeah, Ariana. She said, 'I forgive you, Rika'.>

<You keep that close, Rika. That's the real deal.>

They walked in silence for several minutes before Leslie spoke again.

<You were out for a long time, Rika—four years at least, right?>

<I was in the camps for a year after the war,> Rika replied. *<So, three.>*

<Have anyone special?>

Rika wondered why Leslie was asking. Maybe she just needed something to talk about that would keep her mind off Jerry—though conversation about Rika's love life seemed like an odd choice.

<Maybe,> Rika replied after a while.

<Maybe? How's that?> Leslie asked.

<His name was Chase. He was definitely interested in me—for quite some time, too. But I was too wrapped up in my own head to notice—well, to act on it, at least.>

<What happened?>

<We...I...The night before I was auctioned, I finally...>

Leslie sighed. *<We always wait too long, don't we?>*

Rika nodded silently. That they did.

Their conversation was interrupted by Barne, who was signaling that they were approaching the crash site.

* * * * *

"Looks intact—mostly," Barne said, as he crouched with Rika on the south corner of a dormitory. Leslie was circling around to the north, checking the buildings for hostiles.

"No beacon on it," Rika replied. "I'm going to move in."

"Could be trapped," Barne whispered. "Wait for Leslie to finish her sweep, then you can go play steel hero."

"Drones don't see anything. No comms, though. Going to send one up to see if I can Link with Major Weston's company HQ."

Rika directed a drone to fly up over the site, and once it reached three hundred meters, it made a line-of-sight connection with the drop ship's original landing site.

<Major Weston, this is Lieutenant Rika. We've reached the crash site. No enemy, but it appears empty—barring two casualties.>

<Sorry, Lieutenant, you were off comms for a bit. The platoon survived, and has been proceeding toward our rendezvous. They've run into some trouble a klick to the west of your position, though. I'm sending you their location now.>

<On it,> Rika acknowledged. *<Any further details?>*

<No, we just lost contact with them around the city's museum. Drones have picked up the sound of combat in the area, but the few that tried to get closer got hit by EM fields.>

<We'll find them and get them on their way,> Rika said.

<Good, keep me informed. I might be able to send a B'Muth your way, if it's needed.>

<I'll let you know if that's necessary.>

<Good. Weston out.>

Leslie appeared on the far side of the courtyard. *<North and west side clear,>* she announced.

<I hooked up with Major Weston. The platoon is a kilometer to the west, pinned down in the museum and out of comms' reach,> Rika said to the team.

<Well, let's get moving, then,> Barne replied.

The team moved out of the courtyard, heading west through the university campus. Scenic walks and buildings of all shapes and sizes surrounded them, and Rika wondered what it would have been like to have the time and leisure to spend years in such a place.

She barely remembered her childhood, or much before the war had started when she was twelve. When she was fourteen, her parents had been in an attack on Hollis; Rika had somehow managed to get offworld on a refugee boat. From there she had been shuffled around by the Genevian government until she reached the age of sixteen—when she was able to get out of the camps.

That was what she mostly remembered: fear of the war, fear of the Nietzscheans, and then fear that she wouldn't survive on the streets.

She had only been nineteen when the cops picked her up for stealing food. Never had a chance to attend a school like this, to enjoy her youth.

To relax.

She wondered about visiting Innoa and enjoying its caves. If Basilisk had been there before, maybe they could go again. Perhaps she could find out what it would be like to just *live* for a while.

Before the next time they were in the shit.

Rika pulled her mind away from her reminiscing and back to the present. Distractions like those would be a fantastic way to never see the caves of Innoa.

They neared the edge of the university and could see the stone façade of the museum rising above the surrounding buildings five blocks away. The team formed up behind a high wall with drones monitoring their immediate surroundings.

<*I can hear the weapons fire from here,*> Rika said. <*Sounds sporadic, but I can make out Marauder guns. They're still in there.*>

Barne dropped a holoemitter on the ground, and the museum rose up before them.

<*Looks like it has seven entrances. From the sounds of it, the Niets are still outside, which means they have all those sealed; Marauders must be positioned well enough to keep them from breaching. My guess is that we're looking at between sixty and a hundred Niets, if they can cover all those entrances.*>

<*More, I'd wager,*> Leslie said.

<*Well, if there were too many more, they'd go in through all the windows at once,*> Barne responded.

<*No one ever said the Niets were smart.*>

<*Leslie, Barne,*> Rika said after staring at the holo for a moment. <*I want the two of you to circle around the south. Make a hole on the southwest corner when you get the signal. I'm going to hit the Niets right at the front door. That will pull them back—I hope.*>

Leslie turned her helmeted head to Rika, and shook it slowly. <*You be careful. No more of Basilisk dies on Pyra. Got it?*>

Rika nodded, sending Leslie a warm smile over the Link. <*I got it. No dying. You two need a little mech in your lives.*>

<What's the signal?> Barne asked.

<You really gotta ask?> Leslie replied with a laugh.

* * * * *

Chase leaned around a column and fired his JE34 rifle at the Niets. He didn't think that he'd hit any, but at least they weren't trying to come up the stairs anymore.

<Anyone have any 'nades left?> he asked fireteam three.

<I got one HE,> one of his soldiers called out.

<Toss it here,> Chase replied. *<I have a good angle on a few asshats behind that truck out there.>*

The soldier tossed the grenade to Chase, who caught it and primed it. Chase then pulled a feed from one of the platoon's few remaining drones—most of which had been destroyed by the Niets' EM fields—and looked for the best angle for his toss.

There was a building with an awning across the street. If he could get the grenade to hit it, the 'nade would roll off and land right on top of the enemy troops behind the truck.

Chase pulled his arm back and swung with all the strength his powered armor lent him. From the drone's feed, he saw that the grenade's trajectory was true. It hit the awning and fell out of view.

Two seconds later an explosion flipped the truck over, and Chase assumed the Niets behind it were dead. That had to put the count of enemies at the museum's front door at less than thirty.

Of course, he had only two fireteams at the front; his first was at a side entrance, and the rest of the platoon was spread even thinner.

He'd also had casualties; two dead, and seven others across the platoon in some state of serious injury. Without comms he didn't expect that they'd hold out much longer. He was considering telling the platoon to amass at one of the south entrances and break out of this deathtrap. He could maintain a fiction of a defense at the front door for a few minutes, at least.

So much for finding Rika in the Marauders. Chase shook his head. What a fool's errand this had been. After searching for her for half a year, the only thing he was going to find was a shallow grave on some distant world.

Still, if he could take out a few Niets before he died, that would be something he could accept. If it saved his platoon, that would be even better.

A group of Niets appeared down a side street with a heavy slug thrower. The kinetic weapon had more than enough firepower to tear apart the columns at the front of the museum.

<All fireteams, fall back to squad one's position. At the five-minute mark, make a push out to the memorial building one block to the southwest!> Chase ordered.

Confirmations came over the link and behind them, the two fireteams began to fall back through the museum's entrance.

<You coming, Sarge?> the corporal leading fireteam two asked.

<Yeah, gonna be right behind you guys. Just want to keep them out here a bit longer,> Chase replied.

He could tell the corporal hadn't moved, and Chase looked back at the woman. *<Move, soldier! That's an order!>*

<Yes, Sergeant Chase. Thank you.>

Don't thank me yet, Chase thought.

The fireteams retreated through the museum's entrance as Chase fired from his position; then he moved to another and fired again. He knew the enemy would see some of the Marauders leaving, but with luck, they'd think that the defenders were just falling back through the doors and no further.

He pulled back, closer to the entrance, aware that alone he could be easily flanked amongst the columns. As he slipped behind one, he heard the whine of the slug thrower discharge, and a column exploded five meters to his right.

Another pillar exploded, and he ran toward the door, dodging behind whatever cover he could find as the slug thrower tracked him.

So much for luck, Chase thought as he glanced over his shoulder

At which point he saw the slug thrower explode.

The Niets crewing it were thrown wide as the weapon blew apart in flames and shrapnel. He knew that shot hadn't come from his troops; he tried to raise whoever was out there on comms, but got nothing.

More shots rang out, ballistic rounds that hit half a dozen Niets in rapid succession. An HE grenade exploded where a group of Niets was clustered, and then a car partway down the block flew into the air.

The Niets must have decided that whoever was left at the museum entrance was far less dangerous than whoever was hitting them from behind, and a dozen of them rushed up the stairs and took cover behind the columns. Chase considered hitting them from the rear, when the remainder of their force rose from cover and raced toward the museum's main entrance.

"Oh, shit!" Chase cried out, and ran into the museum, thirty Niets hot on his tail.

* * * * *

Rika was just settling into position when she saw the Marauders begin to fall back through the museum's entrance. She tried to raise them; they needed to stop. A hammer and anvil didn't work nearly as well if there was no anvil.

Shots came from amongst the columns atop the museum's stairs, and Rika prayed that enough Marauders were still present to hold back the Niets.

She eased her weapon over the edge of a building and was about to fire on a pair of enemy soldiers when she saw an a-grav pad float into view—a large-bore kinetic slug thrower resting atop its platform.

Niets never fight fair, Rika grumbled. *Good thing I don't either.*

She repositioned on the rooftop and took aim with her GNR-41C, switching its mode to fire one of her last few uranium sabot rounds, and mentally pulled the trigger.

Nothing happened.

The weapon's jam notice was flashing on her HUD, indicating that the sabot round wasn't seated properly in the chamber. Rika cycled the round out and back into the chamber, and the warning disappeared.

She took aim again while the Niets fired the gun, blowing a pillar apart. Rika fired once more, and the jam notice reappeared.

FAAAWK! she shouted in her mind, and unlatched the chamber cover, sliding it aside. The round was seated properly and the accelerator was aligned.

Then she saw that the jam sensor was cracked. *No wonder.*

Rika quickly sealed up the chamber, disabled the jam sensor, and fired on the Niets' weapon.

The uranium rod flew true, and its sabot dropped off a moment before it hit, tearing the gun apart. Rika moved down the rooftop, firing her ballistic rounds on a dozen other Niets who were hiding behind a stone wall, and then lobbed a grenade at another group behind a car.

Thanks to her two-seventy vision, she saw one of the Marauders still alive in front of the museum's entrance. She tried to signal him, but he turned and raced inside the building.

Fuck...no! Rika swore. Then she saw why—the Niets were all fleeing into the building, apparently far more fearful of her than whoever was still inside.

Rika leapt down from the rooftop and into the street, firing with her JE78 at two Niets who weren't fast enough. Then she lobbed another grenade amongst the columns, trusting its blast to clear a path for her.

Seconds later she was up the marble stairs. Cowards though they were, the Niets would be waiting for her inside the door; even her armor and reflexes couldn't withstand concentrated firepower from twenty weapons.

She glanced at the high windows along the front of the building then ran and jumped through one; shards of glass and steel rained down as she fell into the museum's large foyer.

As expected, the Niets were waiting with weapons trained on the front entrance. She fired a few more rounds from her GNR into their midst as she raced to the dubious cover of some strange twisted sculpture.

Once crouched behind the sculpture, Rika lobbed another grenade out to where her HUD showed the highest concentration of enemies to be. She didn't wait to see if it hit anyone before rushing to a column, which she climbed using the same trick as she had in the bunker—hanging from the capital at its top.

The Niets were firing at the pillar's base, and Rika leaned out and shot a uranium round into the base of a different pillar, then another one. Both stone towers fell as their bases crumbled, raining chunks of marble onto nearby Niets.

Rika had hoped the roof would fall, too, but it seemed to be holding. She was about to take out another pillar when part of the ceiling finally came down. Many of the Niets had retreated back toward the entrance, but the debris still caught a dozen of their number.

She scanned the foyer and saw no movement other than the enemies clustered near the entrance. Rika jumped down from the pillar and clambered over the debris, firing wildly at the Niets, forcing them out of the museum.

Then something hit her back, and Rika spun to see a Niet half-buried by the fallen ceiling firing on her. Before she had a chance to put him down, a trio of shots rang out from further back in the foyer, killing the Niet.

Rika saw a lone Marauder step out from behind a pillar and walk stiffly toward her. His right leg was hit. It didn't look critical—just bad enough to disable the armor's knee joint.

His helmeted head was fixed on her and he lowered his weapon.

<Rika?> a familiar voice came to her over the Link. *<Is…is that you? Rika?>*

Her mind was ready for combat, ready to kill; not ready for this. It took a moment—one that felt like hours—for her to process what she was hearing.

<Chase?>

<Rika!> the armored figure rushed toward her, and she wondered if she was dreaming. Had the Niets killed her, and this was the twisted afterlife that mechs went to?

<How…Chase?>

<Yes, it's me,> Chase's easy laugh flowed into her mind, and Rika felt a strange combination of relief and terror flood through her.

Chase is here, on Pyra, as a Marauder. Did he come to find me? He is going to get himself killed!

The thought turned her attention back to the entrance, certain that the Niets were there, ready to mow them both down.

But no enemies were visible.

<Rika, you there?> Leslie's voice came to her.

Rika shook her head, barely remembering how to form sentences. <Yeah. Front's secure. Sorta.>

<Weston's out here with three B'Muths. The Niets have surrendered. Most of the 'toon looks to be OK; they're just missing their CO. A Sergeant Chase. That wouldn't be the guy you told me about, would it?>

Rika stared down at Chase in wonder, as he cleared his visor and smiled up at her.

<Yeah; yeah, it is.>

MOP UP

STELLAR DATE: 12.23.8948 (Adjusted Years)
LOCATION: City Center, Jersey City
REGION: Pyra, Albany System, Theban Alliance

Rika stood atop a building near a decorative garden in Jersey City's center, surveying the destruction that victory had wrought.

The ground shook as three B'muths walked down a street, their forty-millimeter gatling guns pivoting as the gunners within checked for targets.

Rika suspected there weren't any remaining.

The battle was over.

In space, the Marauders and Thebans had fought the Nietzschean ships to a standstill. Word amongst the troops was that the Niets were so used to a sweeping victory that they relied on overused tactics that the Thebans had been well-prepared for.

Plus, no one had retreated.

Still, Rika had to give the Nietzscheans some credit. They had held on until a Septhian fleet jumped in, apparently responding to drone-borne messages that the Old Man had sent asking for help.

A lot of Thebans were angry with the Marauders. There were already calls for the mercenary organization to be brought up on charges of war crimes by many in the Theban populace.

Luckily there were more Thebans who viewed the Marauders as their saviors—many of whom had apparently been concerned about Nietzschean aggression for some time.

That same group was pushing hard for Thebes to join the Septhian Alliance, and that movement was gaining momentum in the public forums.

Rika considered the irony in that. With Ariana dead and the Niets on their doorstep, that initial mission she had been bought for would likely be fulfilled. Thebes would become a province of Septhia.

Those local politics mattered little to Rika—though she did still keenly feel Ariana's death. But what she felt most strongly was pride—and no small amount of amazement—that the Nietzscheans had been defeated both on the Pyran surface and in space.

It had been a long time since she had seen a victory like that.

A platoon moved through the streets below, falling back toward the muster site on the southern side of Jersey City. It wasn't Chase's but his was close, also moving back to the muster site.

As much as she didn't want to leave his side, Basilisk had orders. There were still buildings to sweep and cover to provide.

At first it had surprised Rika that the Marauders were leaving so soon, but with the Theban regiment moving in from the west, Marauder command felt it was best not to have both forces in the city at once. Too much risk of an incident between the armies.

Rika leapt down from the building and approached Barne and Leslie, who were speaking with Captain Ayer on a street corner.

"I hear you found your long-lost love?" Ayer asked with a smile as Rika approached.

Rika laughed. "Yeah, first freedom, then this. Starting to wonder if maybe the universe doesn't hate me after all."

"He's put in a request to transfer to my company already," Ayer said.

"He's what?" Rika asked.

"Yeah, I've put things in motion to approve it. He seems competent—served with distinction back in the war."

Rika was at a loss for words. In the museum, Chase had told her that he had served in the GAF but they hadn't had time to get into details before being given new orders for the final push to clear out Jersey City.

She wanted to reach out to him, to ask him to tell her everything; they were still in a hot zone, though, and she wasn't going to distract him further. If he felt anything like she did, he was already distracted.

All this after just one night in a bar, Rika thought. *How could it mean so much to me after so little time?*

But she knew there was more to it than that. Chase had pursued her for months, always kind, always supportive. And he had searched for her and *found* her. With all the worlds amongst the stars, he had found her on this small piece of rock, drifting in space.

"Rika, you with us?" Ayer asked.

"Uh, yes. Sorry, ma'am." Rika flushed, glad her helmet hid her embarrassment from her CO.

"Yeah, right. Get your head out of the clouds. I just brought Basilisk back up to full strength; I don't want to have to replace its CO when you get your daydreaming head blown off."

"Filled?" Barne asked. "With who?"

"Seriously?" Leslie asked with a broad smile visible through her cleared visor. "Are you an idiot? Who do you think?"

BASILISK

STELLAR DATE: 12.24.8948 (Adjusted Years)
LOCATION: Commissary, MSS *Romany*
REGION: Pyra, Albany System, Theban Alliance

Rika walked through the *Romany's* mess feeling far more nervous than she would have expected, taking extra care to keep a steady grip on the tray of food in her hands.

Ahead, Chase sat at a table with Team Basilisk and three others that her HUD identified as sergeants from his old platoon. She saw Barne say something, and Leslie groaned while Chase and the man named Ralph laughed.

Chase looked up and smiled at her, sliding over on the bench to make room.

Rika sucked in a deep breath, suddenly feeling much younger and less certain of herself than she should. It felt as though she was in a cheesy vid about a young woman fawning over a boy at a school.

"You gonna stand there all day, or you gonna sit your metal ass down and dig in?" Barne asked around a mouthful of food.

"My ass isn't metal," Rika said with a frown as she sat.

"It's true," Chase nodded. "I've felt it."

"Chase!" Rika exclaimed.

Chase wrapped an arm around her shoulders as she settled.

"Sorry, we've technically only been romantically involved for about two days...spread over half a year. I'm not really sure how to behave."

"Like yourself," Leslie suggested.

Rika leaned into Chase and let out a long breath. "Doesn't matter how you behave. We're together, we're home, and our family is here."

"So, you're sure that you're a Marauder now?" Leslie asked with a twinkle in her eye.

"Yeah, and this Marauder is hungry. These mods don't feed themselves."

"Dig in," Chase said. "I hear this is the last of the real meat. We'll be on vat-grown crap from here out."

"Doesn't matter," Rika said with a smile. "Beats NutriPaste."

"Gah! Tried that crap once," Ralph said. "Tasted like shit! No wonder all you mechs were so surly in the war."

The table fell silent, no one certain how Rika would react. She saw the look of worry on Ralph's face, and knew that he didn't mean to say anything hurtful.

She smiled and shook her head. "Well, you're not supposed to *taste* it. With us, it goes right in the stomach."

"That's Ralph's problem," Casey said with a laugh. "He's like a dirty toddler, just sticking everything in his mouth all the time."

The table broke out into laughter, and Rika closed her eyes, feeling Chase's arm around her. She sighed and didn't even bother keeping back the tears as a feeling of contentment settled over her.

She really was home, and these were her Marauders.

THE END

* * * * *

Follow the continuing adventures of Rika and the Marauders in book 2 of the series: *Rika Redeemed*.

THANK YOU

If you've enjoyed reading Rika Outcast, a review on Amazon.com and/or goodreads.com would be greatly appreciated.

To get the latest news and access to free novellas and short stories, sign up on the Aeon 14 mailing list: www.aeon14.com/signup.

M. D. Cooper

THE BOOKS OF AEON 14

Keep up to date with what is releasing in Aeon 14 with the free Aeon 14 Reading Guide.

Origins of Destiny (The Age of Terra)
- Prequel: Storming the Norse Wind
- Book 1: Shore Leave (in Galactic Genesis until Sept 2018)
- Book 2: Operative (Summer 2018)
- Book 3: Blackest Night (Summer 2018)

The Intrepid Saga (The Age of Terra)
- Book 1: Outsystem
- Book 2: A Path in the Darkness
- Book 3: Building Victoria

- The Intrepid Saga Omnibus – *Also contains Destiny Lost, book 1 of the Orion War series*

- Destiny Rising – *Special Author's Extended Edition comprised of both Outsystem and A Path in the Darkness with over 100 pages of new content.*

The Orion War
- Book 1: Destiny Lost
- Book 2: New Canaan
- Book 3: Orion Rising
- Book 4: The Scipio Alliance
- Book 5: Attack on Thebes
- Book 6: War on a Thousand Fronts
- Book 7: Fallen Empire (2018)
- Book 8: Airtha Ascendancy (2018)
- Book 9: The Orion Front (2018)
- Book 10: Starfire (2019)
- Book 11: Race Across Time (2019)
- Book 12: Return to Sol (2019)

Tales of the Orion War
- Book 1: Set the Galaxy on Fire
- Book 2: Ignite the Stars
- Book 3: Burn the Galaxy to Ash (2018)

Perilous Alliance (Age of the Orion War – w/Chris J. Pike)
- Book 1: Close Proximity
- Book 2: Strike Vector
- Book 3: Collision Course
- Book 4: Impact Imminent
- Book 5: Critical Inertia (2018)

Rika's Marauders (Age of the Orion War)
- Prequel: Rika Mechanized
- Book 1: Rika Outcast
- Book 2: Rika Redeemed
- Book 3: Rika Triumphant
- Book 4: Rika Commander
- Book 5: Rika Infiltrator (2018)
- Book 6: Rika Unleashed (2018)
- Book 7: Rika Conqueror (2019)

Perseus Gate (Age of the Orion War)
Season 1: Orion Space
- Episode 1: The Gate at the Grey Wolf Star
- Episode 2: The World at the Edge of Space
- Episode 3: The Dance on the Moons of Serenity
- Episode 4: The Last Bastion of Star City
- Episode 5: The Toll Road Between the Stars
- Episode 6: The Final Stroll on Perseus's Arm
- Eps 1-3 Omnibus: The Trail Through the Stars
- Eps 4-6 Omnibus: The Path Amongst the Clouds

Season 2: Inner Stars
- Episode 1: A Meeting of Bodies and Minds
- Episode 3: A Deception and a Promise Kept
- Episode 3: A Surreptitious Rescue of Friends and Foes (2018)
- Episode 4: A Trial and the Tribulations (2018)

- Episode 5: A Deal and a True Story Told (2018)
- Episode 6: A New Empire and An Old Ally (2018)

Season 3: AI Empire
- Episode 1: Restitution and Recompense (2019)
- Five more episodes following...

The Warlord (Before the Age of the Orion War)
- Book 1: The Woman Without a World
- Book 2: The Woman Who Seized an Empire
- Book 3: The Woman Who Lost Everything

The Sentience Wars: Origins (Age of the Sentience Wars – w/James S. Aaron)
- Book 1: Lyssa's Dream
- Book 2: Lyssa's Run
- Book 3: Lyssa's Flight
- Book 4: Lyssa's Call
- Book 5: Lyssa's Flame (June 2018)

Enfield Genesis (Age of the Sentience Wars – w/Lisa Richman)
- Book 1: Alpha Centauri
- Book 2: Proxima Centauri (2018)

Hand's Assassin (Age of the Orion War – w/T.G. Ayer)
- Book 1: Death Dealer
- Book 2: Death Mark (August 2018)

Machete System Bounty Hunter (Age of the Orion War – w/Zen DiPietro)
- Book 1: Hired Gun
- Book 2: Gunning for Trouble
- Book 3: With Guns Blazing (June 2018)

Vexa Legacy (Age of the FTL Wars – w/Andrew Gates)
- Book 1: Seas of the Red Star

Building New Canaan (Age of the Orion War – w/J.J. Green)

- Book 1: Carthage (2018)

Fennington Station Murder Mysteries (Age of the Orion War)
- Book 1: Whole Latte Death (w/Chris J. Pike)
- Book 2: Cocoa Crush (w/Chris J. Pike)

The Empire (Age of the Orion War)
- The Empress and the Ambassador (2018)
- Consort of the Scorpion Empress (2018)
- By the Empress's Command (2018)

The Sol Dissolution (The Age of Terra)
- Book 1: Venusian Uprising (2018)
- Book 2: Scattered Disk (2018)
- Book 3: Jovian Offensive (2019)
- Book 4: Fall of Terra (2019)

ABOUT THE AUTHOR

Michael Cooper likes to think of himself as a jack-of-all-trades (and hopes to become master of a few). When not writing, he can be found writing software, working in his shop at his latest carpentry project, or likely reading a book.

He shares his home with a precocious young girl, his wonderful wife (who also writes), two cats, a never-ending list of things he would like to build, and ideas...

Find out what's coming next at *www.aeon14.com*

Made in the USA
Lexington, KY
10 August 2018